Pearls FOR
Margaret

Pearls FOR Margaret

Precious Pearls

BOOK 1

MARJORIE EDDY HARRIS

Pearls For Margaret
Precious Pearls, Book 1

ISBN: 979-8-9869756-0-3 (print)
ISBN: 979-8-9869756-1-0 (eBook)

Editing Services by Midnight Owl Editors
Cover Design and Formatting by Alt 19 Creative

Published by:
Sweet Briar House Press

To Kathleen,
who believed my dreams could become stories

To Don,
who makes dreams come true

A portion of the sale of *Pearls for Margaret*
during its first year of publication will be donated to
Jane Austen's House Museum: Jane's Fund.

For more information, go to https://janeaustens.house/support/

CHAPTER 1

LONDON, 1815

MARGARET STIFLED A SIGH. She tried to focus on buttering her toast, but her uncle's lips smacked while he chewed—audible even though she sat two chairs away at the large dining table. He picked the cold ham from his teeth with his letter opener as he read his correspondence; it was the only flaw which Lady Frances Colborne, Margaret's aunt, had never successfully corrected in her husband. Margaret could have pointed out a few more, but to Lady Frances, arrogance, pride, and disdainful treatment of one's niece were completely acceptable behaviors in a husband.

Margaret stared at the other eight empty dining room chairs and wished her mother was alive, or that Sir Reginald and Lady Frances had produced children, or that they had invited company to stay, which they never did. Then she would not sit here in silence morning after morning, day after day.

She placed her toast back on the plate and focused on the carved Colborne crest in the oak chair across from her and the marble fireplace behind it. She imagined the crackle of the burning wood, warmth flowing toward her. There was rarely a fire at breakfast, even though

London was never warm enough in February. Sir Reginald never felt the cold and never asked Margaret's opinion. Someday, when she was mistress of her own home, she would have warm, glowing fires whenever she wished.

Sir Reginald slit open another letter, totally engrossed in his correspondence—and his chewing.

Her silence would not offend; her uncle preferred her to speak only when spoken to. Since Lady Frances always took her breakfast in bed, Margaret was able to remain quiet most mornings, if not at peace. She was the burden resulting first from her mother's marriage to a mere sailor and then her mother's death. Sir Reginald had never forgiven his sister, Alice, for her choice of spouse, even after her husband had become a captain and retired quite wealthy. Now that she was gone, he took out his resentment on Margaret, who was the undeserved blessing of her parents' union. It would be Margaret, as Lady Frances often bemoaned, and not Sir Reginald, who would receive his sister's inheritance.

Sir Reginald stopped smacking, and his hands stilled. Margaret froze. Sensing something was amiss, she glanced at him from the corner of her eye. His brow was creased, and his faded blue eyes stared at her over a tattered letter, stained at the corner. Her eyes darted back to her plate, and her fork tine scraped the Wedgwood blue when she stabbed a bite of boiled potato.

He began smacking again.

He opened the letter, read the first page, and folded it back up. Placing it face down, he motioned for George, the footman. "Ask Lady Frances to join us."

Margaret's eyes widened at the unusual request. Having Sir Reginald and Lady Frances in the same room often resulted in their combined effort to reform Margaret of some perceived ill. She eyed the door. The Colborne townhouse was large, even by London standards, and afforded more than one hiding place. "Sir Reginald, may

I be excused?" Her normal course of action when she sensed distress was retreat.

"No, you may not." His words were quiet, yet disdainful.

Margaret swallowed down her anger with her hot tea. She hated having her activities and actions controlled. She peeked at him, again. He was reading a different letter. She dropped her gaze to the polished mahogany table around his plate, looking for some part of the ragged letter which had caused the disruption of the morning's rituals, but it was tucked under the rest.

Fifteen minutes passed as slowly as the last century. Margaret pushed her ham about her plate. Her stomach twisted in knots. She dabbed at the corners of her mouth and folded her napkin, both efforts to quell her nerves.

When Lady Frances deigned to enter, Margaret noticed a tendril of her aunt's upswept hair had come loose. She had hurried—uncharacteristically so. Margaret straightened her posture and cleared her expression of any emotion, exactly as she had been taught, trying not to give her aunt a reason to reprimand her.

Lady Frances took a seat across from Margaret and dismissed George. After he closed the door, she said, "Reginald, I demand an explanation for why you summoned me—and at this time of day." She pierced her husband with her gray-eyed gaze, though her tone remained "ladylike."

He handed Lady Frances the letter, the address side facing her. She paused, and their eyes met. Lady Frances unfolded the letter and skimmed it. "This letter is for you, Margaret. From your father." She extended it to Margaret. "Pity your hair is still auburn. It is too… common. I had hoped it would lighten in time. Lady Quintrell's did. Do not let your hands tremble. An accomplished young lady is always calm."

Margaret could not help quivering. Her heartbeat quickened; her smile grew. She ignored the quip about her hair, knowing that it was the exact color her father's had been at her age. She loved the color. But what excited her was the letter. It had been a month since her last letter from her father. Correspondence between London and Lisbon, where her father had returned after Napoleon's defeat, took from two weeks to a month. He was restoring his shipping business, but she hoped, soon, it would be safe for her to join him.

"You will notice he has not addressed the letter properly." Lady Frances tsked. "You are *not* Miss Margaret Pearl Beaton but Miss Margaret Colborne. When we took you in, we *insisted* on this change; still, he flaunts it. As your aunt and uncle, your guardians, we expect *you* to pay more attention to what propriety dictates."

"It is my legal last name." Margaret bit her lower lip.

"Beaton, as we have explained, is not a name of distinction. Colborne is." Uncle Reginald's eyebrows furrowed into one continuous tuft of hair.

"Yes, Sir Reginald." Margaret had never called her uncle or aunt by anything less formal or more familial than their titles. Living with them after her mother's death had been an unpleasant necessity; they were the only family she had left since her father was at sea supplying goods to the British fleet.

"Well, open it, girl," her aunt instructed. "And read it aloud."

Margaret looked up. Having her letters read before they were given to her was not uncommon. Being required to read one aloud was. Why this time? Evidently, her aunt and uncle wished to discuss something *with* her. Still, she waited, unsure if reading her father's letter in front of them was wise. She did not want to hear their unkind words about her father, which happened whenever he became the topic of conversation. She also feared she would be censured if her excitement bubbled out of her. Obediently, Margaret read aloud. She tried to hide her joy beneath the monotonous tone her aunt insisted she use, but her voice trembled and rose in pitch.

My Dear Pearl,

Know of my deep and abiding love for you. I hope you are well.
I have learned from your uncle of your upcoming wedding
to Sir Edgar Fortescue, Baronet, nephew of your aunt—

Margaret tried to focus, but her thoughts and emotions were jumbled; she was first surprised and then quickly incensed. Sir Edgar had only recently paid her any attention, yet her father had received word a month ago from Sir Reginald about *her* engagement. How had her uncle known what Sir Edgar intended?

"Your father knows I am the daughter of an earl," Lady Frances interrupted. "Yet he continually fails to respect my position or that of my husband by addressing us properly." Lady Frances puffed out an exasperated breath. For the hundredth time, Margaret wondered why Lady Frances took her father's "failings" personally. Or Margaret's, for that matter.

"If my sister had not married poorly, we would not be in this situation." Sir Reginald frowned at Margaret and shook his head, a dangerous pursuit since he was picking his teeth again.

Margaret squeezed her eyes shut for a moment to fight down the anger. Their maligning her mother was nothing new, but the sting had somehow increased over the three years since her death.

"Continue." Lady Frances glanced at Margaret and poured herself some tea.

Margaret swallowed and took a breath. Calmly, she continued.

I rejoice in you having found a man of good character, and
believe that if you are marrying for love, as your dear mother
and I did—God rest her soul—

Margaret paused to swallow so her voice would not crack.

that you truly will be as happy as you are good and beautiful. In short, I give my consent.

Her breakfast roiled in her stomach. They had planned a marriage of convenience without consulting her? She would not believe her father was involved; he was not conniving like her aunt and uncle. But marry Sir Edgar? His image came suddenly to her mind: congenial, fashionable but over-dressed, foppish, long-winded. No, she had no romantic feelings for him. Sir Edgar was pleasant, but she wanted to marry for love.

"There. It is as we hoped." Sir Reginald placed his napkin on the table and pushed his chair away. "Your dowry will no longer be a question. The money from your father combined with what we have graciously agreed to bestow upon you will make a fine wedding present to Sir Edgar. Frances, write to your nephew at once. Invite him to dinner, and I will reassure him of Margaret's wealth. No doubt, with this assurance of your inheritance, Sir Edgar can overlook your father's low birth. Now, Sir Edgar will move with more haste."

"Low birth?" Margaret asked, trying not to crinkle the letter even though her hands clenched. She would have to act quickly; if only she weren't alone and unaided. Again.

"Ah, the chit has little mental capacity," Sir Reginald rose from the table. "My dear, you explain to her again how her circumstances—inferior connections but a large inheritance—are tied to her need to marry a suitable gentleman. A June wedding, I think. Now, I must change before I leave for Parliament." Sir Reginald bowed over his wife's hand and sauntered out of the room.

Margaret's mouth dropped open. Less than four months and she would be married. Why such haste? How could she prevent it?

Lady Frances took a long draw of her tea. "Really, have you learned nothing?" her aunt began. Normally Margaret would have steeled herself for one of her aunt's lectures and stinging set-downs, but her desire to finish the letter was stronger. Placing the unread portion face up, Margaret folded her hands in her lap, bowing her head slightly, as if in apologetic submission. But she kept her eyes darting. She skimmed the next few paragraphs and gasped.

Lady Frances scowled. "Whatever is the matter? Have I not taught you—"

"He may arrive within the week?" Margaret smiled, then laughed. "With a present for me."

"Your father is coming?" Lady Frances pulled the letter from Margaret's hand.

"No, his business partner. Mr.—"

The door opened, and Henshem, the butler, announced, "A Mr. Joshua Wynn is here to see Miss Colborne."

"Here?" Lady Frances frowned.

"Yes, ma'am. He is in the library."

"Call Sir Reginald at once." Lady Frances dropped the letter on the table and stood.

Margaret's heart rose to her throat. Her cheek flushed. She would have more news of her father. She quickly gathered the letter and stood to follow, but Lady Frances said, "You may go to the music room to practice either the harp or the pianoforte."

"May I not see him? He has come from my father. I wish to ask how—"

"You will not contradict me. I do not know what has made you so forgetful of your proper place this morning. Clearly, you are too excitable to receive visitors without embarrassing us all. Go to the music room." And with that, Lady Frances swept out of the room.

Margaret fought to control her tears. Only her trembling chin betrayed her. Once in the hall, she tucked the letter into her bodice for safekeeping.

She slowly made her way toward the staircase opposite the library. Fortunately, the library door was ajar since her uncle had not yet joined Mr. Wynn and her aunt. She could hear her aunt's haughty voice, the one reserved for servants or visitors who were beneath her in rank.

Quietly, Margaret approached the library; she halted and peered inside. There stood the tannest man she had ever beheld. Beneath his wavy blond hair, one eyebrow was lifted along with a corner of his mouth. He possessed a commanding air, standing straighter than she had ever seen a man do. Her father had written to her about his new partner, the recently retired naval captain who had captured enough enemy ships and their prize money to leave the service a wealthy man. Yet, her father had failed to mention Mr. Wynn's strong jaw, commanding presence, or lively expression. Her pulse quickened as she stepped toward him. With such a tanned but youthful face, he looked younger than the twenty-eight indicated in her father's last letter.

His faded clothes showed a familiarity with the sun and sea that no Londoner would have known. The salt stains on his shoulders meant he had come straight from his ship or the docks. Margaret wondered why he had come without changing into the attire of a London gentleman. Was he in a hurry? Was there bad news from her father?

He glanced over her aunt's shoulder, and their eyes met.

Margaret averted hers and blushed.

"Here is the young lady now, I believe." With a few quick steps, ignoring the gasp of her aunt, Mr. Wynn came into the hall and bowed. "Do I have the honor of addressing Miss Margaret Pearl Beaton?"

To avoid the embarrassment of looking into his eyes, Margaret stared at Mr. Wynn's chest. This did not, however, make speaking any easier for her, because she noticed the fit of his sunbaked blue jacket over his broad shoulders, down to the trim leanness of his waistcoat. It was a sharp contrast to Sir Edgar's pudgy waist, often festooned in silk brocades.

Her aunt interrupted. "Sir, you have not been introduced to my niece. It is improper for you to address her."

Mr. Wynn looked at Margaret with a kind smile but spoke over his shoulder. "Lady Frances, I have not come to court her but to deliver a message and gift from her father."

Normally, Margaret would have blushed at such directness, but she was too in awe of a man who would speak to her aunt without much deference.

Her aunt's mouth dropped open, and she blinked several times.

Margaret seized the opportunity. "Sir, thank you. Yes, I am the daughter of Mr. David Beaton and would gladly hear your message. Please, go back into the library and sit down."

Lady Frances raised her chin. "Margaret, we are leaving."

"I wish to hear the news about my father." Margaret turned to the footman. "George, could you join Mr. Wynn and myself in the library?"

George's eyes grew wide as they flicked to Lady Frances. She gave the slightest nod and walked away. To the casual observer, Lady Frances's manner belied little. Margaret, however, knew the determined click of her aunt's heels meant trouble. Mr. Wynn might be thrown out at any moment. Margaret sighed. She would hear a lengthy lecture about her lack of propriety later.

"Please excuse my haste," she said, sitting in the nearest chair and leaning in, "but how is my father? Is he well? Tell me everything you remember from when you last saw him."

Mr. Wynn's smile softened. He pulled up a leather-padded chair near her. She caught the scent of sea salt and tar—the way her father always smelled when he returned home from the sea.

"You have his auburn hair and chin, but I assume your green eyes are your mother's?" Mr. Wynn smiled.

She blushed and nodded under his gaze. He cleared his voice.

"Your father stood before me not an hour before I left port. He raked his hand through his graying hair, as you know he does, and said in his booming voice, 'Joshua, my good man. You find my daughter, Pearl, and tell her to her face that she is the most beloved daughter in all the wurld!'"

Tears gathered in Margaret's eyes, and she laughed. Mr. Wynn's portrayal of her father's gestures and Scottish accent was endearing. How she loved her father. How she missed him. The familiar loneliness welled up in her, and the guilt for believing that her father, who had chosen duty to king and country before her, loved her—just not enough to come home to her.

He went on. "'Tell her I am sending her a gift for her wedding and hope she will wear them with pride.'" Mr. Wynn removed a rectangular rosewood box from a leather satchel and handed it to Margaret.

She ran her fingers over the carved top, thinking of how her father's hand had recently touched the box. Overwhelmed with love for her father, she wished she could embrace him. She traced the delicately chiseled rose and bee, for Beaton. *Our family crest,* he had often joked. Her fingers smoothed the inlaid cherry wood border before opening the gold clasp.

The lid popped open, and she looked inside. She gasped. Her mother's necklace, a single strand of pinkish white pearls, gleamed against the black satin. "I remember that Mother left them in Father's care. I never knew why."

"Sir!" Uncle Reginald's voice cut through the room. He stood in the doorway, dressed to meet with the ministers of government, his roundness blocking most of the light. Henshem behind him. "I must ask you to leave. Margaret, go upstairs at once." He motioned to George, who quickly moved to open the front door.

Mr. Wynn raised an eyebrow, but stood and bowed. His smile did not wane; he politely waited for Margaret to step into the hall first.

When Margaret passed, she quietly clicked the box closed and held it low, but her uncle reached out. Her heart dropped and her fists clenched. Sighing, she lowered her head and placed the precious box in his open hand. In the entrance hall, she turned. Catching Mr. Wynn's gaze, she said, "Thank you." She attempted a smile.

Mr. Wynn peered at her with concern.

Dropping her shoulders, she climbed the first few stairs, then paused when she heard Mr. Wynn object. "That gift is for Miss Beaton, from her father."

"You will address me as Sir Reginald." Her uncle said in a clipped tone. "And she is not capable of caring for such a valuable gift. I will protect it. The rest is none of your concern. Now leave at once before I have you thrown out."

"That remark, Sir Reginald, is nonsensical. Her father describes her as a level-headed young lady of eighteen." There was no reply, so Mr. Wynn continued. "Here is the letter Mr. Beaton charged me to deliver to you." Mr. Wynn pulled a letter from his coat pocket and held it out.

Sir Reginald waved two fingers, and Henshem retrieved the proffered letter.

Margaret blushed at the demeaning gesture. Mr. Wynn walked toward the front door with an unhurried manner. George opened it. Before Mr. Wynn left, he looked up at her and winked. He stepped out the doorway and was gone.

Her blush deepened. No man had ever winked at her. She hurried up the stairs. The sooner she reached the music room, the sooner she could re-read her letter in private.

Closing the door behind her, she pulled open the letter and sank into the sofa. Tears gathered in her eyes, but she smiled. A warmth filled her heart. She re-read her father's closing line: *all my love.* No one else on earth ever told her that. Notwithstanding the distance between them or the years of absence, her father loved her. She had worried of late that her father's letters provided fewer details than usual; they were shorter. Even his script was irregular. Had conditions in Lisbon worsened? Was he distracted by business? Had he forgotten how much she needed him?

She re-read the portion concerning Sir Edgar. Regardless of what her uncle had told her about the worthiness of Sir Edgar, her father only wanted her to be happy and to marry for love. Sir Reginald treated her more like a mare for sale at Tattersalls.

She let out a frustrated sigh. How could her uncle keep the pearls? Yes, they had been a gift from Grandfather Colborne to her mother before her elopement. But now they belonged to Margaret. Touching the pearls which her mother had worn had brought a tender reverence for the necklace. How dare Sir Reginald think she would be careless with them.

Margaret remembered playing with a doll near her mother's dressing table. Her mother was preparing for a ball, and her maid placed the pearl necklace around Mother's neck. Margaret was entranced by their lustrous pink glow. Her mother, seeing her fascination, pulled Margaret onto her lap, removed the necklace, and placed it around Margaret's neck. Margaret felt so grown up as she smiled at her mother in the table mirror.

A single tear fell on the letter. Margaret could almost feel her mother's hands on her shoulders. Putting the letter down on the table, she crossed to the piano and retrieved her pocket Portuguese phrase book from its hiding place beneath a Mozart concerto. She opened to the pressed jacaranda blossom, now dried a purple-black color. Another tear fell.

Father had given this to her ten years ago when they'd left Lisbon—to remember their time there as a family.

"You must be brave, Pearl. And patient. Wait for me. I will not fail you." Her father embraced her. The buttons on his navy overcoat scratched her ear as she pressed herself into his arms.

She *had* waited, patiently. Why had her father not come in person? The loneliness hit her like a wave, engulfed her, threatened to drown her. She stood and breathed deeply. She had not seen him in three years. If he had thought she was going to marry, why had he not come himself? He had promised to visit this summer, but if her aunt and uncle had their way, she would be married by then. How she longed to embrace her father and ask for his counsel. How wonderful it would be to accompany him in society—instead of her aunt and uncle. She replaced the phrase book under the music.

Lisbon may have been too dangerous a year ago, but now it must be different. Under British control, the civil unrest borne from seven years of the Peninsular War must be subsiding. Besides, her father could protect her. His shipping business was doing well. Margaret knew some details from skimming her uncle's cast-off copies of the *Gazette,* searching for her father's name and for news of ships arriving at the London docks.

In spite of the advantages of London society, which her aunt and uncle could provide, she wanted more than anything to live with her father. She loved him and shared his adventurous spirit; she longed to walk the streets of Lisbon with him.

Going out with Lady Frances meant visiting one stuffy London drawing room after another.

Now that she understood her aunt and uncle's intention was to marry her off to Sir Edgar by June, her stomach turned. She rubbed her temple. Her mother was gone, and her father was far away. She could only rely on herself now. She had no one else to trust.

She rose and opened the window to look at the small park below, pressing her face into the cool air. A bird flew down from the roof and onto one of the trees. If only she could fly off and leave this house behind her.

That wish brought a distinct hope to her heart, and her smile returned. For the past few years, the grief of her mother's loss, the seven years of war, and the separation from her father had numbed her. Her life was one of enduring, waiting for someone or something to return her life to normal. Nothing in her uncle's house or in London mattered to her. She could leave. She *should* leave.

Fully awake to the plans of her aunt and uncle, she realized she had almost been lulled into a marriage of convenience. If they were so eager to be rid of her, she would leave, just not the way they anticipated. She would no longer blindly obey and wait for a better day. Before she married, before she made any other decision, she would go to her father.

Mr. Wynn would return to Lisbon in a few weeks. All she had to do was convince him to take her with him. She smiled and, sitting at the pianoforte, sorted through the music until she found her father's favorite Scottish air.

CHAPTER 2

"I AM GOING FOR a walk. If either Sir Reginald or Lady Frances asks, Betty and I are taking a turn in the air," Margaret said to George. She tied her bonnet to give her shaking hands something to do.

"But miss… " George said, looking from Margaret to Betty and back. His brow was slightly creased, his mouth open.

"The door, please," Margaret said with a smile.

"Should I ask—" George twisted his gloved hands in front of him.

"Never mind, I shall open it myself."

The color drained out of George's face. He stepped quickly and opened the door.

Outside, Margaret released a shaky sigh. "There, Betty. I told you. Confidence—even pretended—wins the day." She pulled her shawl tighter. The cool morning air seeped into her clothes. The early hour and the overcast gray sky darkened the path. Margaret had planned their departure early enough to avoid Sir Reginald, but still at an acceptable hour. Yet no other ladies were about—only servants returning from errands and a few carriages clattering on the cobblestones. Squaring her shoulders, she reduced their pace. "There is nothing unusual about the two of us going on a walk."

"Oh, miss. I still don' like this. It's too risky. We could still take a turn roun' the square and return inside."

"That is exactly how we will begin. We will walk until we leave Hanover Square and find a coach on Regent Street. I estimate it will take about an hour to reach my father's shipping office near the docks."

"Consider, Miss. It's an undesirable par' of town. Who knows the type of men we might meet?"

"Betty, we will be fine." Margaret lifted her chin and smiled, but inwardly, she had many of the same doubts. Her actions were irregular, if not reckless. The part of town by the docks was known for unsavory elements. She shook her head to free herself from those thoughts. The inconvenience of traveling there, the risk to her reputation, her aunt and uncle's reprimand—it would be worth it to secure passage to see her father. She increased her pace.

Securing a coach had been harder than Margaret had anticipated. She tried to wave down a few and even stepped into the street, but all she got was mud splattered on her day dress. Still, after enlisting the help of a shopkeeper on Beak Street, she had to convince the driver to take them to Beaton and Wynn's Shipping Company on Adams Street. Yes, it was true that ladies did not visit the docks. Yes, her father's business was there. Yes, someone would meet her there. "I will pay you half now, if we can begin," she said, pulling open the strings of her reticule.

"O'course, miss. Pay me after. I just don't want a fine lady like yourself to be in trouble."

She thought she heard him mutter as he closed the door, "Or get *me* in trouble."

Margaret sank back against the seat but gave Betty a wide smile. "All will be well now."

Almost an hour later, the coach slowed.

"Do you wan' I should wait?" the driver asked, his face scrunched while looking up and down the street as he helped Margaret out of the coach.

"No, thank you." Margaret's voice cracked. She paid the driver and turned, nearly stepping on a slumped sailor sitting half on the sidewalk and half in the dirty street. He was evidently asleep or drunk—or both. Then looking over the sailor's head, she blushed. There she saw a half-dressed woman talking with a man.

"Miss Beaton!" A deep voice called from a window above her.

Looking up, Margaret could see Mr. Wynn's face, his forehead crinkled into tight lines, his mouth a heavy frown. Then he disappeared.

Margaret said to the driver, "We will be fine. Come, Betty." They walked up to the front door of the office. It opened before Margaret had a chance to knock.

"Come inside at once!" Mr. Wynn said.

Margaret stepped inside and curtseyed. Betty followed but kept her head down.

"Miss Beaton, I am shocked at your appearance here unaccompanied!"

"Mr. Wynn, I must protest!" Margaret tilted her head toward Betty.

"And you should apologize to your maid for endangering her as well."

"I?" Margaret said.

"Please, both of you, join me in my office." Mr. Wynn cut her off.

Margaret bit her lip and lifted her chin. "Come, Betty." Ascending the staircase, Margaret looked back at the room below; she noticed two other men staring at her and Betty, slack-jawed. The dark-haired man, clearly a gentleman, quickly recovered and nodded politely to her. His bearing was military. Perhaps he was one of the captains. She gave a polite nod.

The other, with bright red hair, a sailor by the looks of his clothing, bowed to Margaret but smiled widely at Betty and said, "Hello." His accent, and his flirtatiousness, revealed he was an Irish American.

Betty blushed and stepped behind Margaret. They followed Mr. Wynn up the stairs.

Mr. Wynn closed the door to the small wood-walled office. His angry expression had deepened. Margaret had not expected this reaction, but then again, she had not considered Mr. Wynn's feelings to begin with. Now, under the weight of his censure, she doubted the wisdom of asking for his help. Yet, he was her father's partner. He could be convinced. The memory of her father strengthened her. Besides, her experience with Sir Reginald and Lady Frances's daily disdain had uniquely prepared her for this encounter. She looked up at Mr. Wynn and smiled slightly.

"Miss Beaton, I ask again, why have you come to this part of town?"

"I thought it obvious," Margaret answered, staring straight into Mr. Wynn's blue eyes. "I came to see you."

Still frowning, he raised an eyebrow.

She raised one back.

The surprise on his face changed; he almost smiled. But he simply retrieved a plain wood chair for her and placed it across from his desk. Then he placed one for Betty closer to the window. The room was small but clean and in complete order. Everything in its place. She followed him with her eyes. When he sat behind his desk, the serious look had returned to Mr. Wynn's face, but he was no longer angry.

Margaret sat straight and held her hands in her lap. Before he could speak, she blurted, "I insist you take me to visit my father. The next sailing would be quite convenient."

"Miss Beaton—"

"It is of the utmost urgency."

"I cannot arrange it that quickly, and it is not convenient for your father's business. We would need to provide you with proper accommodations, meals—you would need to be… chaperoned." He rose and started to pace. "Not to mention the other risks. How do I face your father if you become ill, if we encounter inclement weather, or even—" He stopped and turned to her. "No, without your father's written consent, it is impossible."

She stood, holding her trembling hands. "Mr. Wynn, I sailed from London to Lisbon as a young girl. I did not suffer from illness. Actually, I quite enjoyed it. I am aware of the risks."

"You were with your parents."

"Yes, and now my mother is dead, and my father has been separated from me by war and duty, and I am about to be... I must see him."

Mr. Wynn stopped at the window. Looking out, he clasped his hands behind him.

Margaret could not see his face, could not read his expression. After a moment, she said in a quieter tone, "I have waited, patiently, for the world to return to what was normal and safe, to what it was before the war—waited for my father to come to me, waited for my life to begin again." Her voice cracked, but she swallowed back the tears and said even louder. "I will not wait anymore. I will not be pushed into a marriage of convenience without my father's guidance and intervention."

Mr. Wynn turned to gaze on her, clearly surprised by the revelation.

"If *you* will not take me to see him, I will book passage on another ship." She paused, but Mr. Wynn did not move.

Letting out an exasperated sigh, Margaret said, "Come, Betty. Someone along these streets will be willing to take my money for a passage to Lisbon."

Betty gasped and rose. Her face was very pale.

Margaret stepped toward the door, but Mr. Wynn said, "Please, wait."

His deep blue eyes sought hers. His brows pinched, and she saw concern, even pain. His boyish face looking at her so intently touched something inside her. She wanted to console him, to brush the hair off his forehead or caress his cheek. Her heartbeat increased. She wished she could ask for his story. She realized she was staring and dropped her eyes.

He blinked and motioned for her to sit. Leaning against his desk, he said, "I know something of loss. I will take you to your father, but with the following conditions." He twisted a locket ring on his left hand, then peered at her. "First, you must not come down here again. This is folly."

When she opened her mouth to speak, he raised his hand. She stopped.

"Second, I must gain the approval of your uncle and aunt." Again, before she could protest, he shook his head. "I know how to persuade them."

"Then you must pass on the secret," she said.

The smallest smile came back to Mr. Wynn's face. "You are incredibly like your father. So much so that we will never play cards."

Margaret laughed and stood up. "Oh, we will become friends, Mr. Wynn, you shall see. Any other conditions?"

His face paled. He looked down at his hands and cleared his throat. "Yes. You must be chaperoned while on board. Betty?"

Betty jumped to her feet. "Sir?" Her mouth was open and her eyes wide.

"Will you accompany Miss Beaton to Lisbon?"

"Sir?" She blinked, then turned to Margaret.

Margaret took her hand. "Betty, only if you wish to. I would never force—"

"O' course, miss; yes sir! I never dreamed—that is I would—I'm up in the boughs! Oh miss, pardon my cant, I'm that happy, though, no joke. Oh, sir, I'm not this talk'tive. I'm sure on board I'll be less—"

"Thank you, Betty. I know you will serve and protect Miss Beaton very well." Mr. Wynn gave Betty a real smile. Margaret tilted her head. She was grateful for his kindness to Betty but wondered what it would take to receive a smile like that.

"Miss Beaton," Mr. Wynn said, rising, his smile gone. "I will call you a carriage. Then, I will contact you at your uncle's home when I have more information."

"I depend on it, Mr. Wynn. Do you think, perhaps, that my visit here today could go unmentioned to my aunt and uncle? I do not ask you to lie, but if the subject is not broached… "

"Will they not ask where you have been all morning?"

"Most likely no, but Betty and I did go for a walk before the coach ride."

Mr. Wynn's brows pulled down. "I will not mention it." He bowed and left.

After he closed the door, Margaret heard his exasperated sigh, but her smile could not be held back.

Betty clasped her hands. "I can't believe my luck, miss!"

Margaret took Betty's hands. "It will be a great adventure." Then both girls began to laugh. Margaret twirled Betty around until they knocked a few papers and books to the floor. Laughing harder, they both dropped to pick them up. The door opened. Margaret froze, then rose to her feet.

It was not Mr. Wynn, come to disapprove of them, but the Irish American sailor.

"Yes?" Margaret asked.

The sailor eyed the room and moved around the desk to help Betty pick up the books and place them on the table. "Ladies, so ya are aware, we could all hea' ya dancin' downstairs. Mr. Beaton says to tell ya ladies that your carriage is here."

Betty stood ramrod straight. "We're not both ladies. Miss Beaton's a lady, as you can plainly see, compared to me—"

"But where I come from, a lady is judged by how she acts, so she is. You're both respectable ladies in me book." The sailor, hat in hand, looked directly into Betty's eyes.

Betty blushed deeply, but no smile came to her lips. "I know my place, sir. And I know flat'ery when I 'ears it."

"Good." The sailor beamed.

"Do I detect an Irish and American accent, Mr.—" Margaret stepped in front of Betty to interrupt the sailor, who was now staring at Betty.

He bowed slightly but rose to his full height, still a few inches shorter than Margaret. "Devine, Danny Devine. Yes, ma'am. I was born in Ireland, raised in Boston, and impressed into the British service durin' the war, so I was. But Mr. Beaton freed me, gave me a job, and I'm the best employee he has, I am."

"Thank you, then, for your service to my father."

"Yur… " Danny's shoulders dropped, and one hand smoothed his hair behind an ear.

"Betty, we should go."

"Miss Beaton, I beg your pardon." Danny held open the door. "I'm a blunderbuss, so's I've been tol', but I meant what I said about your father. If you need anything, it would be my pleasure to assist ya."

Margaret smiled at him. At least she had one friend in her father's London office.

Outside, Margaret watched Mr. Wynn pay the driver, give precise directions about the route he should take, and then turn to help Betty and Margaret into the coach.

Margaret leaned out the window and caught Mr. Wynn's eye. "Thank you, Mr. Wynn, for your kind attention to all these details."

"Miss Beaton," he said quietly, placing a hand on the window, "you must be more careful. Please do not travel in this manner again. If something were to happen… you do not know what men are capable of."

"Thank you." She had not expected such gentleness. She looked into his blue eyes. "I promise."

He stepped back and nodded to her, a slight smile returning. To the coachman, he said, "Drive on."

Margaret watched him return inside. He reminded her of her father, taking care of her transportation, seeing to every need. She sat back, the image of Mr. Wynn's face before her eyes, his concern when he had said *If something were to happen.* A small part of her heart expanded, existing for the first time.

She hoped to see that look from him again.

CHAPTER 3

"AH, THIS EVENING WILL be delightful after a month at sea with grimy, flea-bitten men." Foremaster tugged at his white gloves.

Joshua surveyed Foremaster and the ballroom beyond. His only verbal response to Foremaster was, "Hmph." Joshua would rather be swabbing moldy steerage compartments on the ship rather than be surrounded by the prim and proper London ton at a ball. Squaring his shoulders, he glanced again at Foremaster, grateful he did not have to face this ordeal alone.

Joshua trusted no man in the world as implicitly as Foremaster. They had come up through the ranks as midshipmen together, each earning the commission of Captain. Now working for Mr. Beaton, Foremaster was still a captain—by his own volition—and Joshua's first choice whenever he sailed. In fact, they were due to sail to Boston together next week. Unfortunately, Miss Beaton had interrupted those plans. Joshua tugged at his cravat.

A young lady glanced, or more precisely stared, at him as she passed.

Almack's. Joshua would never have guessed he would be standing in the most "sacred" of ballrooms in all of England today, let alone at any time in the next five years. Joshua exhaled loudly, drawing a raised eyebrow from Foremaster.

Sighing more quietly, Joshua took in the room: fine draperies, lighted chandeliers, and the ladies' swaying pastel gowns. At Almack's he stood among the London *ton* at its most refined, but he wished the swaying was from main deck of a ship with the motion of the crew pulling in the topsail. The orchestra located on a balcony above played a Scottish reel, but Joshua wanted to hear the shanties and calls of the sailors at work.

"Ah, a lady in pale blue. My favorite." Foremaster tipped his head in the direction of a dark-haired beauty.

"Remember our goal," Joshua muttered to his friend. He was still amazed that he had gained access to this exclusive ball. Using his grandfather's name and title, revealing details about his own increasing wealth, and, of course, Foremaster's good looks had done the trick, but having to justify his existence to Lady Castlereigh had been degrading.

"Lud, man, it is not a battle." Foremaster flashed a smile and nodded to a bejeweled mama and her simpering daughter who sauntered past them. "But, if I must turn spy, I shall have to get closer to the enemy."

Joshua groaned and looked askance at his friend's close-cut deep-blue coat. He had a military bearing, dark wavy hair, and classic features. Foremaster was a man to be reckoned with. He had chosen to continue as a captain for Mr. Beaton and Joshua's shipping company when many opportunities were laid before him. Foremaster's explanation? He loved the sea. Joshua surmised it was also a broken heart that kept Foremaster away from England most of the time.

Few men could hold their own against Foremaster on ship or in battle; even fewer at a ball. He was a great favorite with the ladies. Already, ladies' fans and heads were moving in his direction. Usually, the added attention that Foremaster brought would grate on Joshua. Tonight, though, most of Joshua's plan would depend on his friend's social abilities.

Joshua pulled his waistcoat straight. "Before I entertain Miss Beaton's request to take her to Lisbon, I need to know what I am getting myself—uh, getting us all—into. The crew will not like the idea of a woman aboard. Please help me ascertain what kind of people her aunt and uncle are. I will interview Miss Beaton. Yesterday, she had the element of surprise; tonight, I do."

"It took a good deal of courage and tenacity from her to come to the docks to find you." Foremaster did not try to wipe the smile off his face. He had been bringing up Miss Beaton's unannounced visit continually.

"Yes, but is she spoiled? Irritating? Foolish? I will not take a chance on folly." Joshua shook his head. "I promised to take her without fully considering all the consequences."

"Yes, you did. Very unlike you." Foremaster chuckled.

Joshua flushed a very unmanly shade of pink. He turned away from Foremaster to search the room. He did not realize he was scowling until he caught an older woman's eye. She sniffed at him and looked away.

Clearing his face and forcing the smallest of smiles, Joshua tried to look interested in the ball, the music, and the people in attendance. Internally, he was not as focused. Mr. Beaton had hinted that Lady Frances had a grudge against him, his wife, and his daughter, though he had not gone into detail. The older man was certainly anxious about Lady Frances matchmaking for Pearl—Margaret, as everyone else called her. This was getting confusing and annoying.

In fact, Joshua was irritated by everything. If only Maria Luisa was here on his arm, enchanting London as she had himself. If only he could hold her in his arms once again, see the enjoyment in her eyes as they danced.

Auburn hair. He followed the lady with his eyes, craning his neck. She turned. No, it was not Miss Beaton, but a different young lady—whose eye he had now accidentally caught. He bowed and moved away quickly. She was attractive, and he could reasonably seek introduction to her—to any young lady. But what would be the point? Since his own family had rejected him, why would he expect anyone here to accept him?

This evening would be longer than attending a court martial—his own! He tugged at the cuffs of his new blue coat. It was close-fitting, more so than he liked. New clothes always bothered him. He could not make them feel right, or make himself feel comfortable the first time he wore them.

Miss Beaton's visit the other day had completely confused him. He did not like being caught off guard. He liked the predictable. Orderly. Safe. At first, he conjectured her behavior was that of a spoiled debutante or of a terribly naïve girl who knew little of the world. How dare she risk coming practically alone to the docks? But her reasons had moved him. Being forced into marriage was reason enough, but it impressed him that she wanted to be reunited with her father. He understood. There were a few people Joshua would move heaven and earth to be with for one more day.

He tugged at his gloves. He admired Miss Beaton's ability to stand up to him but was also unnerved by it. That she was beautiful did not help. She did not look, in appearance, anything like Maria Luisa, except when she stared him down. However, Miss Beaton's joy when he had consented to take her to Lisbon had reminded him of Maria Luisa's happy personality. It had weakened his resolve.

Joshua wiped his brow and replaced his handkerchief. He was sweating—before dancing. He shook his head. He had a mission to accomplish. If Miss Beaton were a vain, spoiled, or conniving young lady, he would refuse to take her or avoid her during the voyage. If she were the opposite—as he hoped she was—he would weather any storm to take her to her father.

He dragged his right foot down the back of his left calf, trying to straighten the leg breeches he had on. While aware that the short pants showed off the athletic cut of his calves compared to the soft, weak men who passed him, he believed it ridiculous that the rules of Almack's required men to wear them. They all looked like lap dogs, waiting for any woman to scoop them up and carry them off.

"Come, Wynn, smile. You look as though we are headed into a sea battle against fire ships."

"That is exactly how I feel."

"Wait, I see the enemy, and he—or *she*—is ours." Foremaster ended with a chuckle. His slight smile only produced more tittering from nearby ladies.

Joshua moved to see Miss Beaton and her aunt, Lady Frances Colborne, walk to the middle of the room. Lady Frances was elegant, but Miss Beaton was stunning. She reminded him of a Greek goddess in her white dress. Her small rib cage—was that what ladies would call it?—was accented with a green ribbon, the same in her hair, the perfect color to set off its auburn color. She turned, and he could see her profile as he moved closer to her. Soft curls framed her brow, accentuating her bright eyes. Her cheeks were slightly flushed.

Around her neck was the beautiful pearl necklace which Joshua had delivered. He let out a breath. The uncle had permitted her to wear it. Good. Still, he could not pull his gaze away from her face until his view was blocked by a gentleman stopping to speak to Lady Frances and Miss Beaton. The man stepped back to acknowledge a friend.

From his profile, this gentleman wore a bright blue coat, floral waistcoat, and silver brocade breeches with matching heels and silver buckles. His posturing showed a desire to flaunt his apparel. When the man laughed, his forehead wiggled his hair, which had been combed up and curled about his head, adding two extra inches to his height. Here was the evening's lap dog.

"I know that man. Sir Edgar. Beaton requested I look him up on the last voyage. That cannot be her uncle," Foremaster said.

"No." Joshua paused. "I believe it is her intended."

Joshua thought he heard Foremaster murmur, "Poor girl," as they moved in her direction,

The man in question crossed to another group of younger similarly dressed and, without a doubt, empty-headed man.

"Lady Frances Colborne," Joshua said as he bowed. "Miss Beaton, may I introduce Captain William Foremaster?" It was bold, he knew, bordering on rude, to introduce Foremaster before ascertaining if the ladies wished for the introduction.

"Mr.… Wynn?" Lady Frances's smile faded as she suddenly recognized him from their previous encounter.

Foremaster interrupted and bowed. "Lady Frances, may I have the honor of this dance?" he asked, smiling broadly.

Joshua watched Lady Frances blush under Foremaster's stare.

"Sir, I had not intended to dance this evening—" She stopped as she noted Foremaster's head tilt toward her. "But I had not expected such an eager partner. Or a handsome one."

"I am honored," Foremaster said, extending his arm to her.

Joshua did not hear the end of the conversation as Captain Foremaster and Lady Frances were engulfed in the crowd.

"Miss Beaton, or am I to call you Miss Colborne? Either way, would you like to dance?"

Miss Beaton's face was divided between surprise and disbelief. Forehead crinkled and mouth slightly open, she asked, "What are you doing here?"

"I am asking you to dance. And it is becoming quite awkward." He raised an eyebrow.

She blushed but, beaming, added, "Yes, of course. I apologize… I was just surprised to see you here. You look very smart in that coat, though you continue to fiddle with it." She took his arm.

Joshua had prepared for many outcomes—from being trapped into vapid conversations, dancing with shallow young ladies, even being kicked out of Almack's altogether if his methods of finding information about Miss Beaton led to… misunderstandings.

What he was not prepared for was the warmth that spread up his arm from her gloved touch. Instinctively, he covered her hand with his own. He looked down. Hers was small and delicate and fit comfortably in his. Suddenly he was overcome with memories: he was back in Lisbon, holding Maria Luisa's hand. The yearning for her was overwhelming. He nearly dropped Miss Beaton's hand, but brought his arm back up.

She peered up at him. A small crease formed between her perfect brows.

Joshua took a deep breath. Relying on his military training, he kept his eyes forward and locked on joining the end of the forming dance line. Arriving, he faced Miss Beaton, but he kept his gaze above her head.

The music started. Joshua danced. It was not graceful, but it was correct. A few moments passed, and his breathing became normal. However, the beating of his heart had not calmed.

"Mr. Wynn?"

He was aware of Miss Beaton's voice. He glanced at her.

"You look pale. Are you well?"

Her countenance had changed from the surprise of earlier. Her brow creased, her eyes blinked a few times, and she pursed her lips. How long had it been since a woman had shown interest or concern for him?

"Yes, thank you." He tried to smile. It may have come out as a grimace. He rolled his shoulders. This mission was not about him; it was about Miss Beaton. He needed to regain control of his emotions. He needed to understand her, understand what he had gotten himself into.

"Do you come to Almack's often?" he asked her.

"Yes. I have come weekly for a few months."

"It appears most of the *ton* is here. Is there much gossip?"

"Yes. Often."

Her eyes were smiling as they continued the steps of the dance. What did that indicate?

"Would you like me to introduce you to Lady Herbert? She is known for being most informed and sharing the *on dit* quite liberally." She was scrunching the sides of her mouth closed.

Confound it. She was laughing at him.

"No, thank you. I… have little grace at small talk."

"You are more like my father than I expected." She smiled and turned with the dance.

Her father? Was he old? Unattractive to her? He was getting distracted again. He changed his tactics. "The man who conversed with you. Was that Sir Edgar?"

"Yes." Her smile disappeared. She broke off eye contact.

Blast. He had not intended to embarrass her. They danced in silence. He tried to remember the questions he had prepared, but the only ones he could remember now seemed slightly offensive to ask. Do you get seasick easily? Are you always this beautiful? Where else have you and your maid gone unaccompanied? Are you in love with Sir Edgar? How could you be in love with Sir Edgar?

"Are you enjoying London?"

Miss Beaton's question brought him back to the reality of his current situation. "Yes. I am happy to be back. It has been some time."

"And do you have family nearby?"

"Yes." Now he grew silent. Since the war ended, he had only spent a few days with his family. Their rejection of him had prevented his return. His grief pushed him on.

He shook his head. This had been a mistake. A dance with a beautiful lady was not conducive to his… interrogation was a harsh term, but that is how he had to view it. Keep it impersonal. They touched hands again. A tingling sensation now traveled to his chest. She smiled up at him. He flushed. How could he think when the steps of the dance were always bringing her back to him, to touch him? What was he thinking? He was attracted to her. *Tarnation!* He needed distance.

"Miss Beaton, may I take you on a drive tomorrow?" he blurted as the last strains of the dance faded. "My tiger can act as chaperone, or you may bring your maid, of course."

She hesitated, and he followed her gaze. Sir Edgar had joined Lady Frances.

Sir Edgar met Joshua's gaze, and though he displayed a bored, glazed-over look, Joshua felt that Sir Edgar was sizing him up. Let him. Joshua puffed out his chest more. Sir Edgar leaned in to Lady Frances and whispered something behind her fan. Miss Beaton saw it, too. Her grip on his arm tightened.

"Yes, you may," Miss Beaton said, her voice strong but emotionless. "Your man will be a sufficient chaperone. Thank you for the dance."

"Thank you." He released her hand. "I will call for you at three o'clock." He bowed to her and Lady Frances.

"Foremaster, I need some air."

"Come, Wynn. You have only danced one dance."

"Stay if you wish, but I will continue to gather information tomorrow."

Foremaster caught his arm. "Maria Luisa?"

"Yes," Joshua said. He did not want pity. He did not want to relive the past. He only wanted out. He bowed.

"Before you go, let me report. My dance with Lady Frances merely confirmed what you had surmised. They are selfish, proud people, but respectable. They intend to marry Miss Colborne, as they call her, to Sir Edgar. But I am invited to tea Friday, if that helps your cause. Evidently, Lady Frances has a niece—"

"Thank you," was all Joshua could muster.

MARGARET NOTED MR. WYNN'S exit. His grimace. He walked straight to the door without a look or a nod to anyone. Several ladies snapped their fans as he brushed past. He did lack social polish, but there was more to it. She was certain he had been distracted a few times while they danced. She wished she could ask him what made him alternatingly brusque and intriguing. She had seen his direct, business-like manner at his office. Today, she had seen him uncomfortable and, well, lost.

Yet there was something in his face, his touch. She smoothed her glove and turned her hand over. Mr. Wynn's touch during the dance had… well, she couldn't describe it. Her hand tingled, her heart raced, her face flushed when he—

"Do you not, Miss Colborne?" Sir Edgar's sing-song voice brought her attention back to his group of friends who had joined them. Before she could respond, he added, "You see, she does not."

The small group tittered.

Margaret smirked and tilted her head. The opening chords of the waltz began. She realized it was her dance with Sir Edgar, but he had asked her if she would rather talk than dance. Not very romantic, but neither was her absent-mindedness in his presence.

Sir Edgar started another story; Margaret did not pay attention to the details. Instead, she watched. His face was expressive when all eyes were on him; unfortunately, his nostrils flared and quivered like a flag waving in the wind when he laughed.

She studied her fan and considered. It was easy to lose the thread of Sir Edgar's ramblings. He was amiable, diverting, and a flattering dance partner, but while he communicated a great deal, very little of it contained any sensible information. She had not fallen in love with him, and worse, he did not exhibit any marked affection for her. She rubbed her temple with two fingers. She did not dislike Sir Edgar, but she had not seriously considered marrying him. She could not seriously consider it now.

Margaret looked again toward the door. Why was she drawn to Mr. Wynn? He was overly serious and irritatingly sensible. Yet, she had also glimpsed a tender, vulnerable part of his soul. One that he hid. She could not seriously consider a man who was distant and difficult. Could she?

Tapping her fan on her palm, Margaret brought herself out of her reverie. She intended to fall in love only once and to love that man completely. Therefore, she expected much of a man she could adore, trust, idolize. She longed for a passionate, lifelong mutual devotion. Age, illness, death—nothing and no one could break it. Just like her mother and father. A man who would not leave her either to the care of her aunt and uncle, as her father had been forced to do. Or to an evening in the company of Sir Edgar without the hopes of a second dance, as Mr. Wynn had just done.

Laughter again. Sir Edgar's nostrils merrily waved. She clasped her hands in front of her dress. She had to be certain to choose the right man with whom to fall in love. Sir Edgar was absolutely not him, but neither was Mr. Wynn.

⸙HAPTER 4

"I DISAPPROVE. YOU MAY not go." Lady Frances put her pen down. She was in the middle of answering invitations—a task she enjoyed and made Margaret sit through.

Margaret noticed the Pomona green dress her aunt had chosen; it matched her eyes and the wallpaper in the drawing room where they sat. Everything her aunt did was calculated to create a grand effect. Margaret respected the command her aunt had of every situation. Elegant but formidable. If only she had kind eyes.

Margaret began again. "Mr. Wynn is a respectable gentleman and my father's business associate." Margaret tried to keep her voice even. Since she had expected resistance, she had waited until the last moments to announce her intention of accompanying Mr. Wynn, and she had entered the room already dressed in her blue-gray pelisse, carrying her matching muff.

"Precisely. Any business he has to discuss should be with Sir Reginald or with your intended, Sir Edgar."

"But Sir Edgar is not my intended. He has not asked—"

"A formality—"

"And I am a formal young lady."

"Do not contradict me in that flippant manner."

"I apologize." Margaret looked down at the carpet. Perhaps she was going to lose this battle.

"Mr. Wynn," Henshem announced.

Both ladies looked toward the door.

Mr. Wynn bowed and began to speak. "Lady Frances, I have arranged to speak with Sir Reginald tomorrow about some business of Mr. Beaton's. However, I do need to ascertain some facts from Miss Bea... er... Colborne as well. I hope you will allow me to both fulfill my duty to Miss *Colborne's* father and take in the sunshine of Hyde Park at the same time. I rarely have the pleasure of seeing London."

He smiled, but Margaret thought his lips were more pained by the effort.

Lady Frances turned over an envelope and paused to read the address before regarding Mr. Wynn. Margaret cringed at her aunt's rudeness.

"Mr. Wynn." Lady Frances putting the envelope down. "You may take my niece out into the sunshine. I can see how having a pretty young lady to display as you ride is an asset. Please, however, do not forget that she has, as you are aware, an understanding with Sir Edgar."

Margaret was seething, but when she saw the dismissive wave of Lady Frances's hand to her, she said, "Thank you," and moved toward the door. She glanced briefly at Mr. Wynn's face and was a bit shocked at the tight-lipped anger which flashed on it. But when he met her eyes, his face softened.

"Miss Beaton, er, Colborne, that is... Miss."

"Danny, how good to see you again. Are you our tiger? You do look smart."

"Yes, Miss. Wore me church clothes today, I did. And a fine pair of horses we rented today for the curricle." He was holding the reins and stroking one of the horse's necks.

"They are." Margaret wished she could pet them as well.

After helping Margaret in and seeing that the carriage blanket was tucked by her feet, Danny sat in the groom's seat behind, which faced the opposite direction. Mr. Wynn sat by her side, holding the reins, and clicked for the horses to begin.

"Lovely weather." Margaret had watched the rain earlier, fearing it would prevent her from leaving the house. She was thrilled it had stopped.

"This drizzle? No sunshine? Gray and cold! Londoners have low expectations of the weather." Mr. Wynn said.

"Pardon me, Wynn, uh, sur." Danny's voice came from the back.

"Danny, you have something to add? Say it." Mr. Wynn shifted in his seat.

"I was only goin' to say how lovely a day it is *whenever* one is able to ride out with a lovely lady. And Boston has more 'weather' than London any day of the year, it has."

"Thank you, Danny," Mr. Wynn said. He leaned toward Margaret. "This is lovely weather for a ride out with you. I apologize that my manners are more accustomed to sailors than lovely ladies. I was just comparing the weather here to that of Lisbon."

"Oh, yes, I love Lisbon. The time I spent there was glorious. Tell me, are the almond trees in bloom?"

"Just starting as we left," Mr. Wynn said. "My favorite is the jacarandas in May. What else do you remember about Lisbon?"

Margaret chatted happily about Lisbon—the food, the people, the language, the music, the flowers—until they turned onto Rotten Row of Hyde Park. Realizing she had talked most of the time, she paused and smoothed her dress. "Thank you," she said.

"For what?" came Mr. Wynn's equally quiet reply.

"For letting me talk. For being… kind. For taking me to the park. I do not go very often. My aunt and uncle, as well as Sir Edgar, do not enjoy it. Fresh air annoys them. But I used to come with Papa and Mama. And then only with Mama. And then… " Margaret trailed off and, looking out to the left, was lost in the memory of her mother's face.

A minute later, she glanced up and caught him looking at her very intently.

"Would you mind telling me about your mother?" he asked.

Margaret beamed. "I would not mind. No one has asked about her for years. In fact, I would love to talk about how my parents met since you claim you will never play cards with me. Father was older and already a captain when they met in London at a ball. During their first dance, she was elated. She described dancing on air and swore her feet never touched the floor.

"A few days later, he arrived at a card party to which my mother had also been invited. At cards, she was his opponent. As she tells the story—told, I mean—she beat him twice in a row. He was smitten, and he began to call on her. Unfortunately, my grandparents wanted my mother to marry… differently. But she was too much in love." Margaret smiled to herself.

"Mother was soft-spoken and gentle with me. She corrected me when I needed it, but I never doubted her love for me. During our separation from Father, she consulted me and relied on my opinion. I miss that. I miss her."

When she looked at Mr. Wynn, she realized he had been studying her intently during her story. A little embarrassed, she changed the topic. "And what of your family?"

Mr. Wynn cleared his throat, sat up straighter, and said, "My grandfather was the Marquess of Thrushford; my father was his youngest son. Fortunately, my father inherited a living from his mother. I have two siblings. My older brother will receive that inheritance upon my father's death, and my sister is married. As a younger son, I needed a profession, and I chose the sea. My grandfather was willing to purchase my commission. Shortly after, he died."

"You admired your grandfather?" Margaret asked.

Mr. Wynn nodded, but looked straight ahead. Perhaps her question was too personal. Mr. Wynn grew quiet.

"Yes, very much," he said.

Another pause followed. Margaret listened to the clip-clop of the horses' shoes. She waved at some acquaintances of her aunts while stealing a glance at Mr. Wynn. Eventually, she asked, "How old were you when you went to sea?"

"I was twelve—"

"Twelve!" Margaret exclaimed. "How difficult for you."

"Not at all. While I did miss my parents, I had already been at school five years. At sea, I found education, physical exertion, and true friendship in the service. On board ship, there is order, but there is also a freedom which I cannot describe."

"I loved the colors of the sea. I was ten when we came to London, and on the voyage, I used to pretend the sea was a beautiful young girl whose emotions could change the color of the water around us. Blue-green when she was happy or playful. Choppy and white peaked when angry. Murky gray when sad or sleepy. I am sure it merely reflected how I felt. I was a handful on board." She laughed and then he did.

"Have you outgrown that, do you think?" Mr. Wynn was holding back a laugh.

"Oh yes, you will not even know I am on board—if my aunt and uncle agree to let me go." She bit her lip, not wanting to focus on the knot that formed in her stomach each time she worried if she would be allowed to sail. "You miss the ocean. I can tell. What happened next? You were still young when war broke out."

"We were actually talking about you, Miss Beaton."

"But you are so much more interesting," she said, smiling.

JOSHUA'S HANDS WERE SWEATY. He had not anticipated how easy a conversation would be with Miss Beaton. And it made him nervous. Or excited. And excitement and attraction were not what he was anticipating, or wanting.

She was different from other young ladies, the ones he usually avoided even before he had met Maria Luisa. Now, his pulse quickened as she smiled at him. Her curls bounced with the motion of the carriage and the brush of the breeze. She smelled of flowers. He had to regain control of the situation. Of himself, actually.

"May I ask how… your mother was received when you returned?" he asked.

The smile on Miss Beaton's face faded. He chided himself for that.

"As Father must have told you, or you surmised, my parents' marriage did not receive my grandfather's blessing. My parents eloped. Before the war, we lived in Lisbon with Father, where I was born. I loved the warm winters, the soft rains, the dry summers. One's childhood always seems rosy, perhaps, but mine was idyllic in every way. Father taught me to swim in the ocean."

"My tutor taught me to swim in a lake near our home. I was terrified. The reeds near the shore tickled my legs, but I was sure they were fish ready to nibble."

Miss Beaton laughed. "Not a very promising start for a sailor."

"No, indeed. What else did your father teach you?"

"Occasionally, we caught fish for dinner. In fact, we fished my last morning in Lisbon. I had not known of the growing conflict between France and England. Later that day—I was ten— father came rushing in, calling on all of the servants to pack our things. My mother was not as surprised as I was, but I remember the sadness in her eyes. I was fearful of leaving Lisbon, of my father leaving us. We sailed the next day, November 29th, 1807, with so many other ships choking the harbor. It felt as if all of Lisbon were fleeing."

Joshua had not been able to look away as Miss Beaton told her story. She looked directly into his eyes, but did not focus on him. A tear was forming in her eye.

Suddenly, the memory engulfed him—Maria Luisa's touch on his arm, the pleading in her eyes, the last touch of her fingertips as he had rushed out the door.

"Mr. Wynn?" Miss Beaton had leaned forward and lightly touched his knee.

He snapped his head up and jerked the reins. The horses pulled, and it took some effort for him to regain control.

"I apologize. I mean, Miss Beaton, should we walk for a while?"

"Oh, I would like that indeed."

A few moments later, after handing the reins to Danny, they were walking side by side. The cool February air cleared his mind. Though the trees were bare and just a hint of sun broke through the fog, the path was crowded. He shivered once. He longed for Lisbon's temperate climate.

Miss Beaton was constantly nodding and acknowledging passersby. Joshua had hoped that walking side by side would lessen her impact on him, but while that had occurred, he had lost her attention—or at least had to share it.

He had not known her for very long, but her conduct, her openness about her parents, her behavior all convinced him that he could trust her on the ship, that he could take her without much risk. He glanced at her and realized that he *wanted* to take her to Lisbon, to restore her to her father. Someone should be happily reunited at the end of this war. He could not do that for Maria Luisa, but he could do that for Miss Beaton.

"Miss Beaton, I intend to speak with your uncle tomorrow and present my best case for taking you back to your father. How would you phrase your argument to him?"

"Oh, thank you," she said, smiling and blushing deeply as she sought his eyes. She laughed a little. "I thank you for asking. My opinion has rarely been sought by my aunt and uncle. Though it is best not to mention that. I do not mean to sound ungrateful." She fidgeted with her reticule.

"No, it would be best to avoid mentioning that information." He paused. "And your trip to the docks."

She looked up at him, and the tension in her brow relaxed. She laughed. "I see you tease me. So many others do not."

He waited for her to continue and noted how her lips pursed as she thought. They were smooth and pink. He studied his shoes.

"Let me think. Sir Reginald. I would appeal to his sense of honor. He believes in all that is good as a gentleman but suffers from the prejudices of our day. Still, I think he will honor my father's request, if you phrase it that way."

"I am all too aware of the prejudices of our day, but I am glad to know that Sir Reginald will act honorably."

"Mr. Wynn," Miss Beaton began, but then paused.

"Yes," he said.

"Thank you for sharing about my father the other day. I do truly want to know how he is, but why did my father stay behind in Lisbon? Why did he not come for me himself?"

"Miss Beaton, your father… " He paused.

She tilted her head and stopped. "What of my father?"

He had almost mentioned her father's illness, something Mr. Beaton had made him promise to not do. He shook his head. "Your father thought it best to let you decide if you wanted him to come. But you have decided to go to him instead."

He knew his words made no sense. She dropped her head and was silent. She did not find his answer satisfactory either.

"I am tired. Would you please take me back?" she asked.

"Of course." He signaled to Danny. The trip back was silent. Joshua could not think of anything to say, and Miss Beaton had no more questions. Even Danny realized the mood of the outing had changed and remained quiet.

The carriage stopped in front of the Colborne's house, but Joshua did not move. "Miss Beaton, we were interrupted the other day by your uncle before I was able to give you a second gift from your father."

Her eyes grew wide, and her lips parted slightly in surprise. Joshua had to look away, stunned again by her beauty. He withdrew a book from his satchel. "It is not as costly as the last, but I believe it is your mother's journal."

"Then it is more precious." She held out her hands. Turning the book over, she pressed it to her heart. "You cannot know what it means to have her words again. To hear her again."

Joshua just nodded, longing for such a keepsake from Maria Luisa. "Thank you, Miss Beaton," Joshua jumped down and then helped her exit the carriage.

"Thank you." She placed her hand on his forearm, gently pressing it. A warmth spread to his heart.

She turned to go, but he caught her arm.

She gazed at him, surprised.

"I will not fail you. I will take you to your father in Lisbon."

"Thank you. I believe you." She gave him a smile and pressed her gloved hand on top of his.

CHAPTER 5

MARGARET LAY IN BED, tucking the light blue coverlet around her and pulling the candle on the nightstand closer. It formed a circle of light near her head in the otherwise darkened room. She had barely kept her countenance during dinner, she was so excited—though she was sure Lady Frances had noticed. Her aunt probably assumed it was the result of spending time with Mr. Wynn, which it was not. Well, not entirely. It was the anticipation of reading her mother's journal—an item which she had sneaked up to her room after the carriage ride, hiding it safely under her pillow.

Finally, in the privacy that night time afforded her, she opened it. Her hands shook a little as she turned the first few pages, revealing a letter written in her mother's hand and addressed to her.

August 23rd, 1811

Dearest Daughter, my Pearl,

I am writing to you as you sleep here next to me. Since my illness has worsened, you have not left my side but for a few moments each day for the past week. Though I worry about your health, it has cheered me to wake and see you nearby. I am grateful for your devotion.

I know that I do not have long to live, and it is unbearable to think that I will be leaving you. There is so much to say, so many conversations to have—not only at present but also in the future.

My own mother's passing left a void in me. I believed she would have tempered my father and brother's reaction to my marrying your father. I wished for her when you were born, when you had fever and ague, when you took your first steps, when you had your first dancing lessons. You oftentimes remind me of her. Your smile and the tilt of your head. How I wish you had known her.

I am sending this journal and my pearls to our London lawyer for safekeeping. Your father will collect them in time and give them to you. The pearls have been a sore subject for your aunt and uncle. They were part of my inheritance—the only part I took as a remembrance of my mother.

These pearls will enhance your physical beauty, and I would love to see you wear them to your first ball, but I hope the journal will be the more valuable of the two gifts.

I wrote it when I met your father and eloped with him. I hesitate to give it to you. Perhaps you may find I was foolish when I was young. But we all are, especially when we are in love. Also, I fear I may have judged Lady Frances too harshly in it. Why she would have ever been jealous of me, I could never account.

I give you this journal because I want you to have the benefit of my experience when you are old enough to be court-ed—when you start your search for your own happiness. Choose for yourself with whom and how you will be happy. You are naturally a pleasant and pleasing child, but do not put another's wishes before your own in the most important decisions of your life.

I did find my happiness, with your father and with you. You both have my undying love. I hope your separation from him will only be for a few months. That is our plan, if all is well in Lisbon. I know that my brother and Lady Frances may be difficult to please, but I know they will look after you. I also hope they will be kind to you. You are most deserving of love and kindness because you impart both so freely.

If there was anyone else to leave you with, I would send you to them, but I must hope that my family will care for you.

I love you, my darling, sweet daughter. God willing, I will watch over you from heaven and be reunited with you when your wonderful and happy life concludes.

Until then, all my love for all your days—

Your devoted, Mother

Margaret's tears flowed freely by the end. She reread the letter through blurry eyes. In her head, she could hear her mother's voice— her tone and cadence. Her mother could not have realized that four years later, Margaret would still be living with her uncle and aunt, who could barely tolerate her. This had always puzzled Margaret; why did they resent her so?

Margaret rolled over on her side and curled up. Her heart, awake with the heaviness of loss, sank in her chest. Placing the letter and journal aside and blowing out the candle, she turned into her pillow and sobbed.

CHAPTER 6

"MR. WYNN," THE BUTLER announced and held the door for Joshua.

Joshua entered Sir Reginald's library and bowed. Sir Reginald was seated behind his large mahogany desk with bookshelves reaching to the ceiling. The leather-bound books were in perfect order, so much so that Joshua wondered if any had been opened in the past decade.

Sir Reginald, motioning for Joshua to sit, continued examining some documents on his desk using a quizzing glass, which was nearly impossible because his starched collar points and elaborate cravat made moving his neck improbable if not painful. To compensate, Sir Reginald peered down his hawk-shaped nose at the papers below.

Noting the rudeness, Joshua grinned. He had anticipated this treatment. While waiting, he studied Sir Reginald. Knowing his opponent's tactics would give him an advantage in negotiations.

A minute later Sir Reginald looked up.

"Thank you for seeing me, Sir Reginald." Joshua looked directly at him.

"Yes." Sir Reginald placed the papers aside and folded his hands on his desk. Raising his monocle, he peered at Joshua for a moment.

Joshua tightened his lips to swallow a chuckle. If Sir Reginald meant to intimidate him, it was having the opposite effect. The remaining tufts of white hair puffed up on the top and sides combined with his eyeball enlarged by the quizzing glass gave Sir Reginald the appearance of a parakeet after having fluffed its feathers.

"What business do you have, sir?" Sir Reginald asked.

"Mr. Beaton charged me with delivering a letter to you. If I am correctly informed by Mr. Beaton, he revealed to you the true nature of his illness but asked that neither you nor I reveal it to his daughter."

Sir Reginald pulled the letter from the bottom of his stack and began to re-read it. "That is correct. Has he seen a doctor? Is he certain that he is… dying? It is the sugar sickness?"

"Mr. Beaton kept his illness from me for a while, but I believed him when he explained the nature of it. I know he has sought medical attention."

"But he should have come to London, to our doctors."

"He is not well enough to travel. It is affecting his ability to walk now. Instead, his daughter has expressed a desire to go to him."

At this Sir Reginald shifted his weight. "She has not expressed it to me."

"Have you asked her?"

"I am not in the habit of being questioned. What matters more to me than the foolish inclinations of a young lady is Mr. Beaton's assenting to her dowry upon her marriage, which was all that was necessary to compensate my wife's nephew for her lack of, shall we say, breeding through her paternal line. Now, he is assured of her worth. She will be well provided for after her marriage."

Joshua gripped the sides of his chair. He could barely keep from blurting out that no woman's value could ever be measured in money, or to defend Mr. Beaton, a common Scot by the *ton's* standards but a fine man. Better in some ways than his own father. But Joshua kept his silence. Since Joshua had also been accused of only pursuing Maria Luisa for her fortune, he knew it was a sore spot for him.

"Travel to Lisbon is risky," Sir Reginald said, pursing his lips. "But she could travel with her husband after their June wedding. That might be best. Sir Edgar could learn about his wife's inheritance. I believe some of the business interests will be left to her husband?"

Joshua shifted in his seat. He knew it was the wrong time to protest Miss Beaton's being forced into an arranged marriage. Instead, he used Miss Beaton's advice. "As gentlemen, society would expect us to reunite a young lady with her ill father—if it can be done safely. The circumstances are not ideal, I grant you, but it is his dying wish and her duty to care for him." Joshua paused to let his words sink in. "As to the risk, I believe her safety and proper accommodations can be assured; it is the honorable course of action. We are gentlemen who understand the world, eh, Sir Reginald?"

Sir Reginald placed the letter down and folded his hands. "Yes, I believe she should return to see him, her father… under certain conditions. I believe we need Lady Frances's counsel in this matter." He rose and pulled the bell.

While Sir Reginald conferred with the footman, Joshua remembered Mr. Beaton's words before he had left.

Joshua stood in Mr. Beaton's office staring out the bow window at the bay. The water glinted with the morning sun. The tide was rising, and he would have to catch it if they were to sail this morning.

Mr. Beaton raked his hand through his graying hair and said loudly, "Joshua, my good man. You find my daughter, Pearl, and tell her to her face that she is the most beloved daughter in all the wurld!" He turned and retrieved a mahogany box from his desk and handed it to Joshua. "I am sending her a gift for her wedding and hope she will wear them with pride. They were her mother's, kept carefully away from her avaricious sister-in-law."

Joshua carefully placed the box in his satchel. "I will hand deliver these to her the moment I land, as requested."

"Also, deliver this, please. It is her mother's journal, written during the time she and I fell in love. She intended Pearl to have it when it was time for her to choose a husband. I am a bit embarrassed when I read how well my wife thought of me. It was then that I first met Lady Frances and

Sir Reginald. I have no proper opinion of that woman." He slammed his hand on his desk. "Which is why I put you on your guard with them. It is a personal score which Lady Frances wishes to settle, and my Pearl may bear the brunt of it."

He watched Beaton twist his wedding ring, which he still wore even as a widower—a habit Joshua knew something about. Then Mr. Beaton exclaimed, "I have to know right away if she is happy." Mr. Beaton sank into a chair. "I should never have left her. I should have brought her here with me."

Joshua shifted his weight and shook his head. "The world here was on fire. She would not have been safe. I am sure you made the right choice for your daughter."

Sighing, Mr. Beaton extended the parchment to Joshua. "You find out what this posy-smelling, lace-ruffled popinjay is up to."

"Yes, I will discover what kind of man Lord Edgar is—and his intentions."

"I meant my brother-in-law, Sir Reginald!" he bellowed. "But of course, figure out how that stuffed brocaded-waist shirt, namby-pamby fop of a macaroni intends to make my daughter happy."

"You have met her intended?"

"No, but my initial guess was confirmed by Foremaster on his last return."

Lady Frances arrived a minute later, dressed fashionably in golden hues yet not overdone. The beauty of her youth had not all faded, evident in the pains she took to accentuate her pale skin and honey-blonde hair. She greeted her husband and Joshua with the same amount of warmth, though her husband with much more respect. Her manner was commanding, but her eye was discerning. She looked at Joshua expectantly as she sat.

Joshua took his seat. Mr. Beaton had correctly described both Sir Reginald and Sir Edgar, but Mr. Beaton had incompletely captured the depths of Lady Frances. He found her to be the most formidable of the three.

She listened to Joshua's proposal with a bored but almost benev-
olent look.

"Absolutely not." Lady Frances did not raise her voice, but the force
behind it was clear. "If traveling by sea were not dangerous enough,
Portugal is still in a state of unrest. Though General Beresford has
been doing his best to bring order and civility, the locals have not been
reasonable enough to comply."

Joshua's mouth dropped open in surprise. He had not expected Lady
Frances to care about events beyond the drawing rooms of London.
He saw that Sir Reginald's mouth was also agape.

"Do not look so surprised. I read the newspaper," was all the
response Lady Frances gave.

"Then you perhaps would appreciate a first-hand account," Joshua
interrupted. "The people of Portugal would be much better suited if
Beresford showed some compassion and helped them to rebuild—"

"Order, civility, obedience—these must come first in any society.
Your questioning British authority leads me to doubt whether you are
the gentleman best suited to sail my niece anywhere," Lady Frances
said quietly.

Joshua realized that Lady Frances was needling him, waiting for
him to prove to her that he was not a gentleman. Swallowing his anger,
he decided to meet "the enemy," as it were, with a different approach.

"My grandfather, Lord Thrushford, taught me to never disagree
with a lady." He smiled at Lady Frances.

"And is your father now Lord Thrushford?" Lady Frances asked.

"No, that title belongs to my uncle. But you are correct: order,
civility, and obedience were many of the lessons that my naval career
instilled in me and allowed me to be promoted to captain. Since I
was paid off and have retired my commission, those lessons have
contributed to my current success."

Lady Frances peered down her nose and sighed. Joshua had no
doubt that she had already researched his past.

Now for his final argument. "My grandfather also taught me the value of family. Miss Colborne needs to see her father before he dies. To that end, we sail in two days. I will make any accommodations on the ship necessary to allow her and her maid to travel in comfort and safety. I have navigated this course many times and can guarantee her safe delivery to her father."

"Yes," Sir Reginald said, as much to Lady Frances as to Joshua. "It is her dying father's wish. As a gentleman, I must honor it."

Lady Frances's mouth became a tight line. She thought before turning to Joshua. "I see you have wisely kept her father's condition from Margaret. We have as well. There is no need to distress her. She is rather emotional at times. You must promise not to reveal it during the voyage."

Joshua was taken aback. He had not expected conditions. "I believe she should have been told from the first, but out of respect for her father, I—"

"Precisely." Lady Frances interrupted. "Out of respect for her father, and for us, you will promise."

"Yes." Joshua's shoulders sagged. He hated the idea of keeping secrets from Miss Beaton about her father. Family relationships were important to him. More so after Maria Luisa's death and the loss of his relationship with his father. If he could prevent a similar tragedy for Miss Beaton, it might help assuage his feelings of loss and helplessness.

"I have another condition." Lady Frances's smile grew. It reminded Joshua of a cat who had just caught its prey.

Joshua's eyes narrowed. "Yes?"

"In order to protect Margaret's reputation from those who are... less than worthy, Sir Edgar will accompany her to Lisbon. Besides, it is only proper for him to meet his future father-in-law before the wedding." Lady Frances smiled.

CHAPTER 7

"SIR EDGAR? TO JOIN me on my voyage to see my father in Portugal?" Margaret blurted this out, partly from her own incredulous surprise and partly because she hoped hearing how ridiculous this sounded might change her aunt's mind. Margaret sank into the chair by the dressing table. Betty stood at attention at the side of the bed where she had been laying out clothing to be packed for the voyage.

"Moderate your tone, Margaret, or you will not travel at all." Lady Frances walked to the bed, inspecting the clothing laid out on it—dresses, shawls, spencers, her riding habit, and pelisse. Margaret loved how their colors blended together like a flower garden.

"Why are you packing your winter gowns as well? Lisbon is more temperate this time of year," asked her aunt, tilting her head.

Margaret bit her lip. She had lived in Lisbon and knew the weather better than her aunt. "I believe it will be cold on the ship." Margaret hoped this accurate statement would keep her from further questions. She had hoped to take most of her belongings, even some of her music, to Lisbon since she planned on never returning to London, at least not to this house.

"No, you will only have room for half of these," Lady Frances said.

"Yes, Lady Frances." Margaret knew she would have to leave some of her belongings behind. But not her most important ones. She eyed her pillow, which safely concealed the journal.

Margaret had been watching Betty pack since they had received word early that afternoon that they would both be sailing to Lisbon. It was hard to tell which one of them was more giddy or more terrified. Their easy laughter and banter had been interrupted by Lady Frances's rare visit to Margaret's rooms.

"As your intended, Sir Edgar will accompany you. He will provide civilized company for you during the journey, protect you on the voyage—both morally and physically if necessary."

Margaret bit the tip of her tongue hard to check her laughter. She imagined Sir Edgar trying to protect anyone physically, and the image only increased her desire to laugh.

Lady Frances moved to the windowsill to inspect for dust. "And he will meet your father. He must be made aware of your... situation. How common your father is. Let us hope he does not reject you in the end."

Margaret bristled at this portrayal of her father. "I hear that Sir Edgar has had his own... problems with rejection."

Lady Frances looked at Margaret, her cheeks flushed a slight pink. "I have taught you to not pay attention to gossip. Sir Edgar is a well-educated, well-mannered gentleman who deserves respect and admiration, especially from someone with your background. I do not understand how you could object when Sir Reginald and I have gone to such trouble. I have personally guided your steps in society, attended to your education in dance, languages, and music, and all the thanks I wish for is your respectable behavior and *appropriate* marriage. It is time you take your place in society as a Colborne. Now that the time has come for you to marry, well, I find you are less grateful and more peevish than ever."

Margaret looked down at her folded hands and drowned out the rest of the lecture. She had heard that Sir Edgar had been refused last season by two ladies of good character and families. Why, she was not sure, but it explained Lady Frances's efforts to repair any damage to her family's name and Uncle Reginald's political career by foisting him on her.

Instead, Margaret's mind settled on a powerful image. Margaret could see her father standing on the dock with open arms. She was running down the gangplank to him. Whatever she had to endure, it would be worth it for that moment. "Yes, Lady Frances. You are right. I am grateful to be going to Lisbon." Margaret bowed her head.

Lady Frances stopped talking and stood blinking. Margaret expected to be chided for interrupting, one of Aunt Frances's pet peeves. It did not come.

Lady Frances leaned over to glimpse her hair in the dressing table mirror. "Your conduct during the voyage will reflect directly on myself, Sir Reginald, Sir Edgar, and your father, which is why Sir Edgar *must* join you. It is not proper for you to go aboard a ship full of men with only your maid. Therefore, I expect you to wait each morning in your cabin until Sir Edgar comes to you. You may not appear on the deck unless you are in his company. The less you mingle with the officers, the better. They are not, for all their wealth, true gentlemen. The sea, Naval service—it brings them into the company of so many common and coarse men that it destroys their natural respect for and appreciation of good company."

Margaret turned her head, indignant at Lady Frances's estimation of Mr. Wynn. She found him a little blunt perhaps, but he had always acted as a true gentleman would.

"Margaret, pay attention. I will know how you act on this journey."

"Sir Edgar will eagerly report—"

"No, I would not ask him. It would be beneath him; besides, he will be busy entertaining you. But I will know. I have made great sacrifices for this family, for your uncle's family name. And I am never thanked properly. Mark me, you will not bring scandal to us without suffering the consequences. Also, I have learned recently that Mr. Wynn has a… past. To that end, I do not want you to become friendly with him. He is your father's employee, nothing more. Now, I will leave you to your packing."

"Yes, Lady Frances."

Margaret watched her turn toward the door. Now was the time to ask. "But, please, may I have my pearls, the ones my father sent me? He will expect to see me wear them." Margaret hoped that her indifferent tone would fool Lady Frances. Margaret wanted with all her heart to wear her mother's pearls, to hold in her hand something of her mother's. She had only been allowed to wear them to Almack's but had had to return them that very night to Sir Reginald's keeping.

"The pearls? They were actually a gift from your grandfather and were meant to stay in the family. I had not—hmm. Perhaps you are right. We do not want to upset your father." Lady Frances paused. "I shall put them in Sir Edgar's luggage. They are too valuable for you to keep track of. There are thieves on board every ship, mark my words."

Margaret's heart dropped a little. At least the pearls would be on the ship. It would not be too difficult to retrieve them from Sir Edgar once at sea. "Yes, Lady Frances. One more thing, please. May I have my pin money for the next two months before I go?"

"Whatever for?"

"For when I am in Lisbon."

"Oh, well, you will only be there a month. I believe your father can provide for you during that time."

"Yes, but it is my mother's money which I inherit—"

"Not until you are nineteen." Lady Frances tossed her head.

"Which is the end of this year."

"Enough. Perhaps one month's advance. I do not want you begging Sir Edgar for money. I will not be embarrassed. I shall have Sir Reginald give it to you before you leave for the ship."

Margaret shook her head as her aunt left. As if she would ask Sir Edgar for anything. And Mr. Wynn was her father's partner, not his employee.

Margaret smiled at Betty, who had started folding the dresses again. She wondered if her aunt had tried to convince Betty to spy. "Betty, what do you think my aunt meant about keeping an eye on things?"

"I dunno know, miss. Purhaps she is paying someone. She told me I'll lose my position if your reputation is sullied." Then Betty winked. "But she won't pay me extra. I'm lucky to be allowed the opportunity 'to travel with your betters.'" Betty ended by mimicking Lady Frances.

"You have an ear for voices." Margaret laughed. She was glad to be rid of Lady Frances's dictatorial manner and heavy conversation.

"What's Lisbon like, miss? Does it rain as much as 'ere?"

"Oh, Lisbon is beautiful." Margaret stood and walked to the bed, smoothing the pile of ribbons. "You've never seen the sun shine so much. It does rain, but it is warmer. And the plants and flowers are everywhere. It has rolling hills and is close to the sea. I loved it as a child."

"But is it safe, miss? Lisbon, I mean? All I've heard is Bonypart's war destroyed it."

"Oh, it is safe. You will see, Betty. Do not fret." Margaret pursed her lips. She needed Betty to be willing to accompany her, but she did owe her the truth. "Lisbon has been affected by the war, but it is rebuilding now. The French are gone, of course. The Queen, Maria of Portugal and Brazil, has not returned from Brazil. Some say she may never do so, but she has placed General Beresford in charge, you see. There are British soldiers there, helping to keep the peace while the Portuguese recover."

"But Cook says they hates us as much as the French. Her brother fought there." Betty folded another dress.

"Perhaps some of them do wish us gone. I know that it has not been completely peaceful or my father would have sent for me a year ago." Margaret bit her lip. "I understand, Betty, if you wish to remain here. It is safer here. But I *must* go."

"O' course you must. And so must I, Miss. You don't think I'd let you, a young girl, go off on an adventure without me? Who will fix your hair and do your wash?" She joked and picked up another dress.

"But you cannot be more than two-and-twenty." Margaret had never asked Betty her age. In fact, she really did not know much about Betty at all, even after the last two years of seeing her every day, multiple times a day.

"Miss, I am a year shy of thirty, but thank you."

"Do you need time this afternoon to tell your family where you are going?"

"Oh, thank you, Miss, that would be most kind. I will visit my mother and step-father. They will be anxious but excited for me."

"You can write them as soon as we arrive in Lisbon, too. So they will not worry."

"Oh, thank you. Perhaps you can write my mother for me when you write to Lady Frances."

Writing Lady Frances. Not eating with her, seeing her, listening to her, only writing to her. Margaret realized that for the two weeks at sea and during her stay in Lisbon with her father, she would be free of her aunt and uncle. Perhaps her father would let her stay with him forever. Margaret laughed again and took Betty's hands and twirled her around. "We are both going to have a holiday and be free!"

At that last word, they both fell on the bed, dissolving in laughter. Margaret caught her breath, but she still wondered who her aunt would have to spy on her. If not Betty, Sir Edgar, or Mr. Wynn, she could not guess whom.

CHAPTER 8

MARGARET SNUGGLED UNDER HER down coverlet, scooting closer to the light of the candle. Opening the journal, she lovingly touched the envelope containing her mother's letter. It had become her good-night ritual—a way to touch something her mother had held and had written just for her.

The previous night she had read the beginning of the journal—a description of the balls her mother had attended, her friends and suitors, and her relationship with her beloved "Reggie," who Margaret could hardly believe was her uncle, Sir Reginald. He must have changed over the years from the "beloved boy" her mother described. Yet, it touched Margaret that her mother had so entirely loved her awkward older brother.

She opened to the page she had marked with a sky-blue ribbon.

February 20th, 1796

Last night's ball was a tremendous success. I still tremble at the events, the memory of which even now quickens my pulse.

Reggie has too long been nervous about dances and social engagements. Though he is five years my elder, I am the one he consults. He is more enlivened by politics than a country dance, but this is most likely the result of nerves at having to talk to a beautiful lady instead of a bearded and beady-eyed old Lord from parliament. I should find it quite the opposite.

Reginald and I arrived for a ball at the Pantheon on Oxford Street. We decided that if he could practice speaking and dancing with ladies under less scrutiny than at Almack's, he could become more confident—meaning navigating fewer mamas of the elite young ladies he wished to court. He is ambitious and wishes to make a good match that will forward his ambitions to become an MP. He plans to seek election next year.

How different is the weight of a man's role than my own. He wants to use marriage as a means of increasing his footing in the world. I am to marry to improve the fortunes and connections of my husband. But what of my own dreams and plans?

I do not speak it aloud, for I do not believe Father will take this particular wish into consideration, but I dearly, dearly wish to marry for love—and if not love, at least affection. Father, however, has his eye set on a few eligible families. I must choose from one of them. Or at least make my suitors believe it was their idea to pursue me. But none of these men inspire even a flicker of love in me.

That was my secret reason for taking Reginald to the Pantheon. I wanted to mingle with other gentlemen without being so closely scrutinized.

The first few dances were a mixture of freedom and excitement. I have always enjoyed dancing, but what young woman does not? It is nearly the only physical exercise, besides sedate walking, which I am allowed.

During my dance with Mr. Plumerford, I came face to face with a tall Navy captain. One could not help but notice his military bearing, strong shoulders, and auburn hair. But what caught my breath were his eyes. His kind, blue eyes. Many men have merry eyes at a ball, some eager ones, a few voracious—as if I am a meal to consume. But no one has ever looked at me with kindness.

I blushed furiously, but I could not help looking at him often during the set. Afterward, I returned to my place next to Reggie. I followed this captain with my eyes, hiding my smile behind my fan. I could not dance with him for we had not been introduced. How could I manage that? After another dance, I realized, however, that I was not the only one seeking an introduction as the captain struck up a conversation with Reggie.

I took a deep breath. My eyes were so focused on their approach that I jumped when I heard a friendly voice at my side.

"Margaret, how lovely to see a familiar face among… all… this."

It was Lady Frances, who has recently chosen me to be her particular friend. I believe, however, that her friendship is more an attempt to gain favor with Reggie.

I immediately curtseyed to her and her spinster aunt, Mrs. DeClare, who wandered off to find a seat. "I had not imagined you would join us." I bit my lip; I had mentioned Reggie's and my outing. I was astonished that she had deigned to attend such a gathering.

She was asking about Reggie when both men joined us. It was a bit awkward as Reggie did not know whether Lady Frances would wish to be introduced. Reggie whispered something to the captain, who waited a few steps back.

What Reggie said or did next, I can scarcely remember. I was lost in the eyes of the captain before me. He smiled and stared back.

Reggie looked at me and squinted. "Captain Beaton, may I introduce my sister, Miss Colborne. And Lady Frances Fortescue, daughter of the Earl of Chilstone."

"A pleasure to make yur acquaintance."

His bow was impeccable. His Scottish accent, irresistible. But I was not the only one who noticed. To my surprise, and Reggie's too, I believe, Lady Frances dominated the conversation with Captain Beaton. I had never seen her in such a mood—almost flirtatious. I attribute it to her wanting to make Reggie jealous. How could she, daughter of an Earl, take an interest in a naval captain?

Reggie had too much pride to stand and watch or play second fiddle. He left to join the party of Miss Johnson. I had no such escape. Nor did I want one.

Captain Beaton, however, was very gallant. He often sought to involve me in the conversation, but Lady Frances made no such effort on my behalf. It was pleasant to notice and be noticed by the handsome Captain Beaton, but surely Lady Frances, with her beauty and standing in the ton, would win the young captain over completely.

When that dance set was ending, I saw Mr. Lewis approaching to my left. I smiled at him, but while he was a few steps off, Captain Beaton said, "Miss Colborne, may I have the pleasure of the next dance?"

I was surprised and pleased beyond measure. I believe I blushed a deep pink. Lady Frances did not mind or even notice. She was soon dancing with Mr. Lewis, taking a place very close to mine.

Standing across from Mr. Beaton was a pleasantly uncomfortable experience. He was very light on his feet, an excellent dancer, and his conversation never waned. All of this was exquisitely pleasant. But his eyes, the way he gazed *into mine—I felt as if he truly saw me. As if he already knew me. My words are not adequate to describe the look nor its effect on me.*

We danced twice that evening. A marked distinction! I was flattered. Many eyes followed us about the room. He was so dashing in his uniform. And he danced with Lady Frances, but just once. Reggie and Lady Frances danced twice. By the end of the evening, Lady Frances and Reggie seemed quite comfortable in each other's company. To my delight, Reggie truly enjoyed Captain Beaton's company—he is witty, knowledgeable, but also a good listener and takes a deep interest in Reggie's political aspirations. The four of us conversed quite often during the evening.

Last night I could barely sleep for thoughts of his blue eyes, the feel of my hand on his arm, his gloved hand placed over mine. It was happiness, pure and sweet, that kept sleep at bay.

Margaret smoothed the page with her hand and sighed. She remembered how her mother had looked lovingly at her father when sitting at the table, and how he had smiled back. Then Margaret tried to imagine Lady Frances wanting to make Sir Reginald jealous. Margaret giggled quietly. Lady Frances and Sir Reginald were *suited* for each other, but Margaret could not imagine a romantic attachment between them. Margaret tilted her head. Sir Reginald had been friendly to her father once. If only they could have remained friends, how different life would have been for them all. And herself. She suspected that friendship had dissolved once Father and Mother eloped.

Margaret closed the journal, preferring to make this first reading, this first discovery of her mother, last as many nights as possible. She kissed it and hid it under her pillow.

CHAPTER 9

SITTING AT HIS DESK, Joshua had written his last business letter before sailing for Lisbon with the next tide. Their shipping company had recently expanded, including an office in Boston. Two of their ships, the *Invicta* and *Próspera*, were halfway from Boston to London by now, full of salted fish, wheat, and tobacco. He *had* intended to meet them; instead, he had left instructions for their cargos to be sold in London before they came on to Lisbon. The *Minerva* and *Liberty* were to return from Lisbon with spices and ivory after repairs.

He had planned with great anticipation to travel on the *Liberty* to Boston to oversee the expansion of their business interests there. He even hoped that in America, he could find a wife, establish a home, and bring Miguel there. At least he could try. Now, all that would be delayed, and he resented the interruption. He almost resented Miss Beaton, which made him feel guilty. And he resented feeling guilty. He pushed away from his desk, his chair scraping against the wood floor.

He breathed out and stretched his arms. He did not have time to waste today. Pulling himself back to the desk, he looked at the last letter, one of a personal nature, which he needed to finish. He had left this unpleasant task to the end. Quickly penning a few lines of regret to his sister, Dorothea, he put the sealed letter aside to be mailed. He exhaled. Was his rejection of her idea too hasty? Leaning his cheek on his hand, he opened her last letter again, his eyes drawn to her suggestion.

> *Mrs. Blaisson is a respectable widow with two young girls. Her situation matches yours since your loss of Maria Luisa. Mrs. Blaisson's husband was in the army, losing his life at Waterloo. With a modest income of her own, she runs her home with efficiency and economy. She is not an emotional woman and is able to manage her household quite well on her own, which would give you the freedom to continue to travel as business requires. When you next visit, you may see for yourself. Concerning Miguel, however, she believes it may be best if he remains with his Portuguese grandmother—*

He slammed the letter down and ran his hands through his hair. He had intended to visit Dorothea and her husband during this trip, but the necessity of transporting Miss Beaton to Lisbon made that also impossible. Yet, he was relieved. He would be spared tea with Mrs. Blaisson for at least another month. Then the guilt returned. He was closest with Dorothea and enjoyed being with her. She had not rejected Miguel, but evidently, Mrs. Blaisson had.

He twisted his ring. While he understood his current need for a wife, the prospect of an arranged marriage to a woman who evidently could function quite well on her own did not soften the blow. Add to that the prejudice against his son, Miguel—well, how could that type of marriage make him happy?

He folded Dorothea's letter and tucked it in his pocket. Perhaps he would visit his family next trip. It had been six months since his last time in England, but he had not bothered to see any of his family then either. Perhaps if his mother had lived, she would have quelled the opposition to his choice of bride.

It was his fault. He had not prepared his family properly. Knowing his father's sentiments against foreigners, Joshua had not written of his courtship or marriage to Maria Luisa. Instead, he had intended to bring Maria Luisa home as his wife after his fortune was assured. Money would help ease their path into society. How naïve, how wrong he had been.

He retrieved his handkerchief from his pocket and examined it. The edge was worn and he would have to rehem a portion, but it was the last one his mother had sewn for him. Before his mother had died, he had enjoyed returning home during leave. Her letters during his years of service had sustained him. He had returned to her and father whenever he could take leave. Becoming a captain during wartime had made those visits shorter and less frequent. The fact that he had not seen his mother during the last two years of her life was a regret with which he had not yet come to terms. Once he had met and married Maria Luisa, he had spent his leave in Lisbon instead of England.

He replaced the handkerchief and, as was his custom, took off and examined his locket ring. He clicked open the gold square, set with topaz, revealing the void inside. He took out the lock of Miguel's baby hair. There in the square well was the miniature pencil drawing of Maria Luisa that he had copied from a larger drawing. He paused for a moment, said a short prayer, and then replaced Miguel's hair. Standing, he shut the ring and replaced it on his finger and moved toward the window. The view of London did not distract him from the images occupying his thoughts. He leaned on the sill.

By the time the letters from his father and sister had found him off the coast of Portugal, he had missed his mother's illness, death, and funeral. Learning of her death had shocked and saddened him, but news shortly after of Maria Luisa's murder at the hands of French troops had pushed him to new depths of depression. He was truly the cause of her death; she had begged him to take them—her mother, Miguel, all of them—on board with him. He had believed it was unsafe, unwise. He had left her crying. Left to do his duty.

He turned and pushed the papers on his desk, the ink, the pen, all onto the floor and, sinking into his chair, held his head between his hands as if he could squeeze the memories out.

For a time, his hatred of the French had made him reckless with his life and the lives of his crew. Without Foremaster's friendship and help running the ship as Joshua's first lieutenant before his promotion, Joshua might have lost his sanity and his command. Foremaster had quelled Joshua's recklessness one evening by reminding Joshua of Miguel. His son's little face had risen above the other images, above the anger. Miguel had his mother's lips and nose, but the boy's eyes were a copy of Joshua's. Miguel, safe in Lisbon with his grandmother, deserved to know his father.

After the war, Joshua had retired his commission. He was done with the senselessness of war. Being paid off, he returned home. By then, Thomas, his older brother, had moved with his young family in London, and Dorothea had married and moved to Kent. He had stayed a short time with each of them, making his way to his childhood home. There, he had been alone with his father and stepmother. The awkwardness of being the only child at home had intensified his grief for his mother. His father's new wife was hosting at table, pouring tea, laughing with his father—everywhere he expected to see his mother, she was there instead. Joshua had not expected the renewal of his grief and loss. He had thought the war had numbed him; his war waged on.

The next morning, Joshua had informed them of his marriage to Maria Luisa, of her death, and of his son, Miguel. His father and stepmother's disdain had not been a complete surprise to Joshua, but it had extinguished any hope of eventual understanding or acceptance of Miguel. The prejudice his father had against foreigners was deep and "justified" by the commonly held opinions of the *ton*. Father had suggested he buy a country estate, find an English wife, and allow the boy to be raised by his own kind. As if Miguel were not his own flesh and blood. Joshua had left that afternoon.

Miguel deserved to be with his father, and Joshua needed to be with him, in a home together. Joshua needed to marry again; perhaps a marriage of convenience would be better. No heart to break. No failure to shoulder. But where could he find a woman who could understand his grief and accept his son unconditionally?

A knock at his office door startled Joshua.

"Everything is in order for Miss Beaton and Sir Edgar's cabins," Foremaster said.

Joshua turned as he heard his friend's voice.

Foremaster looked at the papers and spilled ink on the floor. "A squall, I see? Or were you taking your frustrations out on the inkwell?"

Joshua twisted his lips into a wry smile and began to retrieve the items. "The latter, I am afraid."

"I find a drink of port or rum produces the same relief with less tempestuous effects."

"Yes, after we set sail, I will pour you one myself." Joshua stood and brushed dust off his knees.

"Miss Beaton will take your cabin, as per Lady Frances's request—" Foremaster cleared his throat. "And following your altered instructions, Sir Edgar will share with his valet, Sallow. Strange, that he would agree to serve as a valet to Sir Edgar on this ship."

Joshua shook his head. "After we refused to promote Sallow to first mate, he left our employ altogether. Yes, it is strange."

Foremaster shook his head. "We could not promote a man who was so lax in his discipline of the crew. Or at least those who were his friends. I was amazed he worked for Beaton and you at all. He still holds you responsible for his brother's death on the *Boudicca*."

"Beaton hired him before I came on as partner. Of course, Sallow has always been stiff but polite to me." Joshua raked his hand through his hair. "He is a fair sailor who understands the workings of the ship. I have nothing against the man, though I do acknowledge he holds me responsible for the deaths. Little wonder. I hold myself responsible."

"Not your fault. You did the best you could during the attack."

Joshua shook his head. He would never know how many men's deaths were his fault. "Perhaps he is done resenting me. I cannot imagine why he would agree to serve on the *Rainha Maria* if he still harbors ill will."

"Perhaps she is paying him a great deal."

"From what I have seen of Sir Edgar, he should ask for more money. Again, I want to apologize again for the inconvenience of sharing your cabin with me."

"Nonsense! We will be like midshipmen again and put ink in the steward's tea."

Joshua guffawed out loud. Foremaster and he had received five lashings each for that prank—their only punishment as young midshipmen. But it had been worth it to see the steward, a tremendous bully, with inky black teeth and tongue being laughed at by the other men. "You are a good man and a good friend."

"That may be more true if our passengers are more trouble than we predict. Ah, a rather dignified carriage has stopped on the dock," Foremaster said, peering out the window. "I believe we shall soon find out."

Joshua followed him out to welcome their passengers.

CHAPTER 10

MARGARET BREATHED IN. WHILE the Thames itself did not smell like the ocean and was far from pleasant, the ship held other scents that brought back a flood of memories: salt-laden ropes, earthy wood planks and masts, and the sharpness of pine tar. She closed her eyes and was transported back to the open sea. Her ten-year-old self ran up and down the main deck, which rolled on the water. She chased the seagulls and terns as they swooped and squawked above her in the bright sunlight. The heave of the waves under the ship caused her to stumble and laugh. Then her mother's touch. *Margaret, you are underfoot.*

"Beg pardon, Miss." Betty gently pulled her arm.

Margaret opened her eyes and stepped aside so a group of sailors could swing Sir Edgar's trunk, the last of their luggage, onto the deck beside them using ropes and pulleys.

"Purhaps Sir Edgar is also planning to stay in Lisbon forever," whispered Betty.

Margaret hid her laugh in her handkerchief. It was the only time she had smiled since Sir Edgar had met them in the coach.

"Well," Sir Edgar said, "that was rude to handle my luggage so, so indelicately! Sallow? Sallow? Where is my valet?" Using a walking stick to steady himself and holding a lace handkerchief near his nose, he stepped next to Margaret and Betty under the main mast of the *Rainha Maria.*

Margaret had been avoiding Sir Edgar since they had come on deck five minutes previous. She had heard sailors around her snickering. They had eyed Sir Edgar's hunter green swallow-cut coat with gilt buttons, peach waistcoat, sea-blue knee breeches, and gleaming white stockings which set off his beribboned navy pumps. He was more aptly fit for a stroll through Hyde Park than to sail. Margaret took a few steps away from him.

Danny approached with another sailor. The sailor, passing Sir Edgar, said, "Whoe'er his valet is, he should be sued for malpractice." Danny whacked his friend in the arm as he stopped before Margaret and bowed. "Welcome, Miss Beaton. I'm personally seeing to your luggage." He bowed to Betty, who nodded but looked away.

"Thank you, Danny. I am relieved it is you who will take care of us," Margaret said.

At this, Danny grinned and grew slightly pink.

"Oh, and who is his valet?" Betty whispered.

"Him? Peter Sallow." Danny motioned to a man dressed in somber hues and a worn coat which had known the sea.

Curious. He was not the fine society servant whom Margaret had expected. His tanned face made her wonder. "He's more of a sailor than valet," she said.

"Aye, and worked on this ship until recently. It's a puzzlement. We'll see to your things." At this, Danny pulled his forelock and left with his companion.

When Sallow, who had been conversing with Sir Edgar, stared at her, she turned aside and breathed deeply. It was glorious to be onboard again. She listened to the creaking of ropes and the shouts of men. She tilted her head and held a hand to her eyes as she watched the mainsail being raised—it's loosened form, fully extended, ready to catch the tide. Hope gathered in her chest at the site.

A passing ship hallooed their crew as it made its way down the murky churning Thames to the open sea. Its wake caused a gentle swell to push beneath them. Margaret laughed as the sensation hit her legs and stomach.

"Well!" cried Sir Edgar even louder.

Turning, Margaret could see he was pale if not slightly green. "Sir Edgar, are you well?"

"Well?" he cried. "No, no, no. This will not do. We cannot stay aboard this rocking and pitching piece of flotsam!"

A sailor nearby snickered. Margaret stepped toward Sir Edgar, her hands clasped in front of her. "Please, if you would just go down to your cabin and lie down, this sensation will pass."

"No, I fear it will not!" he cried. "Hallo! You there, return us to shore at once!" He stumbled toward a sailor who was busy hauling a crate below. "I said you there. Ah! He ignored me. Unpardonable. Oh—" Sir Edgar held his stomach. "We must leave this instant! Sallow!"

Sallow whispered something to Sir Edgar, who shook his handkerchief at him and shouted, "I cannot." Then Sir Edgar began waving his handkerchief at Margaret, beckoning her over.

"No! I will not leave this ship!" Margaret cried out.

"We must! We cannot cross this ocean. I cannot endure it. I told Lady Frances that I could not do this. She *convinced* me that meeting your father would solidify our union, but really there is no need. We understand each other well enough. I wished to ask you for your hand this evening, dear Marga—" He heaved but tamped his mouth shut. As he momentarily swayed, swallowing with some effort, he continued, "We are leaving, now!"

As he reached for Margaret's hand, she recoiled. "No, I am going to see my father."

Sallow took a step toward her, "Miss Beaton, I believe—"

"You must accompany me off this ship. Do you not see my distress?" Sir Edgar grabbed her arm.

"Do you not see mine?" She pulled away and shook her head. Her heart was pounding in her ears.

A few of the crew stopped to watch, whispering to each other. One or two laughed.

Margaret's face flushed a deep red. "Sir Edgar, please, send Sallow for Captain Foremaster."

"Another stinking sailor? Not on my life! I will not be forced to converse with anyone else. My mind is made up. Now, come!" Again, he reached for her hand. Sallow stepped forward, holding out his hand.

She retreated a few steps. Sir Edgar walked haltingly toward her with an angry glare. Sallow keep pace on her other side.

Betty stepped between Margaret and Sallow. Her arms were folded. "Oi, you, stop right there."

Margaret's glance darted between the two men to Betty's back. This was getting out of hand. Margaret did not wait. She ran to the ratlines near the starboard side of the ship. These weathered gray ropes, which formed the ladder for sailors to climb at an incline up to the masts, had intrigued her as a child. Now, she draped her day dress mostly over her left arm and swung her boot in the first rung. Her gloves were too slick; she pulled them off and dropped them, feeling the rough rope in her hands.

Sir Edgar lunged toward the rope ladder. She climbed two more rungs before he caught the bottom one, causing the ratlines to quiver. Sallow grabbed the other side. The resulting shaking caused Margaret to gasp out loud, but she pulled her boot up another rung. Her heart was in her throat. Her stomach clenched to keep herself steady as she quickly ascended three more rungs. Neither Sallow or Sir Edgar could reach her.

Sailors above her yelled at her to stop, but her eyes were on Sir Edgar. She climbed seven rungs before the swaying ropes became harder to control. Twisting her arms through the ropes to steady herself, she looked below and behind. The height dizzied her; her breath came ragged and shallow. These ropes angled over the main deck, but if she fell, she would roll down them toward the railing, possibly falling into the water. She had not realized how far up she had climbed. She tried to swallow, to think, to move, but she was frozen.

"Papa, I will fall." Beads of sweat broke out on her forehead. Climbing out on the tree limb to retrieve her cat, Pepper, had seemed so simple. Now, Margaret could not move. Her arms and legs twined about the limb.

"Pearl, do not look down. Focus on my voice." Her father was climbing to her.

Someone called her name. She looked over the deck, which was in commotion; everyone was running toward her or calling out advice.

Sir Edgar was tugging on the lower rung angrily. She felt the rope heaving her. Two sailors grabbed him and pulled him away. Sir Edgar yelled at them, gesticulating with one hand while reaching a handkerchief to his nose with the other. Sallow had backed off to assist Sir Edgar.

Making eye contact with Margaret, however, awakened Betty. She crossed the few remaining feet to stand beneath Margaret and shield anyone from seeing Margaret's stockinged but otherwise exposed ankles.

Captain Foremaster and Mr. Wynn emerged from the quarterdeck cabin and ran to where the men were pointing—staring at her. Both men descended the steps, quickly moving toward her. "Miss Beaton!" Mr. Wynn's voice carried above the commotion.

They locked eyes. His face paled, and she realized the danger she was in.

A deep blush issuing from the depths of her humiliation rose high in Margaret's cheeks. She had not meant to cause alarm; she had promised to follow all orders and behave. They had not even left the dock before she had been impelled to break those promises.

A tremor on the ropes broke Margaret's thoughts. The sailors descending the ratlines above her were causing the ropes to sway.

Her right foot slipped. A small cry escaped her lips. The rope burned her palm as it slipped through. Margaret clenched the rung below in her hands and pushed harder with her left foot in an effort to prevent herself from falling. Panicked, she kicked at her skirt to find another foothold. Success. Drenched in sweat, her stomach muscles tight and burning, she trembled from her clenched hands and pointed toes.

Captain Foremaster's voice thundered above the rest. "Silence!"

Immediately, the crew quieted and froze. The only sounds now came from the docks where onlookers pointed at her. She tilted her head back. Wide-eyed young sailors above her stared but did not move. The motion of the ropes quieted to a soft tremor in her hands. Her arms ached and her legs shook.

Captain Foremaster, on the main deck below, strode toward her. "Miss Beaton, do not move." Captain Foremaster's voice was calm, betraying the quick motion of his feet. "I am coming to get you." Captain Foremaster's face was tight. Margaret did not see fear or anger, but determination. Mr. Wynn was at his side, passing a now slack-jawed Sir Edgar whose silk handkerchief had fallen to the deck.

Margaret's face flushed hot with embarrassment and effort. She was losing the moment. Once they helped her down, they would comply with Sir Edgar just to rid their ship of her.

Captain Foremaster stepped onto the ropes behind her and slowly ascended.

She was ready for the tremor in the ropes, but her stomach still clenched. Margaret sought the face of Mr. Wynn, who was directly below her.

Making eye contact, he nodded reassuringly to her. His face was concerned, but not angry.

"Please," she mouthed, and her eyes darted toward Sir Edgar and back to Mr. Wynn.

Mr. Wynn's gaze followed hers to Sir Edgar and back. A slight nod of his head relaxed her. She could move again.

Captain Foremaster placed his hand on the back of her left ankle. "Move your left foot down. Yes. Feel the next rung. Good. Now your left hand. Right foot."

Margaret began to move down slowly. Captain Foremaster stood on the deck as she came to the bottom rung. "Thank you, Captain Foremaster," she whispered.

"Wynn, will you be so kind?" Captain Foremaster steadied the ropes with one hand, the other on her arm.

"Certainly. Miss Beaton, will you allow me?"

"Yes, thank you." Margaret's body shook, the fear and effort taking a toll.

Mr. Wynn placed his hands on her waist, lifted her off the ropes and into his arms, wrapping his right arm around her waist. She felt weightless. Clinging to his chest as he swung her free of the ropes, she could feel his heart pounding. Or was it her own? She gazed into his eyes. He placed her on the deck. The men let out a collective exhale, and the usual sounds and activity on deck resumed.

"Thank you," Margaret said as she slid her hand out of his.

A retching sound caught her attention. She spun her head and saw Sir Edgar vomit all over his polished court shoes.

CHAPTER 11

JOSHUA KEPT A HAND on Miss Beaton's back. She was still trembling.

Sir Edgar yelled. "Miss Beaton, I insist! You will come off this ship at once. I cannot make this journey, and you may not go without me." Sir Edgar shook his right shoe, which was soiled with vomit, as if he were dancing a jig. His shoe came off and somersaulted through the air. "Sallow, my shoe!"

Mr. Sallow walked toward the shoe.

Joshua nearly laughed, but seeing the dismay of Miss Beaton, he checked himself. Her face was quite pale, her eyes squinted.

Clenching his fists, Joshua's anger intensified. How dare Sir Edgar order her around and embarrass her.

"I will not. I am sailing to see my father," she said, her voice quiet but cracking. Turning to Captain Foremaster, she looked him straight in the eye and asked, "May I remain on board, Captain?"

"Yes, but you and your maid will go to your cabin immediately." Foremaster's entire face was a mask of anger. Joshua understood it well. No one was allowed to speak back to the captain, and Sir Edgar had thrown a fit which the entire crew had witnessed. His behavior was an inexcusable affront. How Foremaster had managed to control his anger thus far had surprised Joshua.

Miss Beaton dropped her head and, with Betty's help, went in the door under the poop deck to their cabin.

"NO! You may not leave!" Sir Edgar shouted toward Margaret. Then to Foremaster, he said, "You will deliver Miss Colborne and myself, with our luggage, off this ship at once." Sir Edgar paused to breathe heavily into his handkerchief.

"For the last time, I will not remove a lady against her will. You are *not* her relation. And you are making me miss the tide. Enough. Mr. Kernsby, employ the canvas sling and remove Sir Edgar from my ship." Foremaster turned and ascended the stairs to the wheel house. Sallow followed him. Joshua was not pleased to see Sallow on board and wondered why he was not helping Sir Edgar leave instead of pestering Foremaster.

With a signal from Kernsby, six men surrounded and pushed Sir Edgar onto the middle of the canvas sling, spread out on the deck. Amidst Sir Edgar's "unhand me" and "how dare you," they lifted the sides of the canvas and secured them to the four-legged bridle which kept it from closing completely around Sir Edgar. Only his shoulders and head were visible, and the fist he was now shaking; he looked like a cat caught in a knapsack. The men snickered.

"You have no right to do this! I am Sir Edgar Fortescue, younger son of—wuh." Sir Edgar threw up again, spraying the main deck and scattering the men, a few of whom cursed Sir Edgar's parentage. The sling basket swayed as Sir Edgar swung up in the air and off the ship, to the wonder and astonishment of all who passed by on the dock or boardwalk.

He was placed, not too gently, on the ground and fell in a heap. Untangling himself, Joshua heard him exclaim, "You have not seen the last of me."

Joshua had no compassion for the man. But he did wish Miss Beaton had been there to see Sir Edgar fall on his backside.

Foremaster and Kernsby were giving the orders to prepare the ship. The crew became engrossed in their tasks. It always pleased Joshua to watch a ship's crew work. It was like viewing fencing or fisticuffs, full of physical challenge and agility. All working together to bring the ship to life. At last, the order was given to cast away. The lines were cast off, and the ship, loose from its bands, slipped away, gliding like an elegant woman at a ball. The soft swell beneath them was her exhale. Joshua breathed deeply, too.

Turning for a last look at Sir Edgar as the ship pulled into the middle lane of the Thames, Joshua waved. Sir Edgar, shoeless and smudged with dirt, shook a fist at him. Joshua had not expected to see Sir Reginald alight from a carriage.

"Captain Foremaster, I insist. Come back," Sir Reginald yelled.

Joshua looked to the wheelhouse. Foremaster had not heard. They would catch the tide.

Joshua shook his head and turned his back. The afternoon's events had been memorable. They had been worth delaying his trip to Boston. This story would be told and retold by every man present. In fact, he would pay for a round of rum for the crew tonight.

Then he thought of Miss Beaton. His anger returned. If he could prevent it in any way possible, he would see that Miss Beaton never had to marry that stuffed brocaded-waist shirt namby-pamby fop of a macaroni.

ℭHAPTER 12

CROSSING THE ATLANTIC

MARGARET CAUGHT A LAST look at the Thames and the foggy coast of England through the large windows at the back of her cabin. She sighed. She had wished to be on deck for all of it. Her final goodbye.

There was a knock at the door. She stood and quickly wiped away any tears as Betty answered it. It was Mr. Wynn. She tried a smile, but his reaction to her face told the tale. Mr. Wynn had spotted her tear-stained face.

"Miss Beaton… I wanted to see if there is anything you need?"

"Thank you, no. But I think it best if we take our dinner here tonight."

"Of course." He twisted a ring on his finger. Then dropping his hands, he said, "You should know that your uncle arrived with Sir Edgar just as we had pushed off from the dock, demanding that we return. But we had caught the tide, and Captain Foremaster was too angry at Sir Edgar to give them any heed."

"Oh, dear." Margaret frowned and bit her lip. "May I ask, did Sir Edgar's luggage remain?" She knew it was an odd request, confirmed by Mr. Wynn's raised eyebrows. "You see, my mother's pearls were packed in his portmanteau."

"Oh, I understand. Actually, in our haste to catch the tide, we did keep Sir Edgar's luggage. I can have it moved to your room." He turned to leave but added, "I am sorry that Sir Edgar tried to bully you. No gentleman, no man, should ever force a lady to act against her will."

"Thank you." She felt a blush creep up her neck and face.

He paused again. "Most women might have cowed to such a request. I admire your strength of character. Your father would be quite proud of you."

Blushing more furiously from the compliment, she smiled weakly. "I apologize for my rash decision to inspect the crow's nest before sailing."

"You nearly made it. Just another 90 feet or so."

She laughed. "Touché. I thought I might glimpse Lisbon from the top."

"If anyone could, it would be you." He bowed and departed but stopped part way down the passageway. "If it is any consolation, I do not believe Sir Edgar will ever wear those shoes again."

Margaret tried to swallow a laugh. "Thank you. It is."

About five minutes later, there was another knock. Margaret stood, hoping to see Mr. Wynn again. But it was Captain Foremaster.

"Miss Beaton," he said, declining to enter. "I will not have you put my men or yourself at risk. I do not care who your father is. In this case, you being the daughter of one of the owners makes it worse. If you were injured during this voyage, your father would be well within his rights to fire me. Therefore, I request that you stay in your cabin as much as possible."

Margaret nodded but could not speak. The lump in her throat was too large to even swallow. The color drained out of her face. Though he had not raised his voice, his tone had conveyed his frustration—at the situation or at her, it did not matter. Her humiliation was complete.

"Good night." Captain Foremaster left.

Margaret sat on the bed, holding the covers in one hand and her mouth with her handkerchief as she sobbed again.

"There, now, miss." Betty cooed and rubbed her back, but Margaret could not stop, not for half an hour.

When Tom, the cabin boy, brought their dinner, Margaret did not look up.

Betty placed the tray on Sir Edgar's luggage and uncovered the meal. "Oh, no, miss. I feel—" Betty barely made it to the pail in time, her first taste of seasickness.

Margaret stood and found a towel. Kneeling beside her, Margaret handed it to her and said, "Oh, Betty, we are a pair."

For two days, Betty was unable to do little more than sleep and sip some tea. While Margaret was not as negatively affected, she felt the pull of the sea on her stomach and head. It was difficult to walk in a straight line during the swells.

"Will this pass, miss, or will it las' the entire two weeks we are at sea?" Betty asked from the bed.

Margaret dabbed Betty's pale forehead with a rag soaked in cool water. "Dr. Giles believes in another day your seasickness will end; then we can go up and get some fresh air. For now, try to rest. I believe he will check on us again later."

Betty closed her eyes.

Margaret pulled her mother's journal from her trunk and sat back in her chair—the only other furniture in the room besides the bed that she and Betty shared. Since reading the journal often brought Margaret to tears, she had only read her mother's journal when Betty was asleep.

March 18, 1796

I met Captain Beaton in the park today as I walked with Reggie, which is not entirely a surprise since I had mentioned at Thursday's ball that I would walk here today. My desire to be in his company is only increasing. I know I am falling in love with him.

Lady Frances and he were talking as we approached. Reggie seemed surprised to see her at the park—and with Captain Beaton. When she saw us, she turned to Reggie, almost completely ignoring Captain Beaton and me. I looked at him. His lips were pulled into a straight line, but he shook his head. Then he smiled and asked if I would care for a card game. I laughed.

This is not a mere fancy on my part. When Captain Beaton talks about his family, I am charmed. He loves his sister and his parents so much. When he shares stories about his life growing up, I am delighted that he had an idyllic childhood. I can imagine him out of doors from dawn to dusk, exploring the world. When he talks of the sea and his adventures fighting, I am mesmerized. He has a deep desire to make something of himself after his service to King and Country, and I believe in his dreams.

Add to all this his desire to know of what I dream. What my delights are. No man has ever asked me, but I wish to travel and see something more than London drawing rooms. I wish to be loved and to love, deeply and tenderly. To have children. Of course, I have not expressed the latter two thoughts as I would blush to say them aloud to him.

Margaret hugged the journal to her chest and beamed. Reading her mother's words, Margaret realized they mirrored her own feelings and desires. It emboldened her to think that her mother had pursued her dreams—just as Margaret was trying to do now.

Margaret retrieved her handkerchief and patted her forehead. The afternoon heat that accumulated in their closed cabin had been slightly alleviated by opening two windows. Their cabin was part of a larger area that spanned the back of the ship and had large windows, but the space they occupied had been reduced using moveable wood panels to give them privacy and allow for the dining room to be a separate area. A locking door had been added to the far right, and more panels created a narrow hallway outside their door. Margaret had learned from Dr. Giles that the other adjacent cabins were used by himself and then Captain Foremaster and Mr. Wynn.

Margaret and Betty had taken dinner in their cabin the past two nights; they had listened to the murmurs of Captain Foremaster and the senior officers at dinner on the other side of the partition. She could distinguish Mr. Wynn's voice as well. She had been invited but had claimed she needed to stay with Betty.

She pursed her lips. If she was honest with herself, it was embarrassment that had kept her from accepting their invitation. Her face grew hot again as she remembered Sir Edgar's public censure of her. Some of the sailors had laughed, but she had stood defiant and silent. Then had come the humiliation of Captain Foremaster's clipped command to go below, which had left no doubt of his anger and disappointment in her. She was grateful that he and Mr. Wynn had refused Sir Edgar's plan to force her to leave.

Margaret looked over at Betty, who finally slept. She was sorry Betty was suffering. Yet to her surprise, Margaret found she did not mind the chance to change places and care for Betty and herself. Dressing herself, arranging her own hair, even washing some of their clothes made Margaret realize how much she was capable of and how invaluable Betty was to her everyday comfort and happiness. She sighed and closed her eyes for just a moment.

A knock at the door caused Margaret to jump and Betty to wake.

It was Tom, the cabin boy, who asked, "Please, miss, have you any dishes? Do you need some fresh wash water?"

"Thank you, Tom, we do. You are very thoughtful and diligent."

The boy shifted his weight on his feet and dropped his head. Margaret knew from the tip of his red ear that her compliment had found its mark. She handed him the dishes, and he ran out, nearly bumping into Danny Devine, who had brought a bucket and a mop.

"Danny, I know you are invaluable to Mr. Wynn on land, but what is your role on the ship?" Margaret asked while he mopped, hoping to take his attention away from Betty, who lay with her face to the wall.

"I've been a sailor for years, I have, and know every job on a ship, but this voyage, I'm the stewar' and specifically tasked with takin' care of our guests, meaning you'selves."

"Thank you. But I doubt you have time with your duties. In fact, mopping may not be a regular job of yours."

He might have reddened a little. "As I said ea'lier, miss. My job is lookin' after you fine ladies. And seeing as you're stayin' in the cap'n's quarters, I like to keep it extra clean."

"The captain's quarters?" Margaret's voice rose. "I had no idea we were inconveniencing him."

"No inconvenience, miss. He's taken up in Mr. Wynn's. I put up his ol' hammock. They're like school mates, talkin' to the wee hours, they are," he said, laughing and shaking his head.

Margaret's blush deepened. Both Mr. Wynn and Captain Foremaster had been put out by her presence, on top of her behavior when first coming on board. Her shame sank deeper into her heart.

"Now, I believe Miss Betty there has yet to gain her sea legs, so I do. May I suggest some remedies? Ginge' tea and fresh air."

Danny's ginger tea did help Betty's stomach, but it took a little convincing to get Betty to go above deck.

An hour later, Margaret guided Betty out onto the quarterdeck. They found the nearest wall, supporting the upper deck where the wheelhouse was, and leaned against it. The heat of the wood warmed them, but their faces caught the full breeze. It pulled at Margaret's hair and rippled the ruffles on her pelisse. The ship was making good time with a full wind.

Margaret blocked the sunlight with her hand. The ship stretched out in front of them. The main deck below was obscured by the billowing sails and numerous ropes and ratlines which secured them to the deck. Some of the forecastle deck at the very front was visible. The sun shone, its light glinting off the ocean. Margaret blinked rapidly. Its clarity and warmth were a contrast to London's fog and damp. She held Betty's hand and laughed. "I feel so light. The sun is too bright."

"I've no words, miss."

Margaret placed her arm around Betty's waist and sighed. "Here we shall be happy. Free. We can be ourselves."

"But miss, I've neve' been anyone else."

"Then I shall be more like you." Margaret gazed up.

The sails of the main and fore masts were billowed like clouds, floating and flapping above them. Pure white against the blue sky. Margaret closed her eyes, content to feel the warmth of the sun on her face and be lulled by the motion of the waves. Some of the crew were aloft maintaining the ropes on the masts; others were swabbing the forecastle deck. The sounds around her were rhythmic, hypnotic—the slap of the water, the calls of the men, the creaking of the wood, the flapping of the masts. She breathed out slowly, allowing a smile to pull at her lips.

"I never tire of the sounds," a male voice near her ear said.

She opened her eyes.

Mr. Wynn bowed. "I wondered when you would emerge." He smiled.

Betty squeezed Margaret's hand and let go, making her way to the rail. Behind Mr. Wynn, Margaret caught the eye of a passing sailor, who nodded to them both, but kept her eye as he passed, pulling his forelock. "*Rainha*."

Margaret turned to Mr. Wynn. "Did he call me 'queen' in Portuguese?"

"Um… yes. The ship is named the *Rainha Maria*, but your conduct on board as we set sail—I believe some of the men approved of how you held your ground against… " His voice trailed off, and he looked down at his hands.

"I confess, I feared that I would not be welcome on deck because of my behavior," Margaret said.

"On the contrary. Most of the crew want to thank you for ridding them of Sir Edgar. They believed he was going to bring… bad luck."

"More so than two women on board? I know what a superstitious lot sailors can be."

"I believe your pluck has earned you a bit of esteem among the crew. But tell me, how is Betty?"

"She is improving, thank you."

"And do you require any more help?"

"No, Danny and Tom have been quite helpful. And actually, I have discovered how resourceful I can be. I am enjoying it immensely. I have a sense of freedom here that I did not know in London."

"Yes, the sea can be a great equalizer, but also a stern and unforgiving mistress."

"How so?" Margaret looked up to see Mr. Wynn's brow creased.

"She can separate you from loved ones and hold you back through storms or doldrums."

"But she can also reunite you with loved ones, as in my case."

"Yes." His eyes refocused from the horizon back to her face. "If you are well enough, would you be willing to take your dinner with the officers tonight? I believe Captain Foremaster fears he was too rough in his speech to you the other day."

"I assure you, he was not." She smiled. "Yes, please let them know I will join you. But first, I have a favor to ask."

CHAPTER 13

JOSHUA STOOD IN THE dining room, which during the day functioned as the captain's office, but was transformed each night. The table was set for five tonight. He shifted his weight, again, and twisted his ring, then noticing, clasped both hands behind his back.

"Wynn, no need to stand at attention just because I enter the room," Foremaster said as he came in, a wry smile on his lips.

Joshua gave his friend a warning glare.

"Are you nervous about dinner tonight?" Foremaster asked with a smile, ignoring Joshua's sternness.

"Hmpf." Joshua was nervous, but he hated that it was obvious. He knew that Miss Beaton was coming to dinner because an hour earlier, he had helped her open Sir Edgar's luggage, looking for her pearl necklace. Both had laughed at the quantity of shoes Sir Edgar had packed. Underneath them had been the mahogany case with her pearls. Her smile at seeing her father's gift had lit a part of his heart which had remained untouched for years. He had forgotten the satisfaction that could be found in making a woman smile. In fact, he could not get the memory of her face out of his mind.

He rolled his shoulders. His attraction to her unnerved him. Though five years had passed since Maria Luisa's death, he still felt committed to her; he always would. It was part love and part sorrow, but so much guilt. The guilt was crushing. Until meeting Miss Beaton, he had not looked at another woman with interest, but no man who could not or would not save his first wife deserved a second. Miss Beaton would reside either in Lisbon with her father or eventually back in London. He was bound for Boston.

Joshua was relieved when the first mate, Mr. Kernsby, and Dr. Giles joined them. "Is everyone well, doctor?" Joshua asked.

"Yes, I believe so. I confess, I feel that I should be paying you for the privilege of this voyage. So far, a toothache and a sea-sick maid, nothing extraordinary."

"Careful not to jinx us, sir," said Kernsby. "I remember a voyage to—"

The door opened, and Miss Beaton entered. There was a brief moment of stunned silence; the men bowed and she curtsied. As Joshua straightened, he stared into Miss Beaton's green eyes. She smiled. He swallowed.

While he had expected Miss Beaton to join them for dinner, he had not expected her to appear as if entering Almack's ballroom, her hair swept up to reveal her delicate neck and the lustrous pearl necklace clasped around it. Joshua reddened and dropped his gaze to her waist, which was framed by her lithe arms and soft skin peeking out from the top of her long gloves. He dropped his gaze to the table.

Captain Foremaster regained his powers of speech first. "Miss Beaton, welcome. We are all glad you could join us this evening."

"Thank you, Captain. May I apologize again for disrupting your ship before leaving port?"

Her words were soft-spoken, and a slight blush crept up her neck. But she looked Foremaster straight in the eye.

"No, Miss Beaton, I fear I did not temper my tone—um, my words, to address a lady. I so seldom have the opportunity onboard. Please sit." Foremaster motioned to the seat next to him and cleared his throat.

As Joshua pulled her chair out, her white muslin dress brushed against his hand. He took the chair next to hers.

"Miss Beaton," Foremaster continued, "may I introduce you to first mate, Mr. Kernsby. I believe you already know Dr. Giles."

"Good evening."

Kernsby nodded, but Dr. Giles asked, "How is Betty feeling this evening?"

"Much better. Thank you. I am sure your help has made the difference."

"I remember a voyage to Spain where seasickness overcame a good many of the crew." Joshua noticed that Margaret's smile did not falter, even during Dr. Giles's story. He was glad it did not interfere with her appetite. Mr. Sallow and young Jim entered and served them dinner of boiled potatoes, beef with gravy, and fresh rolls.

Sallow had stopped behind Miss Beaton's chair, his eyes focused on her pearl necklace. She glanced at Sallow briefly and stiffened. Joshua stared at Sallow, who backed up and then gazed straight ahead. "Thank you, Mr. Sallow, Jim. If we need you further, we will call for you."

Foremaster raised an eyebrow at Joshua. Joshua knew he was overstepping his place at the captain's table, but he tilted his head toward Miss Beaton, who let out a breath and lifted her fork for the first time. Foremaster gave a small nod.

Clearly, Joshua had missed something about the encounter with Sir Edgar and Miss Beaton. Sallow had willingly accepted the change of his role from valet to second mate after Sir Edgar's hasty departure, insisting he would rather stay on board. Joshua found that curious, but Sallow's presence was disturbing to Miss Beaton. He was determined to find out why.

MARGARET WATCHED SALLOW LEAVE and let out a shaky breath. She took a bite of potato, but her appetite had fled. She had assumed Sallow had left with Sir Edgar. The memory of him trying to entrap her with Sir Edgar made her shiver. She glanced up and hoped no one had noticed.

The men ate quietly for a time. Margaret steadied herself and smiled. She was grateful that Betty had made impressive work with her matted hair. She had hoped to put forth a more genteel impression than the one of her splayed like a flying fish caught on the ratlines a few days earlier. She touched her mother's pearl necklace to calm herself. Somehow, the pearls gave her a boost of confidence.

She ate daintily. It was not her first dinner at a table with a fiddle rail, meant to keep dishes from sliding off the table in a storm. But having to lift her wrists over it to retrieve her forked food was a trick. She smiled as the wine in her glass tilted gently back and forth.

It was also not her first dinner with a captain and his guests. She had been privileged, at the age of ten, to enjoy dinner at the captain's table when her parents brought her to London. She wished her parents were here now, but Margaret determined not to dwell on the past. Her purpose tonight was to gain the information she needed. Before she could convince her father to let her stay with him, she needed to know what conditions were like in Lisbon. That would help her frame her arguments.

After a few minutes of listening to talk of the weather, wind speed, and mending one of the topsails, Margaret looked at Captain Foremaster and said, "I am looking forward to seeing my father, but I also long to see Lisbon again. Tell me, has much changed since the end of the war? Is it more peaceful now?"

Captain Foremaster dabbed his lips with his napkin. "It is recovering well economically, but politically, there is still much unrest. Most of us here saw action in Lisbon, but the action moved north during the later battles." Then with a smile, he added, "I know of a certain midshipman who acted magnificently during the chaotic evacuation of troops from

Corunna. As darkness fell, he saw two other vessels near to ramming his, the *Boudicca*. Rushing up the forecastle with only a lantern, he grabbed hold of the figurehead and then, hanging over the water and certain death, I might add, if he had fallen, began waving his lantern and yelling like a madman in English, Spanish, and Portuguese. The other ships' men were astonished to see him dangling so."

Mr. Wynn choked on his wine. The other men laughed.

"What?" Margaret gasped.

Clearing his throat, Mr. Wynn said, "He was a fool, to be sure."

She turned to Mr. Wynn. "No, it was pure bravery,"

Mr. Wynn looked down; his neck flushed red.

Turning back to Captain Foremaster, Margaret asked, "What happened to the midshipman and the ship?"

"The starboard ship heaved to, and quickly avoided us, but oars from the other ship scraped the brass buttons off the midshipman's sleeve before he could climb clear. It was a close one; the men banged the oars against our ship and took the ear off the figurehead mermaid before their ship could be turned."

"No!" Margaret exclaimed. Again, she was at a loss for why the other men, excepting Mr. Wynn, were laughing. Mr. Wynn tugged at his cravat.

"For the rest of my time on the ship, all the men either rubbed the spot of the missing ear or the buttons on Midshipman Wynn's other sleeve for good luck."

"Mr. Wynn?"

He nodded to her. "Yes, I was the fool." Then he peered at Captain Foremaster. Margaret could not understand their unspoken communication which ended with the captain giving a slight nod to Mr. Wynn.

"How, then, did you both become captains?" Margaret asked as pie was served for dessert.

Captain Foremaster leaned back. "I was first transferred to the *William* as third lieutenant and then back to the *Boudicca* where I served under Captain Wynn. In 1814, I was promoted captain and transferred to the *Perseverance*. My friend here remained on the *Boudicca*; his was a battlefield promotion." Captain Foremaster's smile faded.

Margaret followed his look of sadness and turned to see Mr. Wynn studying his empty plate.

"Which I only held until the end of the war and could be paid off and retire," Mr. Wynn said, folding his napkin.

"He convinced all of us here to join him in your father's trade and transport business. And all of us, to a man, would rather sail with him than any other." Captain Foremaster raised his glass to Mr. Wynn.

"Thank you. Excuse me," Mr. Wynn said as he rose.

Once the door closed, Captain Foremaster said, "Miss Beaton, forgive me. I believe I have embarrassed my friend. The battle which claimed the lives of our former captain and first lieutenant was especially brutal. Wynn never speaks of it. He became captain during it. In the opening moments of battle, a barrage of cannon fire from the French caught the *Boudicca's* mainsail; the first lieutenant was crushed by a falling mast. Then the French set one of their rowboats aflame and sent it crashing into the stern. The fire spread up, and the captain and three other men were badly burned fighting it." He swallowed a sip of wine.

"Wynn saved the ship by aiming the cannon fire into the other fire ship's hull beneath the waterline. While it sank, a second French ship attacked. Wynn had the port cannons fire low, followed by the stern cannon turned to fire high across the ship. The last caught the mainmast. It was quick thinking that saved most of his men, but the other ship sank, taking most of the enemy with it. Many lived, but many died that day due to his actions." Mr. Foremaster stared at his folded hands.

Margaret pushed the last bite of pie around her plate. "Does he blame himself for the enemies' deaths?" she asked.

"No, but for not being able to save all of his own. And perhaps for surviving when others did not," Captain Foremaster answered.

Margaret swallowed, surprised to find her mouth dry. She understood the sorrow and the guilt of surviving. When her mother had become ill, she had been unable to keep her alive. All the doctors, herbs, and tinctures had failed. Margaret had sat up with her mother, night after night, listening to her coughing fits and irregular gasps for air. Always hoping to keep her mother alive until Father arrived. But with a war raging, the letters coming or going from a ship were never predictable. In the end, Father had not come.

Margaret blinked rapidly, remembering standing over her mother's grave. Surrounded by people but feeling utterly alone, not knowing how to endure.

"Miss Beaton?" Captain Foremaster had gently placed his hand on hers, just briefly enough to break her link to the past.

Margaret flinched slightly. "Yes." She peered into Captain Foremaster's eyes. She was grateful to see the small pinch of his eyebrows and the kind set of his mouth. "I am sorry. I was caught up in a memory. My mother." Margaret studied her pie and found her appetite had fled. She placed her fork down. "Thank you for dinner. I promised Betty we would take the night air. If you will excuse me."

CHAPTER 14

WRAPPED IN SHAWLS AND holding onto each other's arms, Margaret and Betty stepped haltingly toward the railing, timing their steps to match the rise of the waves. Lantern light helped them make their way across the dark deck. The sliver of a crescent moon could be seen with a wisp of clouds blowing past. The sea was rolling more vigorously underneath them, as a gust of wind whipped some of Margaret's curls loose. "Come feel the cool night breeze on your face, Betty."

"That's a bit more 'n a breeze. Are we safe, miss?"

"Safe for now." Mr. Sallow bowed to Margaret and held a lantern aloft. "*Rainha*." His lips formed a smile but his eyes squinted at her.

The blood rose into Margaret's cheeks, but it was indignation, not fear. Ignoring his last comment, Margaret asked, "What do you mean, Mr. Sallow?"

"We are in for a squall tonight. Best keep yourself tucked in safe. These decks is no place for a lady. It's dangerous."

"A more likely danger is for me to meet a bully here on deck." Margaret raised her chin. Sallow stepped back. Shock momentarily registered on his face. "My actions and words have only ever been meant to aid and serve."

"Then do so at some distance in future." Margaret pulled her shawl closer around her. Sallow bowed deeply, but Margaret did not like the way he eyed her figure; his gaze returned to and paused on her neckline.

"Those are beautiful pearls."

"Good evening," Margaret said. She began to walk off, but Mr. Sallow stepped in front of her.

He leaned in so only she could hear, even with the wind. "As I served dinner, I heard some of the stories Captain told. The famous Mr. Wynn, yes, but you know he has secrets."

"Good evening." Margaret said, louder. She was finished with Mr. Sallow. She did not care if she was rude. In fact, *he* was imposing on her.

Mr. Sallow followed her and Betty, then said, "But now, you know how sailors exaggerate." He bowed as he passed on, but added, "He's got secrets, same as all of us."

Margaret opened her mouth to confront the man, but he had disappeared under the mainsail.

"Is anyone botherin' ya?"

Margaret turned to find Danny at Betty's elbow. They stepped closer to the glow of light from the lantern near the mainmast.

"No." Betty's voice squeaked a little.

"I've no good opini'n of Sallow, but it does no good to say so now. We are here on the ship together for two weeks. Please let me know if you need… any… protectin' or the likes." Danny produced this speech while staring fully into Betty's lamplit face.

"Thank you, Danny," Margaret said. She almost walked on, but something about the lack of light and Mr. Swallow's behavior had raised an alert in her mind. "Danny, it is so dark tonight that I would appreciate you staying nearby."

"Of course. A pleasure, miss, and an honor." His eyes again stayed on Betty's blushing face. He stood straighter.

Margaret motioned Betty toward the railing. The sounds of the sea could be heard more than seen, except when the boat rolled to one side and the reflection of the lantern lights streaked across the dark waves.

"Not too close, Miss." Betty hesitated.

Margaret pulled her arm. "Just two more steps to get clear of the sails. I promise it is worth it. Turn so our backs are to the moon. Now, look up."

Betty gasped. "Why, I neve'. The stars are even comin' up from the sea!" she squealed.

"Aye, Miss." Danny came closer. "If you stand here and wait, they'll move abof' ya."

"No, you are lyin' to a po'r girl." Betty sniffed.

"I would never lie to you, nor make fun. Not Danny Devine. I've seen enough foolishness with folks makin' fun of me, my accent, my being an American, and Irish at that, I have." Danny stood to his full height and shouted, "Of which I'm proud!"

Margaret bit back a smile as she heard other sailors on watch or around the decks groan or curse at him. A man cleared his voice loudly behind her, and the men quieted. When she turned, she saw Mr. Wynn.

"Taking the night air?" he asked.

"Yes, Betty sat in the cabin while I dined. It hardly seemed fair. I also knew that she had never seen stars like this." She raised her head to find Danny directing Betty toward the forecastle deck for a better view. Margaret followed but slowly.

Keeping pace with her, Mr. Wynn said, "You are very kind to Betty. More than many young women of your… circumstance."

"Station or privilege, I think you meant." Margaret laughed. "Yes, I have been blessed with money and position, but since my mother's death and my separation from Father, I have learned what loneliness is—what it is to be ignored. But do not pity me, Mr. Wynn. I do not wish to imply—"

"Not at all." He reassured her. "Miss Beaton, may I ask—I do not wish to make you uncomfortable; however, I—"

Margaret laughed slightly. "Mr. Wynn, I believe *you* are the one who is uncomfortable."

"Yes." He paused. "Why does Mr. Sallow make you uncomfortable?"

"Oh," she said. "I hoped my reaction had gone unnoticed. When Sir Edgar was asking me to leave the ship—before you and the captain arrived—Sir Edgar had Mr. Sallow help him. They were both walking toward me, and I felt—I know it was foolish, but I felt trapped."

"Please, Miss Beaton, say no more. You do not need to relive it on my account." He wiped his forehead with the back of his hand. "I believe I understand. If only I could rid the ship of Mr. Sallow, but we will not make land until Lisbon. Nevertheless, I swear he will not come near you. Not anymore."

His face was a mask of anger. "Mr. Wynn, please, I believe you mistake the matter. He never touched me. I only thought I was… threatened."

"You should *never,* ever have to feel that way. It is unpardonable, what Sir Edgar and Sallow tried."

"But again, sir, I believe Mr. Sallow was only following orders from—"

"That does not make it right! Following orders? How many crimes have been committed with that as an excuse?"

"Please," Margaret placed a hand on his arm. She did not know how to comfort him, but she wanted to—deeply. "I believe you are remembering something because of me. I would not wish that. Besides, I had words with Mr. Sallow moments ago. I believe he understands my wishes fully."

"You? Had 'words'?"

Margaret smiled. "My aunt's society lessons were dreadfully boring and unconscionably arrogant, but I believe for once, just once, my ability to set a servant in his place has been useful. I daresay, I even surprised myself. It is the sea which has emboldened me."

He chuckled. "Remind me to never fall out of your good graces, or to meet you on deck at night if I have. You would have made a fearsome midshipman, Miss Beaton."

"Oh no." She shook her head. "I would 'a made a fearsome cap'ain,'" she said, imitating her father's Scottish accent.

"Touché!" He laughed again.

She loved to hear his laugh. That *she* could make him laugh. Stopping where she could still see Betty and Danny, Margaret pulled her shawl closer and looked up. Mr. Wynn also silently gazed at the sky full of stars, sparkling in varying degrees of brightness. The night sky was mesmerizing. In silence, they listened to the ship breaching wave after wave—the rhythmic bouncing of the water against the hull. Darkness and the impression of privacy gave Margaret courage, so she turned slightly and searched Mr. Wynn's face. It was in shadow, with lantern light spilling over his shoulder outlining his hair, his broad shoulders. Her heart pounded and ached, full of compassion. "Will you allow me to thank you?" she asked.

"Thank me?"

"Yes, for your service in the war. I heard some of the details from Captain Foremaster."

He did not respond for a time. Then cleared his throat and said, "Cannons booming, black powder, swords clanging, sweat pouring down me, panic rising like bile, blurring anger into madness—the memories never leave me."

"But," she paused. "They would have killed you. You acted to save your crew and yourself."

"Kill or be killed. What civilized nations we claim to be." He scoffed.

"We are… if there are men like you."

"Thank you," he said.

"Thank me?" she asked, looking sideways at him.

"Yes, for a softer view of myself than I have considered in many years." He stopped. They watched the night in comfortable silence. "Orion is rising from the sea." He pointed, and Margaret stepped closer to his arm to see. His breath tickled the side of her neck. He blocked the breeze for her, yet she still shivered from the delight of his nearness.

"You are cold." It was more statement than question. He wrapped her shawl higher up on her shoulders with both hands, then recoiled. "I beg your pardon." He stepped back.

She turned but could not make out his face in the darkness. "I am not offended." She placed a hand on his arm and cocked her head slightly. She wished for light so she could peer into his eyes. Her heart wished to take away his guilt and sadness, all that the war had burdened him with.

He did not pull away, but statue like, still shrouded in darkness, he watched her. He placed his hand on top of hers.

"It is all right," she whispered. She hardly knew what she meant until she had spoken it. Her heart beating faster, a warm smile spread across her face. She had never received the tenderness of romantic affection before; now it engulfed her. Here before her was a gentleman, a trusted ally of her father, a decorated hero. Yet he was thoughtful and gentle, a man with deep and worthy feelings. Images of him flashed before her—his tanned face in her uncle's study, defending her in front of her uncle, the touch of his hands during their dance, their conversation in the carriage, his arms carrying her off the ratlines. Every quality she had dreamed of in a man was fulfilled and standing before her. She blushed. Perhaps he *was* her one and only love.

He took her hand in both of his and gently rubbed the back of it. Even through her glove, she could feel his warmth. It was nothing to compare to the fire shooting up her arm.

Then gently, he lowered her hand and dropped it. "No, it is not. I am not—" He stepped back. "Good night, Miss Beaton." He turned and left.

The breeze chilled her even as her blush deepened. Embarrassment replaced her happy feelings. She had been terribly forward. What must he think of her? She moved to the railing and looked into the obscure murkiness of the sea, grateful for the darkness.

"I think it's time to go below, miss." Betty had rejoined her.

Holding her arm, Margaret allowed Betty to lead her.

"No use leadin' anyone on," Betty whispered. Head high, she looked straight ahead.

Passing under a lantern, Margaret saw Danny watch them leave the deck. "No," she said to Betty. "No one could mistake anyone's intentions tonight." She sighed as the door closed behind them.

Safe in their cabin, Margaret lay the pearls in their case at the bottom of her trunk, then sat on the end of the bed so Betty could remove Margaret's hairpins.

"Betty, do you ever think about being in love?"

"Me, miss? I dunno. I haven't had much time for it."

"Falling in love?"

"Thinking. Both, I dare say! I've been in service ten years, and at twenty-nine, I'm an old maid." Betty laughed and began to brush Margaret's hair.

"I can do that." Margaret took the brush and sat on the chair so Betty could have the bed. "You lie down and rest."

"This feels strange, me watching you work."

"No, you are helping me. Now tell me. What do you know of love?"

"Oh, miss. If this is because that Danny Devine was talkin' nonsense in the moonlight—"

"He was?"

"Oh, it was nothing. I promise."

"I am not surprised. You are a lovely young woman. Of course, Danny is interested."

"Now, miss, let's not have a misunderstandin'. I'm not aiming to catch myself a beau. I value my position—"

"Of course, Betty. Please, be at ease. It is—I trust you, Betty. I value your opinion. We are the only two women on this ship, and I need to—well, I have always believed that I would fall in love, deeply and truly. And that after I did, I would never recover, never love another. I would be true to it, always."

Betty smiled.

Margaret waited, hoping for some reply. "Is that silly?"

"No, it's a beautiful dream. I hope it comes true for you."

"But…"

"But life's not always that fair or perfect. My mother married again after Father died. I was purhaps three. I never knew he was my stepfather until I was ten. Even then, I wasn't confused. I knew somehow that mother loved them both. That love didn't die with my real father, but it didn't suffocate mother either. She could love again."

Margaret put the brush down. She smiled back at Betty. "Your mother and stepfather raised a good woman. Thank you."

Half an hour later, Margaret lay in the dark, listening to Betty's quiet breathing and feeling the sway of the ship on the waves. Instead of lulling her to sleep, they pulled her from thought to thought. Could she really be falling in love with Mr. Wynn? He had taken her hand, caressed it, but dropped it. Had she embarrassed him? Herself? What if he did not feel the same attraction, the same regard?

Her stomach sank with the next pull of the ocean under her. Mr. Sallow had hinted about secrets—Mr. Wynn's secrets? She had only known him for little more than a week. It was foolhardy. How could she feel this intensely for him with so little an understanding of him?

She rolled over and decided to not fall in love. Not yet. It was too risky. Margaret wanted to only love once; she had to guard her heart until she was certain love would be returned. Wasn't that wise? Why did her heart reject her mind's appeal for patience and caution? Why did it pound as she remembered his touch as he had held her hand in his?

She lay on her back and shook her head. No, she would find her father, and the two of them would settle in their quiet way. She would be content. She would finally control her own path; no one could do this for her or even with her. Sighing, she conjured up an image of walking on the beach with her father. Sleep slowly washed over her.

The dream changed. She and her father rocked in a boat in a small bay. The sea grew rough, and rain fell from a leaden sky. Father brought a hand to his head and peered off to the right, far away. A voice cried out. The boat rocked. Margaret grabbed the sides. When she looked up, Father was gone. The voice cried again. Rain pelted her. She twisted, looking at the churning sea all around the boat. Nothing. No one.

"Father!" she screamed. And woke up.

CHAPTER 15

MARGARET'S EYES OPENED TO darkness as she sat up. Had she screamed? Where was her father? Where was she? She heard a shout again. The ship lurched; she grabbed the sides of the bed to stay in it. "Betty? Betty?"

"Yes, miss."

"Did you hear—"

Before Margaret could finish, the cry came again. "Maria Luisa!" It was a man's voice from a nearby cabin.

Margaret jumped up and grabbed her shawl. The ship lurched back, and it threw her off balance. She stubbed her toe into the chair. She fumbled to the dresser attached firmly to the side wall. Finding a match, she lit the candle.

"*Espere por mim!*" the voice cried above the creaking of the timbers.

Margaret knew it was Portuguese: "Wait for me." But who was calling out?

The candle flared. Betty grabbed the door as she and Margaret spilled out into the passageway. The ship was tossing.

"Wake up, man!"

It was Captain Foremaster's deep voice from two cabins down.

Margaret knocked. "Is everyone well?"

The door flew open.

Margaret gasped and stepped back. Mr. Wynn stood before her, both hands pushed against the doorway to keep his body steady. She held the candle up and peered at him. He was wide eyed but focused on the wall behind her; perspiration glistened on his brow. His hair had fallen in his eyes, his nightshirt rumpled and partially open revealing the muscles of his neck. She blushed at the pounding of her heart as she saw the strength of his upper body. She pulled her shawl closer and looked away. "Are you well, sir?" she asked, lowering her voice.

The sea rose again beneath them and dropped. Margaret slid back and fell against the wall. The candle, landing on the floor, sputtered out.

"Where am I?" Mr. Wynn asked.

The doctor's cabin door opened across from Mr. Wynn's. Holding a candle, Dr. Giles stepped out, fully dressed. Margaret's face reddened at being found in her nightdress in the passageway.

Betty retrieved their candle and lit it using Dr. Giles's.

Captain Foremaster now appeared behind Mr. Wynn. "Nightmare. Sorry to have awakened you. Please—"

"Of course." She and Betty stepped out of the doctor's way.

"A sedative, I think?" The doctor passed under Mr. Wynn's arm, entering the cabin.

Mr. Wynn blinked several times and rubbed his face with his hand. "Miss Beaton?" he asked, as his eyes finally focused on what was in front of him. His face was a mask of pain.

Margaret's stomach dropped. "Good night, sir." She and Betty scurried back toward their cabin, leaning against the walls as the angry sea pitched the boat.

Once inside with Betty, Margaret sobbed a few times. Then she crawled into her bed and pulled the covers up close.

"What is it, miss? Are you upset?" Betty asked.

"No, just… embarrassed."

"Oh, no cause. It was a simple misunderstandin'. I was with you, and your shawl kept you modest."

"Thank you, Betty." Margaret rolled over toward the wall. A large tear slipped toward her ear. She remembered Mr. Wynn's words: "Maria Luisa! *Espere por mim!*" He had called for Maria Luisa by her Christian name, a Portuguese name. He was not calling for his mother or sister. For all Margaret knew, Mr. Wynn was betrothed. Why else would he have asked that woman to wait for him? He must love this Maria Luisa, with all his broken heart. His desperate tone tore at her.

How could she have been so simple? Mr. Wynn was at least ten years older than she. He had traveled Europe, fought a war, and experienced life. Why had she believed that he might fall in love with her, and fall in love for the first time?

She squeezed her eyes to stop the tears. *Maria Luisa.* Margaret stared up in the darkness, her heart shuddering, her breath shaking.

JOSHUA SWALLOWED THE SLEEPING draught. "Thank you." Embarrassed, he slipped into his hammock. The doctor left, and Foremaster blew out the candle.

"Foremaster?"

"Hm?"

"What did I say this time?"

"You asked Maria Luisa to wait for you."

Silence. Joshua did not want to say more. How could he admit to anyone that he had failed his wife? That he had left her to die?

Joshua exhaled slowly. It was the same dream, the same memory.

His ship would sail the next morning. He held Maria Luisa, crushed her in his arms, breathed the scent of lilac in her hair, tipped her head back and placed his lips on hers—

The ship lunged, and he felt his hammock sway. He sat up in bed and raked his hand through his hair. The memory tore at him; first it fed him false hope, then ate him alive with longing. He squeezed his eyes, but the memory returned.

He kissed Maria's temple, her eyes, then her lips—slowly, deeply. He wanted her to know the depth of his love for her. Since their marriage a year earlier and the birth of their son two months ago, he had only seen her a few times when his ship had come into port. His arms encircled both her and his son, Miguel. He did not know how long it would be before he could hold her again. He kissed Miguel, whose entire head fit in his palm. Then cradling her head in his hands, he kissed her forehead once more and tried to step back. She clung to him, crying into the shoulder of his uniform.

"Não nos deixe. Levenos com você."

Do not leave us. Take us with you. *Her words seared into his heart. He thought it through again. He could not take Maria Luisa, her mother, and an infant on board a crowded man-o-war, possibly into battle. What if they were attacked? Sank? What if they were captured? The French could be brutal. He pulled back and gazed lovingly into her eyes. "You will be safe here in this convent. I will come for you when I can."*

What a fool he was. What a logical fool to follow his head instead of his heart. To deny her his protection.

"Meu amor. Minha vida. Eu te amo."

"I love you, too. I will come back to you." He kissed her and left. Looking back, he saw his mother-in-law holding his wife as she sobbed.

Joshua slipped out of his hammock and dressed. Outside, he was pelted with rain. Ascending to the poop deck, he greeted the helmsman. Resting against the mizzenmast completely drenched by the storm, Joshua let a few tears flow. Water lashed his face. The boat lurched again, and water washed across his boots when the ship tilted starboard. *Just as the water from the overturned baptistry had met his feet at the convent.* Why did everything remind him of Maria Luisa, of his worst day on earth? Touching Miss Beaton's hand, feeling an intense attraction to her, feeling her compassion had brought the memories back.

He ran inside the church. "Maria Luisa!" Stepped in the water of the overturned baptismal font. No holy water left to cleanse anyone. Two broken pews were pushed against the wall. Splintered bottles and bloody rags littered the nave. The stench of filth assaulted his nose. The ornate walls and gold-leafed statues behind the altar still gleamed, a strange contrast to the destruction of the rest of the chapel.

His heart pounded. Sweat dripped off him. He ran. "Maria Luisa!" The door to the cloister was off its hinge. He bounded up the stairs. "Maria!" Nothing. No one. "Maria!"

He looked out Maria Luisa's chamber window onto the courtyard. A nun lay face down. Only her wimple moved with the breeze. He bolted for the stairs.

Joshua pounded his fist against the mast holding him upright. The pain of his hand exceeded or at least distracted his heart from the pain of his loss. He had been foolish. He had let his guard down. Only a few hours ago, he had lost himself in the sweet, trusting, naïve face of Miss Beaton; he had forgotten his sorrow, his failure. Her eyes had locked on his, revealing her gratitude, her trust, perhaps even the beginnings of affection.

He had lingered, held her hand. Miss Beaton had found the part of his heart he had believed lost or banished, drowned in his tears for Maria Luisa. Now awake, his heart gushed out all of his guilt and brought it, warm, to the surface. His love, his loss—it was fresh again.

He knelt over Maria's broken body, pulled her bodice closed, pulled her skirt down over her ankles. He cradled her head in his arms. A guttural roar tore out of his throat. Another. And another.

Then he jumped up and whirled. "Miguel!" Where was his son?

Tears flowed down his cheeks with the rain. He had failed. It was his fault Maria Luisa was dead. He had not saved Maria or protected himself from heartache and loss; it would be the same with another, now. How could he ever allow himself to care for, to love, another woman? How could he face the unknown terrors that a life of love would inevitably bring? No. He may marry someday for convenience. He might have a companion, friendship, but he would never risk love and failure again, and pain—inevitable pain.

He twisted his ring. Miguel and his mother-in-law had escaped, hidden. They had lived, survived. Maria Luisa's sacrifice had saved them. He should have been there; he should have died, not Maria Luisa.

He stamped his feet to warm them and shook the blood back into his numb hands. The rain had softened; the storm was moving on. The boat jerked less. He found his footing again. Slowly, he made his way down and through the tossing quarterdeck and below. The effects of the sleeping draught, which he had fought, began to overtake him. He would sleep and avoid Miss Beaton. That would be better. Let her forget any growing feelings for him, if indeed she had any. It would be less painful for them both now than for him to disappoint her later.

Rubbing his eyes, Joshua stepped out onto the quarterdeck. Four bells. It was six o'clock in the morning and twilight was beginning to remove the darkness on the quarterdeck. He had slept fitfully, but not well, tossing in his hammock. He arose and dressed.

The storm had passed and a gusty breeze was drying out the ship. Wet rope, tar, and pine filled his nostrils. He rolled his shoulders. Climbing the steps to the poop deck, he nodded to Mr. Sallow at the wheel. Joshua turned, surprised to see Miss Beaton down on the main deck wrapped in a shawl, looking up at the mainsail. She smiled weakly at him but moved away.

Clearly his plan to avoid her would not work. He descended and walked to her. "Miss Beaton, I fear that last night, I inconvenienced you and many others." His words applied to both times he had been in her company. Would she understand that? He looked directly at her. She did not look away.

"Please, do not be uncomfortable." Miss Beaton's smile disappeared.

"I was not inconvenienced. I realized the truth quickly enough. It is painful, though, to watch someone wake from a nightmare. I apologize for having intruded, for having woken you." She crossed to the rail.

Touché, he thought. He joined her and gazed out at the cloudy gray sky and lead colored sea. Little white caps formed from the wind, and the ship rolled more gently under his feet. "Nightmares, yes. Residue from the war."

She raised her eyes to his, her brows creased, and shook her head. "I understand sadness and mourning."

He creased his forehead. Did she understand him? She met him at every turn with a depth of faith and compassion that he had lost, or believed he had lost. "Thank you."

"Who is she? Your Maria Luisa?" Margaret stared out at the waves.

Joshua paused. He had not considered sharing this. His emotions were raw; he was unsure of himself. But perhaps his explanation could end any expectations Miss Beaton might have because of his behavior. "My wife." He swallowed. "My deceased wife."

"Oh." Miss Beaton said and turned her head away. A minute passed with only the sound of waves slapping the hull and the wind whipping the sails. Joshua shook his head. She would reject him now because he had married a Portuguese lady. He should not have been surprised that Miss Beaton also suffered from the prejudices of London. Why did it hurt more than usual?

"Will you tell me about her?"

Joshua's eyes widened. He peered at Miss Beaton. She looked at him, but her face was blank; she wore the society mask so many women adopted. He sighed. Why did it matter? What good would it do? But he needed to speak of Maria Luisa. He shifted his weight and placed his hands on the rail.

Closing his eyes, he was once again in Lisbon, six years ago. "I attended a ball in Lisbon. Strange how in wartime the most mundane events, like a ball, make one feel normal. The French had moved north;

Lisbon was relatively safe. Maria Luisa was there, and we danced. She did not look down on me as an Englishman, but tried to speak to me in English. We laughed at our attempts to speak each other's languages. She was beautiful and kind. I was smitten."

He opened his eyes and waited for a reaction. Miss Beaton was completely still despite the motion around her. She gazed out at the ocean with both hands on the rail. She said nothing, but simply held onto the railing to steady herself against the constant dips. The spray dampened her curls and blew a few strands in his direction.

He rolled his head and took a breath. "She was the daughter of Dom Duarte Marques-Almeida and Dona Benedita Maria Abreu-Santos. Her family, she had a brother and sister, did not leave with the queen and her court to Brazil. Her father, a wealthy noble and patriot, stayed to fight for his country."

Joshua leaned against the rail and allowed himself to get lost in memory. "I called on her the next day since I had a few days of leave. Her father met me in his library and explained that no fortune-seeking Englishman was welcome to court his daughter. What could I answer? I was a second son of a second son—I had no inheritance. I was a second lieutenant at the time, though tragically, within the month, I would become a captain. I had not earned much money from my time at sea, but we had captured two prize ships. I bowed and turned to leave when Maria Luisa entered her father's study and asked us to tea with her mother. Her chin held high, there was a fire in her eyes. A determination. Reluctantly, her father agreed."

"At tea, Maria Luisa's mother asked a number of questions about my family, my experiences and background. Between their broken English and my poor Portuguese, I answered as best I could, but I left hopeless of ever seeing Maria Luisa again. However, the next day, I received an invitation to a party given by a friend of her family's. Maria Luisa attended, accompanied by her mother, and I was allowed to call on her."

Joshua paused. The memory of Maria Luisa's dark hair and flashing eyes against her white gown slowly faded. "After my promotion, I continued to see Maria the three times I was in Lisbon. Six months later, Dom Marques asked me point blank what my intentions were, and if my family would protect and love Maria. I was shocked but elated. I promised I would, and my family would. We were married three days later before her father and brother, Rafael, left with the Portuguese forces for the front."

"Months passed. I saw her when I could, but my ship was positioned farther north, supporting troops, fighting French frigates. It was relatively safe in Lisbon, but when Maria Luisa's father died, she wanted to be closer to me. She hoped I would be there when our son was born." He kicked his toe against the hull. "I was not."

Miss Beaton inhaled. The spell of memory broken, he looked over at her. Eyes closed, her lips were drawn in a thin line. Her head bowed slightly.

Joshua gripped the rail. "You are shocked that I have married a foreigner and had a child with her."

Miss Beaton lifted her tear-streaked face to him. "I am saddened that a child has lost his mother. I understand that pain. Your offense is misplaced." She turned to go.

He reached out for her forearm and held it gently. She relented and stopped. Over her bowed head, he said. "I apologize. I have too long expected disgust and disdain for my life's choices. But I should have expected a charitable response from so kind a lady."

"Thank you." She hesitated. "I understand the disdain of society. My parents' union was not acknowledged or accepted by my mother's people." An uneasy silence settled between them.

"Please, may I finish?" He tried to look into her eyes, but she nodded without looking up. Instead, she returned to the railing, her gaze on the sea. The impending sunrise was reflecting pink on the silvery gray-blue of the ocean. He had not spoken of these events to

another soul, not in this way, and somehow the confession of it un-
burdened him. He could not stop. No. More than that, he *wanted* to
tell her everything. He hoped she would understand him. He needed
her understanding.

He needed her.

He took a breath. "I relented and took her, our son, and her mother
to Oporto on my ship. They had money and convinced the nuns of the
Carmelitas to let them stay in their convent. Months passed. As the
fighting intensified, it was harder to get leave to see them. On my last
visit, she begged me to take them with me, but I knew I was headed
into danger. I pleaded with her to understand. She cried as I left."

Joshua scraped his boot against the wooden deck. He stood up
straight. He gazed at the sea and swallowed down his emotions, his
tears. The silence was only broken by the churn of the sea below them
and calls of the men in the rigging above. At the single bell of the
watch, the sun broke the surface of the deep blue horizon.

"What happened?" Miss Beaton asked quietly.

The sun's rising was blinding; he blinked and looked down at his
hands. He sighed deeply. "My ship saw some action, but I was safe. That
is when I heard—" He cradled his bowed head in his hands. "Oporto
was attacked. The convent was broken into by French soldiers. It was
chaos. Some nuns prayed; some ran. Maria distracted the soldiers
away from her room where her mother was hiding with our son. My
mother-in-law informed me when I finally found their hiding place.
There were few survivors."

"Killed?" Miss Beaton's head came up sharply. "When?"

"Five years ago." He pounded the railing with a fist. "The French
were brutal. She sacrificed herself to save her mother and our son."

Miss Beaton retrieved her handkerchief and wiped her eyes.
Blinking several times first, she turned to him. Her face was grave,
her mouth turned down. She nodded once and then spoke. "You

remember her when she was fearful and frustrated with you. But that was just the once. What was she like during the rest of her life?"

His jaw dropped. He had not considered that over the years he had focused so much on his own pain and Maria Luisa's last words to him that he had not remembered the joyous times. "She loved to laugh." A small smile flickered on his lips. "She loved to dance and host parties, sing to Miguel, and walk with me in the garden. Ah, she loved flowers." A tear formed in his eye. How had he forgotten all of that? Why had he forgotten?

"And is that her in the ring?" Miss Beaton gently took his hands. He hadn't realized they were shaking.

Joshua studied Miss Beaton's face. It was a mask of agony, tears running down her cheeks. The ring. Careful to keep Miguel's hair from flying away, he clicked it open. At first his heart pounded a guilty thump for showing it to another woman, but as Margaret held his hand in both of hers to gaze into the face of Maria Luisa, he was comforted in a way he had not thought possible.

"She is very beautiful." Miss Beaton withdrew her hands. "Is that her lock of hair?"

"Miguel's." He closed his ring carefully and examined her face. She did not look up.

"I am glad you found your true love; I am sorry she was taken away." She pulled her shawl tightly around her shoulders, then stopped. "You are no more at fault for her death than I am for my mother's. We have lost them, but not forever. And not even for the present. Why, Maria Luisa is alive in you and in your son. You will have her love for all your days." Her voice cracked. "Excuse me." She walked toward the door to her cabin below.

CHAPTER 16

MARGARET AWOKE. LIGHT SEEPED under the cabin door. It must be mid-morning. Opening the curtains, she saw the sun glinting off the sea.

After leaving Mr. Wynn at sunrise the previous day, she had stayed in her cabin, telling Betty she was unwell. Betty was kind and quiet. Margaret could not find the words to explain, not even to herself, the roiling emotions that fought for her attention. Surprise, disappointment, love, sorrow, loss, mourning. Last night she had been restless, not falling asleep until early morning. When Betty had risen, Margaret had sent her on deck for fresh air, then tried to sleep again.

Margaret sat up in bed and pulled her legs up to her chest. She let the sea rock her, the way her mother had when she missed her father.

She rubbed her eyes to loosen the skin where her tears had dried before sleep had relieved her. Loss. Eternal loss. Heart break. The emotions lay in a lump where her heart should have been. Listening to Joshua had torn open her own wound—those long days of watching her mother suffer, watching her mother weaken. Losing her mother to illness at the age of fourteen, had left her unmoored.

Her father had not received their letters in time. He had not come to the funeral. She had sat alone in the first pew. Her father's family was dead. Her mother's only sibling, Sir Reginald, sat behind her with Lady Frances. Singing. A sermon. The coolness of the outside. The smell of earth in her hand just before she dropped it onto her mother's coffin.

Then she was living with Sir Reginald and Lady Frances. Any hope of affection or comfort from her aunt had been dispelled in the first minutes of Margaret's stay in their house.

At first, Margaret dreamed her father would come. But then the war continued, years past, and Margaret had her first season. A new hope grew next to the one she had for her father. She might meet a worthy man, they would fall in love, and together, they would find her father. They would have a home and children. He would be her one and only love. She, his.

Here in the dark, Margaret recognized that Mr. Wynn was a worthy man. He had always treated her with respect, kindness, and friendship. No wonder she had feelings for him. She had been starving for such attention. Together, they were traveling to her father. But—he had fallen in love already. His heart had been given. Margaret's pulse raced. Maria Luisa had been killed. That horror fell on Margaret again, and the tears flowed. How could he stand it? To know that Maria Luisa had suffered? To be parted from her?

Listening to his story, her heart melted. She had wanted to take him in her arms and comfort him. To place her hand on his cheek.

Instead, alone in her cabin, she held her head in her hands. Clearly, Mr. Wynn had loved his wife, still loved his wife. She would not change that if she could.

But how could she change her own heart? Set herself free? What about her dreams of a first love? The love her parents had shared? Those ideas now were like the dreams of a child: sweet but unsubstantial in the light of reality. Her compassion for Mr. Wynn was more than simple Christian duty. It was a longing to comfort someone the way *she* needed to be comforted. To address the wrongs and losses of life with an equal. To heal together. He could understand her in ways that others could not. And she, him.

Except, he was still in love with Maria Luisa. And always would be. She turned her face into her pillow and sobbed.

JOSHUA STOOD NEAR THE wheel. The sun glinted off the starboard side of the ship; it was nearing sunset. He sighed.

"Afternoon, sir."

"Sallow." Joshua said. The man passed and looked askance at him. Joshua shifted his weight. He realized that others would notice that he had spent more time on deck today than usual. He knew he had stayed, hoping for a glimpse of Miss Beaton. He had found himself hoping to glimpse her at dinner last night, or on deck after, or even in the early hours of today. No white skirt glided on the deck. No sign of her had disturbed the rhythmic sounds of the sailors' songs and calls as the ship rocked up and down.

It had been over a day since she left him on the deck. Danny reported last night that Miss Beaton was indisposed and would not join the officers at dinner. Today, Joshua had seen only Betty on deck.

Miss Beaton was avoiding him and everyone else. The look in her eyes, the pain, the mourning at their last meeting—he wished he could spare her that. What was she thinking? Why had she stayed in her cabin the entire day? Perhaps he had caused her new grief? Her heart had been broken before with the death of her mother. She had been truly shocked to hear of Maria Luisa's death. Perhaps he had been too straightforward. Miss Beaton was a lady, not a sailor, not a soldier.

He walked to the stern of the boat for privacy, knowing that Miss Beaton was in the cabin just beneath him. He was as close to her as he could be. Leaning on the rail, he noticed the wake. The chop of the white caps was fiercest near the ship. But as the ship passed, the water calmed until only a streak of glossiness remained on the surface far into the distance. He could see where they had sailed, and it was peaceful from this distance.

He inhaled the sea's freshness. He had lived in the churn of Maria Luisa's death, keeping the pain fresh, keeping it close. Now, he realized time could heal him, bring him distance and peace. Maria Luisa's influence would always be felt in his life, but he did not have to let the pain of her loss eclipse the joy of her life.

Looking over the taffrail, he could see that the curtains of Miss Beaton's cabin were open. He did not want to see in. He simply needed to know she was well. He needed to see her.

How had she seen into his heart, touched it gently, and left it beating stronger than before? He had never shared so much about Maria Luisa before, even with Foremaster. Miss Beaton had listened and reached for him. She had forgiven his rude assumptions about her. She had not recoiled from him when he had admitted to having a foreign wife and son. Half English, half Portuguese. Most women of the *ton* would have rejected him, his choices, his son, just as his father had, but she had not. They had shared a moment of tenderness over his son.

Joshua ran a hand through his hair. His feelings for Miss Beaton transcended his attraction for her youth and beauty. It was deeper. It was more. There was respect and friendship. Now when hope for a future, a life, was alive within him again, Miss Beaton had left. And all that sound and motion on board which had distracted Joshua from his grief for years could not help him now as much as Miss Beaton's presence, her touch, could.

How could he apologize? How could he set things right?

CHAPTER 17

"JUST APOLOGIZE. BUT BOW first." Foremaster grabbed his hat and turned to leave their shared cabin.

Joshua shifted uncomfortably in his hammock.

"Unless you are… afraid?"

"Of course, I am afraid."

"Wise." Foremaster raised an eyebrow. "There is nothing as terrifying as an unattached young lady. Even when they choose you, you can never be certain." He brushed his hat with his sleeve.

Joshua sighed. Foremaster had been bitterly disappointed by the now Mrs. Barrowclough.

Foremaster opened the door, then looked at Joshua directly. "Still. It must be faced."

Joshua groaned as Foremaster raised his chin and left. Foremaster had repeated the advice they'd heard constantly as midshipmen. *It must be faced.* No task, no matter how distasteful or daunting, et cetera, et cetera.

Rolling out of the hammock onto his feet, Joshua walked to the small mirror in the cabin above the shelf with the shaving blade. It was a bit tricky to shave on ship, but he had years of practice. As he examined his reflection, he pondered the earlier question. Was he afraid of Miss Beaton? Her face rose before him—the green eyes, auburn waves of hair, the soft smile. The touch of her hands on his, the look of sadness in her eyes as she gazed at Maria Luisa's picture. Yes, he was afraid—of *hurting* her. No man would wish to cause such a sweet lady to cry, to be distressed. He had already done that once. How could he avoid doing it again?

He had wandered the deck for an hour in hopes that Miss Beaton would come. Five more minutes, and he would knock on her door. He would apologize today.

The blue waves were tinged with silver as the noon-day sun glinted off them. A stiff breeze whipped at his hat and filled the sails. They were making excellent time, probably five knots.

"Mr. Wynn, good afternoon."

He whirled around, caught off guard. Miss Beaton and Betty were arm in arm. She curtsied. He bowed. She passed on. *Strange.*

The ladies made their way to the railing but kept walking, evidently making a turn around the main deck.

"Danny." Joshua called as Danny exited the wheelhouse.

"Sir."

"I need you to intercept Betty. I need to speak with Miss—"

"O' course." Danny was gone before Joshua could finish. *Also strange.*

Danny walked toward the ladies from the opposite side of the deck while Joshua went down the middle, over the coiled lines by the main mast, to come up from behind.

"Miss Beaton, Miss Betty. A fine day to you." Danny stopped in front of them and bowed.

"Uh, Miss Beaton." Joshua cleared his throat and removed his hat.

Miss Beaton turned without releasing Betty's arm, but Danny extended his arm to Betty, and she took it. Miss Beaton placed her hands together in front of her and gave him her placid society face. She did not speak.

Clearing his throat, he said, "I have not seen you on deck recently." That did not sound like an apology. *Blast!*

"I have been otherwise engaged." She blinked twice at him.

He twisted his hat in his hands. "I am sorry."

"What?" Her face took on a look of concern.

He gazed at her, into her eyes, wide with concern. This was the real Miss Beaton, not society's polished lady.

"I should not have burdened you with my grief, with its details. It was unpardonable. Forgive me." He looked up.

Her brows contracted. She bit her lip. "I was not—there is no need. I mean—" She had not turned away. Then she blushed and stared at her hands.

"Can we be friends again?"

"Friends?" Her voice cracked and her face pinched but so briefly that a second later he was not sure it had happened. "Of course," she said.

He blew out a breath and offered his arm. "Shall we stroll the main deck?" She took his arm and heat rose splendidly up it. He breathed in again. "I wanted to thank you."

"Thank me?"

"Yes, I—it is an odd thing to explain, but you did not judge me for marrying Maria Luisa, for having a half-Portuguese son. I—I am grateful."

MR. WYNN'S SMILE MELTED her. Margaret had come above deck, resolved to keep Mr. Wynn at arm's length, but now her hand was placed gently on his forearm. The closeness sent shivers through her.

"Are you chilled?" He pulled her shawl over her shoulder as naturally... as he would have done for Maria Luisa.

"Yes. No!" She turned to find Betty. "It is the wind."

"Let me call Betty."

"No, I do not want to ruin her time on deck."

"Then I will walk you in." They proceeded in that direction when he chuckled.

"You are laughing. What do you find amusing?"

"I find *you* both refreshing and surprising, Miss Beaton. At the moment, I am delighted that you care so much for your maid's happiness."

"Do you?"

"Yes, when I was a young boy, I came upon my nursemaid crying. It was then that I realized she was more than just *my* personal servant." He spoke about his childhood, his mother, having to leave at a young age for school. Margaret was amazed. He shared so freely what many in society would not have shared, or at least not so soon. He was open with her. True, they had not known each other long, but if they had been courting in London, she would have learned about a tenth of this. Yet, in a few weeks of courting, Society would have pushed her to make a match with much less information about a man's character.

She was laughing at his antics when the bells sounded.

"We should go in, but Miss Beaton, tomorrow I would very much like to hear of your childhood." He extended his arm.

Margaret took his arm but blushed deeply and walked more quickly. She needed to get away from the irresistible pull which drew her toward this man who—only this morning—she had decided was still in love with his departed wife. This man, with whom she would not fall in love, whom she could never marry, now blocked the wind for her with his muscular frame and tenderly adjusted her shawl. His nearness caused her heart to gallop like Poseidon's watery steeds.

"Thank you," she said as he opened the door for her.

"Will I see you at dinner?"

"Of course." She tried to smile, but the twitch of her lips was a weak effort. "Goodbye." The door closed behind her, and she made her way to her cabin. Grateful to be alone, she fell on the bed. Fresh tears slipped one at a time from the corners of her eyes. *Friends?* He'd uttered that word and part of her heart had broken. Either it broke in two or broke free from the restrictions she had tried to place on it. Or both. She knew that in spite of her romantic notions and best preventative efforts, she had fallen in love with Mr. Joshua Wynn.

CHAPTER 18

MARGARET AND BETTY STEPPED onto the main deck the next day. Margaret blinked several times, trying to adjust her eyes to the shine of the sun. It glinted off the ship's surfaces. A breeze lifted the curls on her neck and pulled a few strands free from her bun. She breathed deeply and sighed. She and Betty walked the main deck, but near enough to the rail for support when the swells beneath them rolled. The worn rail was warm and smooth in Margaret's hand.

Sailors at work would stop or rise to pull a forelock. Margaret nodded back. She was looking for Mr. Wynn. She was hoping for Mr. Wynn. They had both been rather quiet at dinner the night before. Afterward, he had accompanied her and Betty as they'd walked under the stars. He'd stayed only a few silent minutes before he had bid her goodnight and retired to his quarters.

In the calm hours of early morning, Margaret had lain awake thinking of Mr. Wynn's history. She was not repulsed by Mr. Wynn's son being half-Portuguese, but she wondered if she and Mr. Wynn ever married, could she truly love someone else's son as her own? She had never considered such a possibility. Could the boy like her?

She rolled over in bed. A more pertinent question rattled again inside her brain. Friends? What had he meant by friends? And he had certainly meant it. His smile, the way he'd leaned toward her. Friends? Was that all he considered for the future? For her? She should be glad. At her father's, she would see Mr. Wynn often, meet in company often, travel in the same social circle. But how would she feel, knowing that her emotions were stronger than friendship toward him?

Her mind wound around many issues as she lay in the dark waiting for sunrise and the day's activities, which would fill her mind with something else. In the end, her thoughts came back to the most important question: could she ever trust Mr. Wynn to truly love her after he had already loved someone else? If so, she would be happy. She could accept him, and his son. They would live in Lisbon with her father, of course.

Could she help him see the possibility of being more than friends? She had to try. They were halfway through the crossing. In one more week, she would be in Lisbon. While she had his attention now, she must make the most of it.

Those thoughts returned in the bright sunlight of the afternoon. She had let her mind run ahead, too far ahead. Margaret nodded at Danny, who passed them, very slowly. It brought Margaret back to the present. She should focus on what would come in a few days. Could she make a life in Lisbon? Either with her father or with Mr. Wynn. She spoke enough Portuguese to not fear learning the language more completely. Living with her father would certainly make that an important skill. Would she be accepted by Mr. Wynn's friends and associates? The British were not popular in Lisbon at the moment.

"Afternoon, *ladies.*"

Margaret turned, but it was Mr. Sallow who smiled and bowed as he passed.

Margaret shivered. He caused the hair on her neck to stand up. Grateful to be going in the opposite direction, Margaret looked toward the wheel house. Captain Foremaster was there. He saw her outstretched hand and waved. She sighed and rolled her shoulders back. "Let us head in," she said to Betty.

Near the middle of the ship, Margaret tilted her head back. The sails were full, and the ship was cutting through the shining water with a gentle bounce. The waves slapped against the side of the ship, releasing a bit of spray into the wind. Moving one hand over her eyes, Margaret gazed out on the deep blue of the ocean. It stretched to the horizon, leaving Margaret feeling insignificant and awestruck.

"Excuse me, Miss Beaton. May I have a word?"

Margaret turned to see Danny Devine, cap in hand, before her. She glanced at Betty to her right. Betty's head was down, her face bright red, hands fidgeting with her reticule.

"Yes, Danny?" Margaret returned her attention to Danny, who was also looking at Betty.

"Er… " He cleared his throat and looked Margaret straight in the eyes. "I wish to court Betty, so I do. As an honorable man, I asked if there was anyone whose permission I should ask first. She said to ask you."

Margaret's eyes widened. She looked at Betty, whose hopeful face was bright red. Margaret gave a small smile and a slight nod to her maid. Betty returned the nod. That gesture melted Margaret's heart. Margaret's mind flashed to scenes that she and Betty had shared. Dancing in Mr. Wynn's office, laughing on the bed while packing, Betty standing beneath Margaret on the ratlines, Betty placing her mother's necklace on Margaret.

Betty had grown quite dear to her. She had followed Margaret on this journey without hesitation. How could she repay such friendship and loyalty? She wanted the very best for Betty. Margaret examined Danny. Was he good enough for Betty? Her eyes narrowed a bit. What would Margaret's father say to this? "Mr. Devine, you have my permission to court Betty—" She noticed his growing smile. "On three conditions."

His smile faded, and he shifted his weight. "Thank you, um, what may they be?"

"First, it must always be in my company. Second, you must explain to me your situation and position and why you believe this... um, courting would be beneficial to Betty. And third, you must ask permission from both Captain Foremaster and Mr. Wynn."

Danny's smile returned. "And I have already done such a thing by askin' Mr. Wynn. Thank you, miss. When I am done with my watch, I will relate to you my situation."

"Tea tomorrow will be more appropriate. In the dining room, when you are off watch."

"As you please." He replaced his cap, and with a bow to both ladies, he strode off. Betty giggled as she watched him go with a new bounce in her step.

"Oh, miss. How can I ev'r thank you?"

"Betty, are you sure?"

"Yes, miss. Coming on this ship and meeting Danny, I realized that I will not always be content to work as a maid. That, I might find—" Betty opened her mouth, but then shut it and curtseyed. "Mr. Wynn," she said, looking over Margaret's shoulder.

Margaret turned and was face to face with him.

"A word, Miss Beaton?" he asked.

Betty curtseyed and made her way to the railing, looking out over the sea, but this time staying in ear shot. Margaret did not mind.

"I believe Danny just approached you about courting Betty."

"Yes, and I have given my approval... with conditions."

JOSHUA RAISED HIS EYEBROW. which brought a smile to Miss Beaton's face. "So have I. What were yours?" he asked.

"That he court her in my presence, after making an account of himself, and that you and Captain Foremaster also give approval."

"How very similarly our minds work," he said. "I added that it must be for thirty minutes or less each day under my watch, unless, of course, you invite him to tea."

"Of course." She nodded. "I believe I will need to invite you to tea as well, then."

His eyes widened, then he dropped his gaze to his shoes. "Miss Beaton, I gladly accept, as Danny's chaperone."

She laughed, then added, "For a moment, I thought you were going to say as Danny's second. You accepted as if agreeing to a duel."

"I meant no disrespect—"

"Do not make yourself uncomfortable, Mr. Wynn. If tea does not go well, I will see you with pistols at dawn."

Her mouth twisted as she left. She was laughing at him, but as politely as she could. He shook his head. A half-hour of tea he could manage, but chaperoning Danny and Betty? Uncomfortable did not begin to describe his reaction.

Danny had done what Joshua had wanted to do, had planned to do that evening after dinner—speak his mind and make a formal declaration. Now, Joshua would feel ridiculous asking Miss Beaton. *So, Danny has given me an idea, Miss Beaton. Perhaps I can not only be Danny's chaperone but court you as well?* Preposterous! Besides, on this ship, she was under his protection. He would not take advantage of that, of her.

Still, if he did not declare himself, he would feel like a fraud, spending time with Miss Beaton under the guise of friendship and duty, all while trying to woo her. No. He would have to wait. And waiting is what had gotten him into this mess.

CHAPTER 19

"COME IN." BETTY BOBBED a welcome to Mr. Wynn and Danny as they entered the dining room. Margaret noticed a becoming blush on Betty's cheek. She looked over her head and caught Mr. Wynn's eye. She had hoped he would also be diverted. Instead, his brow contracted and his eyes were pinched. He appeared rather... somber? Pensive? Nervous?

"Me darling," Danny began until he caught Margaret's raised eyebrow. "Er, I mean, Miss Betty." Danny cleared his throat.

"Miss Beaton, Betty," Mr. Wynn, hat in hand, was running his hand through his blond hair.

Margaret smiled at him. "Please, sit down." Margaret began pouring the first cup. "Mr. Devine, where in Ireland did you say you were born?"

"Sligo. On the West Coast. We lived near the city of Grange. I had the sea for my front door and Benbulbin, our green mountain, out the back. So many days, I'd climb up its west slope and look out at the sea. A sparkling jewel it seemed to me. I would dream of sailing away to the west. It was an enchanting place to be young, it was. At home, I'd smell my ma's cooking over a peat fire." He sighed. "But tweren't any opportunities for us. I was ten when my parents brought us to Boston in search of freedoms denied us by the... British. Pardon my frankness. I have no hardness toward you ladies."

Danny went quiet, fumbling with his teacup.

"And your parents? Do they live in Boston?" Margaret took a sip.

"Me father died when I was nigh twelve. That's when I first went to sea, to support me ma and two sisters. They worked where they could. My mother took in wash; my sisters worked as scullery maids. For five years, I learned the skills of sailing, I did. Then, our ship, flying the American flag, was attacked and boarded by the British. They heard me accent and immediately pressed me to serve his Majesty. Next I knows, I'm a sailor for the British Navy until the end of Napoleon. The very government me family tried to escape! Four years with no pay to send home while me family suffere'."

Mr. Wynn cleared his throat, and Danny stared into his cup. Margaret, taking a bite of buttered bread, glanced at Betty. Her head was bowed, but a red blush rose to her forehead.

Danny cleared his throat. "Then me luck changed, it did. I was fortunate to serve under Captain Wynn, as he was. When he got out of the Navy, he offered me a job. Me! Why, I was that proud. I bought me mother and two sisters muslin and sent it to them with me firs' pay." Danny chuckled and grinned at Betty. She had raised her head slightly.

"Danny was one of the best sailors, the hardest working of my men. Considering the distasteful circumstances surrounding his *employment* in the British Navy, his desire to make something of himself impressed me."

"That's how we Devines are—hard workers." Danny smiled again at Betty. "I am to follow Mr. Wynn to Boston to set up an office there, I am. With the pay, I can afford to set up a household… if I were to find a woman kind enough to work beside me." He blushed and sipped his tea.

"I am glad to hear it," Margaret said. "Danny, I am sorry for the circumstances which brought you under British command."

Danny looked up, eyes wide. He gave a soft smile, and said, "Thank you, Miss Beaton. Purhaps me words were a bit… strong, but I have only spoken the truth." After a few moments of silence, he said, "Miss Betty, I've a letter from my sister which came last month. I wish you to read it." Danny unfolded the letter and placed it between them.

Betty's eyes grew wide. She stared at Margaret

Margaret immediately understood. Betty could not read. Why had Margaret not realized it before? The past week had taught Margaret much about Betty's life, but what did she really know about Betty? Why hadn't she asked more questions? Listened more? Margaret had still been focused on her own self. She determined to learn more about what Betty wanted to do and become. To start, Margaret would offer to teach Betty to read the next morning. "Danny, perhaps you wish to read your letter to Betty. Mr. Wynn and I need to discuss Lisbon. If you do not mind us talking at the other end of the room?"

"Aye, miss. I mean thank you, Miss Beaton."

Betty smiled gratefully at Margaret and then turned her whole attention on Danny's face as he began to read.

"That was tactfully and kindly handled." Mr. Wynn was looking at Margaret with a half-smile, but his expression was curious. They stood by the side board at the end of the table. It was a small room, as evidenced by the murmur of Danny's reading, but they could talk quietly.

"I never realized that Betty could not read. If she wishes to learn, I will teach her. We have five more days without much to occupy us until we make Lisbon. We can make a start if she wishes."

"You are curious, Miss Beaton." His eyebrow raised.

Margaret blushed, then raised an eyebrow at him, causing him to laugh. "I have a story to tell you about growing up in Lisbon."

"I am eager to learn how you behaved as a child." He offered her a chair.

"Oh, we need to sit?"

"Yes," he replied, joining her. "I anticipate being shocked."

She laughed. "Are my manners so poor now that you believe they have always been so?"

"Just the opposite. I believe you have had a radical change of behavior, and I must hear all of it."

"My father and I were fishing one afternoon."

"Worse and worse," he sighed dramatically.

She continued with her story of touching her first slimy fish and nearly causing her father to fall in the water. By the end, Mr. Wynn and she were both laughing, tears rolling down his face. Margaret was pleased she could make him laugh. "You remind me of my father when you laugh. Truly, we should play cards." She leaned in and cocked her head.

"Yes, actually I—" he paused, then shook his head. "Um, Danny, I am sorry to interrupt, but we should be going." He bowed toward Margaret, but the smile was gone. A flash of frustration flickered past his eyes. He stepped to the door and bowed.

Margaret curtseyed and he left. She turned toward the wall and blushed. Her first attempt at flirting with Mr. Wynn had made him uncomfortable. Why? How she wished she could confide in her mother, to talk over her feelings and gain from her mother's experience. Danny kissed Betty's hand before he left. Margaret wished she and Mr. Wynn could have parted like that.

She sighed and sat while Betty called for Tom to clear the tea things. In a few days, Margaret would have her father to talk to, confide in. A happy smile spread across her face. Her father. The closer the ship got to Lisbon, the more excited she was to see him, but the more awkward she was beginning to feel. What would it be like after so many years?

And what could she do about Mr. Wynn? Sometimes she believed he was open to the idea of courting her, of their mutual happiness. But perhaps she was seeing what she hoped to see.

"Oh, miss," Betty said as they closed the door to their cabin.

Margaret turned to Betty, whose face shone. Margaret reached out her hands, and Betty took them.

"He's in love with me, he says. I almos' don't believe it. Now, don't smile at me. I knows enough it's not calf-love like Johnny the stable boy looking at me whenever I happened out of the London house. I believe it is love." Betty sighed.

"And do you love him?" Margaret asked.

"Not at first, but then, yes. I believe I am beginning to."

"Then I am pleased for you."

"And, may I be pleased for you as well?" Betty looked up at her from the corner of her eye.

"Oh. I? Well, Mr. Wynn is difficult to read. I do not believe he is ready to move on."

"Hm. As you say. I can help you dress for dinner."

Margaret suspected that Betty did not believe her assessment of Mr. Wynn's unreadiness to love again. How Margaret would like to believe that, but if she did give in to her hopes and he was not, well, she would be heartbroken. Better not to hope.

Margaret opened the trunk. "Betty, I thought we put my pearls in the bottom of this trunk."

"Yes, we did." Betty put down the brush and mirror.

"I cannot find them." Margaret's heart sank. She pulled up the corners of her day dresses where she had placed the wood box, on top of her night dress and extra shawl.

"Let me empty it." Betty knelt beside her. Together, they took out each piece.

Margaret let out her breath in relief. There on its side was the wood inlaid box, the carved bee sitting on the rose.

Betty handed the box to Margaret.

It was empty.

CHAPTER 20

"GONE?" CAPTAIN FOREMASTER STOOD near the dinner table.

"What?" Mr. Wynn stepped toward her.

Dr. Giles's mouth was agape, and Mr. Kernsby, brows knit, pulled his head back.

Margaret had closed the door to the dining room before revealing her pearls were gone. Her cheeks flamed at the comments of the men. "Yes, sir." Margaret twisted her hands. "We have searched our cabin, unpacked every trunk. We would appreciate some help searching our things again." The pit in her stomach dropped further. Her heart beat in her ears. She wanted to wake from this nightmare.

Captain Foremaster's lips pulled into a stern line. "Yes, we can begin there. We will then search my and Mr. Wynn's cabins, Dr. Giles's, Kernsby's, and on down through every inch of this ship until they are found."

"Captain, certainly you are above reproach. I would never suspect—" Margaret placed a hand to her collar bone.

"Miss Beaton, before I subject the crew to a search, I will have my own rooms examined."

Margaret moved as Captain Foremaster jerked the door open. "Danny!"

"Aye, Cap'n." Danny's voice carried from the hallway.

"Tell the cook to hold dinner; then return, please. Wynn, will you follow me? Miss Beaton, lead on."

Captain Foremaster held the door for her, and Margaret led the two men to her cabin. She opened the door, and Betty stood up from the bed. Her face was crumpled; tears flowed freely.

"Betty, who has been in this room since last night?" Captain Foremaster's voice was even, but his question was direct.

"No one, sir. Miss Beaton and I were here in the morning. After breakfast, we went up on deck for an 'our. I came down to do laundry. Danny brought me wash wa'er, but he neve' came in. I hung the laundry. Miss Beaton came down to rest. Then we took tea in the dining room with Mr. Wynn and Danny. After we came down to dress her fo' dinner. Miss Beaton reached into the trunk, and they were gone, sir." Betty's voice trembled, and her hands shook.

"Miss Beaton, were you both absent for an hour in the morning and another in the afternoon? At what hours?"

"About eleven this morning and again at four. As Betty said, for about an hour each time." Margaret pulled Betty to her and put an arm around her.

"Thank you. Then you both searched?"

Margaret glanced around the room. Every item was slightly askew or dumped onto the bed. "Yes, twice."

"And is this the box?" Captain Foremaster asked.

Margaret nodded.

"May we enter?" Captain Foremaster asked.

"Yes." Margaret and Betty stepped out into the hallway. Mr. Wynn stepped past her to enter and sought her eyes. Looking into his, her heart lifted slightly. Mr. Wynn's eyes communicated sympathy. He nodded reassurance.

Captain Foremaster and Mr. Wynn quickly removed and replaced every piece of clothing, bedding, and luggage. Margaret's face burned as they searched her under garments.

"Miss Beaton, I can confirm your pearls are not in this cabin. We will now search the cabin Wynn and I share. Please accompany us."

Margaret and Betty followed down the hallway.

"Danny, if you will, please, search our cabin." The captain opened the door.

"Aye, sir." Danny entered and methodically began to empty every item from Captain Foremaster's trunk into his hammock. Then he moved to Mr. Wynn's belongings.

Margaret's eyes found her shoes. Her embarrassment was complete. Twice she had inconvenienced the captain, disrupted his ship, and this time cast a shadow on him and his crew. How could she have been so foolish or careless to leave the pearls in an unlocked trunk? She had been too trusting. Aunt Frances had been correct about her inability to care for such a treasure. The idea that she would never hold her mother's pearls again sickened her. She placed a hand on her stomach.

"Sir?" Danny pulled his arm out of one of the trunks, a string of pearls in his hand.

"What?" Mr. Wynn stepped toward the trunk. "That is impossible. I never—"

Captain Foremaster, his jaw slack, turned. "Wynn, what—"

"Gentlemen." Margaret interrupted. Her voice trembled, but she pretended confidence. "Clearly, this is a joke or a trick being played upon myself. I do not believe for one moment that Mr. Wynn could…" She paused. "I am grateful to have them returned. Thank you for your assistance." She slowly extended her hand, and Danny gently but quickly placed the pearls on her glove.

None of the men spoke or moved. Captain Foremaster's brow was still wrinkled. Mr. Wynn exhaled, but his face glowed deep red.

"Captain, perhaps we should return to dinner as usual. I am sure Cook is beside himself." Margaret tried to smile at her joke, but her lips barely lifted at the corners.

Captain Foremaster nodded and stepped into the hallway, asking Danny to inform Cook. The others followed him toward the dining room.

Margaret moved to follow; her thoughts whirling. Who would play this trick on her? Did her aunt really have someone on board in her pay? Margaret trusted Captain Foremaster and Mr. Wynn, of course, and Danny and Tom, but if not them, then who?

"Miss Beaton, thank you." Mr. Wynn's voice was level and serious.

Margaret stopped and turned. She held the ends of the necklace in front of her. "Will you assist me?" She turned her back to him and extended the necklace in both hands near her neck. He took the ends of the necklace from her hands. His breath was warm on her neck as he engaged the clasp.

She turned around. "I assure you, I have already forgotten the incident."

"I assure you, I have not." Mr. Wynn's jaw clenched, but he motioned for Margaret to pass and then followed her.

Her mind raced. Who on the ship would wish to discredit her, embarrass her? "Do you know who might have played such a… trick on me?" She whispered, but she was sure Mr. Wynn could hear. "My aunt intimated that she would know what I did on board, with whom I would associate. I suspect she is paying someone… "

"Not on you, Miss Beaton. On me," he whispered back.

Margaret's eyes widened. If a member of the crew had tried to discredit Mr. Wynn, possibly ruin her esteem for him, his pride and his honor would be wounded. What might he do if he caught the man? Her heart leaped in her throat. She turned. "Please, do not seek redress on my account."

"My actions, madam, are my own." His voice was firm, but his eyes softened as he looked into hers.

"Then… " She smiled and raised an eyebrow. "Will you accompany me to dinner?"

He sighed, his first show of relief. "It would be a pleasure."

CHAPTER 21

THE NEXT AFTERNOON, MARGARET sat in a chair on the main deck sketching, studying the forecastle deck and sail. She had done so for an hour. Betty had sat beside her for a time, but then Danny had come to visit for his half-hour. They stood talking by the railing.

Sketching and managing the roll of the sea and tug of the wind was a bit difficult, but Margaret had adapted. She held her sketchbook against a more solid book with her left hand and worked her pencil with her right. The wind pulled at her hat, but the chin strap held. Still, she had to stop occasionally and tuck her hair back under it. The fact that she did not care if her drawings were artistically done helped. Her true purpose was to study each member of the crew.

That morning she had come on deck shortly before the change of the watch. Then she'd come up again four hours later. Sketching away, she focused on faces. Some of the crew she recognized, but for most, she had no idea of their names. She was studying them: their attitudes, stance, and demeanor, especially their reactions to authority. Blond, brunette, black hair—blue, green, brown eyes—several races and languages—the crew were a microcosm of the world. Margaret was embarrassed that she had not seen them, not truly regarded them before. These men kept the ship afloat; they were bringing her to her father. She had been naïve and snobbish, and it made her uncomfortable.

If she had believed she could identify the guilty party simply by studying faces, she was wrong. Some men were older, their weathered and tanned faces belied their spry climbing of the ropes or pulling on the lines. Others limped; one had a few fingers missing. Several men were more serious, their faces never altering. None of the men acted tense or uncomfortable. Most joked and laughed, sang and shouted as normal. She did, however, note how Tom, the cabin boy, hunched over and hurried from the wheelhouse down to the main cabin. She would have Betty send for him later so she could ask him what was amiss.

Her short list of men who would have access to her cabin without arousing suspicion included Captain Foremaster, Mr. Wynn, Dr. Giles, Mr. Kernsby, Danny, and Tom. Cook could have gained access, but she had not seen him once this voyage.

She had immediately removed all from suspicion except Tom. She knew it was wrong to suspect him just because he was young and poor, but he was vulnerable and could be coerced. Mr. Sallow, whose oiliness had more than once made her stomach turn, might have been on that list, except he had been removed from any duties near her cabin.

Two sailors on occasion took the wheel: a man named Jonesy and a tall, weathered bearded fellow. She was trying to capture the latter when Betty walked up and stood behind her.

"Are you done visiting?" Margaret asked without looking away from the sailor.

"Yes, miss."

Margaret stood to stretch and looked at Betty. Tears were pooling in her eyes. Margaret closed her sketch book. "I believe it is time to get out of the sun and have a rest."

Betty gathered the pencils and sketchbook. Margaret waited for her and took her arm. Betty stared straight ahead as they crossed the deck. Once in their cabin Margaret asked, "Betty, what is wrong?"

Betty said between sobs. "Oh, miss. We have quarreled. I do believe Danny will give up on us complete."

Margaret pulled her onto the bed to sit next to her. "Now, now. Betty, I do not believe a man as entirely in love as Danny could act in such a manner—"

"You don' know what I said to 'im." She cried harder.

"Let me bring you some tea." Margaret stepped out in the hall and called, "Hello." No one responded, so she walked toward the stairs leading down to the galley. Normally, Betty would have gone, but Margaret would not make her go in her current state.

The galley was a cramped but efficient room. Pots, pans, dishes, and knives were all ordered and ready. Barrels of flour and sugar were open. Steam and heat flowed toward her, as Cook was bent over opening an oven. "Pardon my intrusion, Cook."

The sweaty sailor whose girth perhaps testified of his excellent cooking skills looked up at her. Shocked, he stepped away from his hot stove to bow. "I can't tend you proper, miss. You ain't to be down here."

"I do apologize, but I could find no one above. Is Tom about? Or Danny?"

"That boy," Cook grumbled. "Someone will be up direc'ly."

"Thank you. We would like some tea."

He muttered under his breath, no longer focused on her.

"Thank you for the excellent meals," she added. He grunted a response but also a nod. She returned upstairs. Margaret noted that Cook could be added to her list, but doubted he had any free time. She waited outside her cabin door listening to Betty's sobs. She wanted to comfort her but also wanted to let Betty have a moment's peace and privacy. Margaret waited outside the cabin, studying the wood paneling.

"Yes, miss." Tom came running.

"Tom, would you please bring up some tea? I believe Miss Betty is unwell."

Tom's head shot up. "Please, miss, don' be cross with 'er. She had nothing to do with it. It truly ain't—" He dropped his head.

"Tom," Margaret knelt on the ground to look up into his eyes. His eyes grew wide, a bit shocked by her behavior. "I am not upset with Betty, or you, or anyone on this ship. A prank was played either on Mr. Wynn or myself, but it ended properly. Betty is unwell from too much sun. Would you ask Cook for some tea?"

Relief flooded his face. "Yes, miss. Betty is always kind, you see. And Danny says, oh, well, I shouldn't repeat that."

"I bet you hear things on ship, being… young and all." She did not want to offend him by mentioning how little attention others likely paid him. She had often felt invisible in her aunt and uncle's home.

"I never talk. I never would. He'd—I'll fetch the tea." Tom ran off.

A few minutes later, he returned with the tea. "I washed me hands."

Margaret, who met him at the door, could not see signs of cleanliness on the backs of them, but trusted the insides of his hands were clean. "Thank you for thinking of that. Now, Betty is asleep, so let us bring in the tea quietly."

Betty had rolled toward the wall. After he placed the tea things down, Tom made for the door, but Margaret took his arm. "Tom, may I shake your hand?"

"Yes, miss." He rubbed it vigorously against his trousers first.

She held it and knelt again. "Would you be willing to help a lady?"

"Surely, miss." His eyes darted about the room, confused.

"Thank you. I believe you may know something of what happened with my pearls last night."

His eyes widened.

"Now, I would never put you in an awkward position. And I know you would never speak out against a member of the crew."

He vigorously shook his head.

"That is why I wish to show you a picture. If you nod, I will understand that *I* have guessed correctly as to prankster of this joke. You see, you will not have said a word."

Tom's eyes glazed in thought. Then he nodded.

Margaret took her sketchbook, opened it to a page, and placed it carelessly on the bed, taking a step back, she folded a tea towel.

Tom's eyes grew wide. Margaret did not like the look of fear there. Tom nodded twice, turned, and fled.

"What was that about?" murmured Betty. She rolled over and sat up.

"Nothing to worry about. First, take some tea, and then rest. I mean to walk on deck again. If you would like to practice the letters we worked on, I can leave a pencil and paper."

Betty said, "Thank you, miss."

"Please, I think you should call me Margaret."

Betty's lips turned up in a slight smile which brightened her tear-streaked face. "But only in private, miss, um, Margaret."

Margaret smiled as she picked up the sketchbook. She needed to find Mr. Wynn, immediately.

CHAPTER 22

"PERHAPS YOU DID NOT see my sketch well enough." Miss Beaton turned the paper so Joshua could see the picture. Clearly, it was Sallow that she had drawn.

"Please." Joshua gently took the sketchbook and closed it. "We cannot accuse a man on a whim. A ship has many ears, and it will do no one any good to start rumors. It is time to prepare for dinner. We should go in." He stepped to the side to let her pass, but Miss Beaton kept one hand on the railing and the other on her sketchbook. Her look was defiant. Even now, Joshua was drawn to her.

Joshua acted calmly, but his anger had not abated. Since the previous night, rumors of the "prank" had undoubtedly passed through the entire crew. If the culprit were not caught before they reached port, Joshua knew some might believe *he* had tried to steal the pearls. He'd racked his brain, reviewing each member of the crew, trying to determine whom he had offended or who had a complaint against him. He knew them all.

Cook had asked for a loan before sailing. Instead, Joshua and Mr. Beaton had advanced his wage for this voyage. Perhaps the man needed more money or was dissatisfied with the arrangement. Jonesy and Carlos had had a drunken brawl the night before their departure but could not recall why they'd fought each other by the time they'd sailed. Chippy always grumbled. Dagoo kept to himself. Mince always joked and sang. The crew was very much as it always was.

Except for Sallow.

It had been a surprise to both Foremaster and Joshua that Sallow had agreed to act as valet to Sir Edgar and sail on the *Rainha Maria* after quitting sailing with them a few months prior and because of his past resentment of Joshua. But Sallow had been pleasant and accommodating the past week and a half.

Sallow's name had remained on Joshua's mind throughout the day, but since Sallow was well liked by many of the crew, any of whom could be on duty at the moment, he did not want to discuss his suspicions openly.

Yet, he did not wish to distress Miss Beaton, whose stare was becoming frustrated and icy. She had surprised him. Again.

Miss Beaton's lips formed a straight line. "A whim? I am not accusing anyone or starting rumors. I am putting *you* on your guard. And this is the only appropriate place for us to talk without chaperones."

She was speaking as loudly as she dared, but she might easily be overheard. Joshua glanced uneasily over his shoulder and then up to the yard arms and ratlines above them. Looking back into her green eyes, he said rather loudly, "Please, do not distress yourself." Then quieter, he added, "It is not enough proof."

She lowered her voice a bit more. "I have given all I can. I have a witness. There must be a reason for this man to dislike you or to want to see you harmed."

"I will not contradict a lady." Joshua took her hand. "Truly, I thank you for your concern, but—"

"But you refuse to take me seriously. You, like so many others, will discount me." She turned to leave.

Joshua reached out and took her into his arms and spoke into her ear. "I do not discount you, but I fear being overheard. I agree with you. Now push me away hard and make your way to your cabin."

"I certainly will!" She pulled back, surprised, stomped on his foot, and pushed him back. He actually fell into the railing as he watched her, sketchbook hugged to her chest, make her way to the door.

"Blast!" he said. Straightening up, he began to head back to the door.

"Too bad, sir," Sallow said with a bit of a grin. He sauntered over and leaned on the railing. "High-spirited and high-born ladies, eh?"

"Be careful of whom you speak. You on watch, then?" Joshua peered at the man.

"Yes."

"Be mindful. It looks like a storm is coming." Joshua walked off.

"Aye, sir." Sallow respectfully pulled his forelock and moved on toward the bow.

CHAPTER 23

MARGARET LAY ON HER bed fully clothed, pushing against the wall with one hand and gripping the storm rail which ran alongside the bed. Betty held a similar position at the other end of the bed. She and Betty had raised it along the side of the bed earlier in the evening when the storm had awakened them. They had dressed as a precaution, ready to move to a safer location if necessary.

Margaret doubted she could sleep anyway. Her emotions flitted between being frustrated with Mr. Wynn's refusal to accept her proof against Mr. Sallow, to being surprised when Mr. Wynn had taken her into his arms, to the satisfaction she experienced at pushing him away. Aunt Frances would have been shocked at the change in her. What had happened to the proper young lady who was too timid to stand up for herself? She chuckled.

Mixed in with all those emotions was her relief that he *did* believe her. His whispered assurance had softened her reaction. She shivered, remembering the sight of Mr. Sallow out of the corner of her eye as she had walked off. His presence had chilled her. What if he had overheard?

When Margaret had returned from walking with Mr. Wynn, Betty had been huddled in bed. She had not wished to talk yet about what had occurred between her and Danny. Margaret had dressed herself for dinner quietly, hoping to speak with Mr. Wynn and Captain Foremaster after. The storm hit during dinner, sending Margaret to her cabin with Betty.

The darkness of night and the storm engulfed her. Not only did the storm keep her awake, but her interaction with Mr. Wynn kept her mind spinning. Mr. Sallow was behind the discrediting of Mr. Wynn; she knew in her heart it was true. She could not figure out why. Could it be jealousy or the animosity one man might feel toward another who had been more successful?

Also lingering uncomfortably in the back of her mind was the thought of Lady Frances. Perhaps she had hired Mr. Sallow to keep watch on Margaret's activities, to prevent her from becoming close to Mr. Wynn. She shook out her arm and repositioned herself.

Another recurring impression kept her heart beating—the power of Mr. Wynn's arms and the warmth of his breath near her ear. Being held by him once made her wish to fold herself into his arms again. Albeit, under different circumstances.

The ship lurched and Margaret's stomach with it. For an hour it had rocked but not in the peaceful roll of forward motion. Storm waves jerked the ship one direction, only to suspend it, then slam it into the water below. Then the waves would rise and jerk the ship again.

Both Margaret and Betty had lost the contents of their stomachs into the bucket which was now nestled in the bed between them.

"Man overboard!" A voice echoed into the hallway outside their door. Another door slammed nearby.

Margaret sat up. "Betty, did you hear that?"

"Yes!"

The yelling and commotion outside their door continued. Margaret peered out but saw nothing in the dark until Dr. Giles rushed past with a lantern.

"Who is it?" he called.

"Danny!" Tom's treble voice was unmistakable.

Betty gasped and staggered to the door, holding a lighted candle.

"No, Betty!" Margaret stood and moved toward the door, but Betty had already made her way into the hall.

"Is it true? Is it Danny?" Betty called to Tom who was taking blankets to the dining table.

"Aye."

Betty rushed for the doorway leading out to the quarterdeck.

Margaret struggled after her. "Betty, wait!"

When Betty opened the door to the deck, water, wind, and pelting rain struck Margaret. She inhaled and coughed. She held her hand before her eyes to shield them from the onslaught. Pushing her head out the doorway, Margaret saw Betty to her left, gripping the rope which held canvas to the door, preventing the water from seeping in from the deck.

A lantern near the door provided some light, but the rain pelted her eyes. The deck was besieged by waves which crashed over the railing and streamed toward the opposite edge. Another group of men on her left worked to heave something up from the side of the ship. Captain Foremaster, holding a lantern, shouted orders. Above on the poop deck, Margaret could see Mr. Wynn's figure with Jonesy, the two of them fighting to keep the wheel from turning.

"Come back inside! We cannot help him." Margaret yelled in Betty's ear; the wind whipped the sound of her voice away.

"I cannot bear it!" Betty cried out. "I told him no, that I wouldn't marry him. How can I live without him?" Betty's face crumpled in agony as sobs racked her body.

Margaret waited until the ship righted, then she grabbed Betty and pulled her toward the door. Betty grasped her as they moved, and Margaret pushed her inside when the ship tipped again. Margaret grabbed the door handle; it slammed shut with Betty safely inside, but a wave washed Margaret's feet out from under her. She could not hold the weight of her own body. Her hand lost the handle and she slipped. She gasped as she was engulfed in the frigid seawater.

She screamed until the water filled her mouth, choking her; her body scraped down the deck to the right feet first at too great a speed to stop herself. Even with the shocking cold of the waves, the skin on her arms and back burned as she slid against the wood. Her hands flailed, but there was nothing to hold on to. She was fast approaching the side of the ship. Could she stop herself without going over the railing and into the sea?

JOSHUA SAW MISS BEATON'S figure sliding to the edge. "Help her!" he screamed. He moved around the wheel and took the stairs two at a time, holding both railings to steady himself. The ship rolled the other direction, and she stopped momentarily. Her figure, soaked and still, was barely lit from the lantern. She lay unmoving on the main deck before him.

Joshua sucked in his breath. The ship shuddered and rolled again. Margaret slid away from him, back to the port side, head first. Before Joshua could reach her, Captain Foremaster had her in his arms. Joshua joined him, and they staggered together toward the hallway door.

The door slammed behind them. "Is she hurt?" Joshua's voice cracked.

Miss Beaton coughed and sputtered. "Not entirely," she said weakly.

The men held her head to the side so the sea water could come out of her freely.

"Oh, miss!" Betty's tears flowed down her wet face as she met them in the hall.

"Take her." Captain Foremaster placed her in Joshua's arms and turned for the door.

"How is Danny?" Joshua asked.

"He caught the forestay and secured himself to the side. We thought he would be drowned there. The men almost had him when I heard Miss Beaton scream." Looking at Betty, he said, "I am certain they have him now." With that, Foremaster exited into the storm. The door slammed behind him.

Joshua looked down at the pale and limp figure of Miss Beaton. She shivered in his arms. Her eyelids fluttered. "Betty, we must get her dry."

Entering the cabin, Joshua laid Miss Beaton on her bed and knelt beside her, rubbing her hands. Betty covered Miss Beaton with a blanket to hide her soaked and shredded dress. She removed Miss Beaton's shoes.

"Thank you," Miss Beaton said. Her eyes flickered open but shut quickly again.

Joshua gazed into Miss Beaton's face. Her eyes were open, and some color was returning to her cheeks. "I did not save you." He glanced away. "You should rest."

He moved to stand, but she placed her hand on his. "Do not leave me." Her eyes closed and she breathed out, but she did not release his hand. The sea still rolled, but the storm had lessened. The rocking was more predictable.

Joshua was torn. "I do not wish to, but I need to summon Dr. Giles and see if they need me on deck."

Tears streamed out of her eyes. "Duty. I understand. Go."

He kissed her hand and tore through the door.

Half an hour later, he knocked gently. Betty answered. "Danny is recovering."

Betty gulped back a sob but smiled.

He stepped in. Miss Beaton's wet clothes were gone, and she was tucked into a blanket. He knelt. Taking a cloth from Betty, he began to pat dry Miss Beaton's hair.

Miss Beaton winced.

"Betty, did Dr. Giles come?"

"Yes, sir, and he helped me change her and gave her a sleeping draught. Oh. I'm sorry, miss. Your calf is scraped up so. It's all my fault." Betty's tears streamed.

Without releasing Miss Beaton's hand, he said gently, "Betty, go change into dry things so you do not become ill. Use my cabin. I will wait here with Miss Beaton until you return."

Betty gathered dry clothes and left.

"Mr. Wynn." Miss Beaton's voice was quiet. "Is all well?"

"Yes. The sea is calming. Danny is recovering."

Her eyes remained closed.

"I am sorry I had to leave you." He held her auburn hair in the towel.

"I am sorry, too. You and my father, both men of honor and duty. Still, it comes at a price."

Joshua hung his head. He had failed her twice that night. But the ship was safe; that had to count for something. She was alive. He was sitting beside her.

She shivered. He grabbed the other dry blanket and laid it on her. As he tucked it around Miss Beaton, her shoulders winced. "How extensively are you hurt?"

"My nose is quite well." She began to laugh, but the pain stopped her.

"It is a beautiful nose. I believe the sleeping draught is beginning to work."

"Yes." She quieted.

He wiped his eyes with his hand. Miss Beaton lay so still. It was Maria Luisa all over again. He squeezed his eyes shut. His heart swelled. He loved Miss Beaton as tenderly as he had ever loved before. He held his breath. He loved her, but he had been unable to save her. He had failed. Again.

She opened her eyes. "I am in some pain. Will you help distract me? Please, tell me about my father."

Joshua's heart lurched. How could he keep her father's secret without breaking faith with Miss Beaton? This certainly was not the time to explain. "The first time I met your father, he was hailing my ship to resupply. We had been weeks without food and supplies, chasing the fight as best we could. Your father stood on the forecastle of his ship yelling encouraging words to us, congratulating us on successes, and telling us of the fresh—well, relatively fresh—meat we would have." Joshua chuckled. "I could have kissed his boots."

Miss Beaton smiled. "It has been so long since I have seen him."

Joshua stroked her fingers one at a time. He swallowed hard. How would she react when she learned of her father's illness? Her time with him would be limited.

She continued softly, "The last time he came to London, we went to Mother's grave. It was hard for him to stand there—six months after her death—knowing he had missed her illness, her death, her funeral. He hugged me to his side as I cried and said to me, 'Pearl, tears for a season, but love for all time. We do not truly lose the ones we love. We love her and she knows it still. Heaven will not be heaven without her there.'"

"He is a wise man."

"Do you think of Maria Luisa waiting in heaven for you?"

"Yes."

"That is good."

Mr. Wynn brushed the hair from her forehead. "And I know that Maria Luisa does not wish me to be alone or unhappy for the rest of my life."

"Mr. Wynn, I have not been entirely honest with you."

"What?" He could not fathom what untruth Miss Beaton might have told, what secret she might have kept. He was the one being dishonest, keeping a secret from her.

"I have imposed on you. I convinced you to take me to Lisbon under false pretenses. I never intend to return to London, but to live with my father in Lisbon." She paused and yawned. "Why did Father not come to London himself?"

Joshua opened his eyes to see Miss Beaton looking up at him. "I will tell you every detail when you are better. For now, you must rest. We will arrive in Lisbon in four days."

"Lisbon." A smile lingered on her lips, and she closed her eyes.

He leaned in and kissed her forehead.

She sighed. "My mother used to kiss me like that when I was hurt or scared," she murmured, eyes closed.

He leaned over her and nearly kissed her lips.

"I am back, sir." Betty entered and quickly turned her back. "Should I retrieve more blankets?"

"No, Betty." Joshua stood and held the wall to steady himself. "You attend to Miss Beaton. I will send Dr. Giles to see to her wounds." He passed Betty and stopped to whisper. "We must guard against infection and fever." He paused. "I will give you news of Danny when I learn anything."

"Thank you, sir."

Joshua moved into the hallway and met the doctor coming in from the rain "Dr. Giles, how is Danny?"

The cabin door behind him flew open, and Betty stood there, her eyes wide, her face drawn.

"He will be well if he has not swallowed too much sea water. He has been rolled over a barrel and given rum and treacle water. For now, he is resting in a warm hammock. Now, Betty, to Miss Beaton." The doctor entered and closed the door on Joshua.

Joshua entered his cabin and leaned upon his hammock. He had nearly lost Miss Beaton, but in that moment, he had discovered his love for her was deep and sustaining. He would never love again without the fear of loss. Even so, there was one truth: he knew that the pain of living without her would be worse than the pain of losing her.

CHAPTER 24

TWO DAYS HAD NEARLY passed since the storm. Margaret lay on her stomach on her bed while her scratched skin was open to the air. Dr. Giles insisted that her back be cleaned with salt water. That was excruciating, but it would prevent infection, so she must bear it. Then her skin must be allowed to air dry before applying an ointment. But the scrapes were not deep and within a few days would scab over. She would be well soon.

"Does it hurt?" Betty fanned Margaret's back.

"It itches incessantly. Any news about Danny?"

"Nothing at the moment."

"What happened between you? Can I help?"

Betty put the fan down. "He asked me to marry him."

"Oh, Betty. I am so happy—"

"I told him no."

"But why?"

"He's Catholic." Betty sighed. "He says I have to be Catholic so we c'n be married in the church with all his fam'ly. In Boston. I told him we could be married in a few weeks in London with my ma and sister present. He said we should be married in Boston and start our life together there. I said Boston was full of Americans and fools, that

I was scared to go. I said I wouldn't go to Boston for all the Danny Devines in the world." A sob caught in her throat. "He shook his head and walked away. Then he goes and nearly drowns, and I couldn't think but what if he dies thinkin' I didn't care?"

Margaret waited a few minutes while Betty gathered herself. Quietly, Margaret asked, "Have you spoken with him yet?"

"No. He was drying out for a day. I asked Mr. Wynn to pass on my good wishes. Danny only said, 'Thank her, sir.'" Another sob caught in Betty's throat.

"Betty, do you love him?"

"Yes, miss! Somethin' turrible."

"More than your family? More than what your family thinks?"

"Yes, but I still care what my fam'ly thinks."

"I know because you are good and loyal. If Danny is the same, and I believe he is, would he be willing to put your wishes before his family's? Does he love you?"

"I thought he did. I believe so."

"Then it is just a matter of pride. I know a bit on that subject. I have some of my own to contend with."

"You, miss?"

"Yes." Margaret smiled. "Get me dressed, and I will call for Danny."

"But the doctor says—"

"Hang the doctor, Betty!"

Betty laughed. "I wonder what Lady Frances would thin' of you now? 'Such shocking behavior! Proper young ladies do not use cant nor do they slouch. Currently, you are doing both.'"

Margaret laughed at Betty's imitation of Lady Frances's voice. "Lady Frances warned me that being at sea changes people. She would relish the thought that she is correct." Margaret had changed, but only for the better. Speaking her mind, acting for herself, treating others better—it all suited her.

"Danny, I wish to have a word with you." Margaret sat up straight, not letting her back touch the chair they'd borrowed from the dining room. She could ignore the pain for a few minutes. She could ignore the pain much longer if she could help Betty in any way.

"I can't stay long. We're cleaning up from the storm." He held his hat in his hand but refused to look at Margaret or Betty. His skin was pale, and he rubbed one eye.

"Please sit down. You look as tired as I feel." Margaret moved with Betty's help to the bed. Both ladies sat there.

Danny had started to protest, but Margaret said, "Please, I insist."

"Thank you." He sat on the chair, but still examined his shoes.

Margaret studied the stubborn Irishman and realized the depth of his disappointment. Betty's head was bowed.

"Danny, are you proud of your Irish heritage?"

Danny, surprised, looked her directly in the eyes. His eyebrows pinched. "O' course, miss."

"Did the British—we, I should say—force your countrymen to follow our rules and to give up your land?"

"Yes, miss." The confusion was evident on his face now.

"Do you agree that we should apologize and promise not to force you to do those things?"

"Yes." His eyes were wary.

"Then I apologize, Danny. We should never have forced you. Betty? Do you agree?"

"Yes." Betty stood and faced Danny. "I apologize, Danny, for any ills I have caused you."

He rose and took Betty's hands. "The wrongs were not yours."

"But I have caused you pain. I said things—"

"So did I." Danny reached for Betty's hand.

"Danny," Margaret said quietly, "do you feel that Betty should be forced to change her religion to marry you?"

"No, miss." He glanced from Betty to Margaret and back. "I hope someday you might consider it, but I will not force you to it, I won't." He took Betty's hands in his. "Elisabeth Brown, I love you, heart and soul, I do. Will you do me the honor of becoming my wife? When and where you'd like?"

"Yes! I will!" Betty bounced on her toes and threw her arms around his neck.

Margaret smiled and turned away. She could get accustomed to speaking her mind. In fact, she had something to say to Mr. Wynn.

CHAPTER 25

"WE HAVE NO PROOF." Joshua looked at Foremaster. "Just Tom's nod at Miss Beaton's sketch." He stood by his hammock while Foremaster stood across from him in their small cabin, arms crossed, leaning against the wall.

Foremaster shrugged his shoulders. "Sallow's name is the only one I had considered even before Miss Beaton's, um, proof. Kernsby and I will talk with Tom later today. Kernsby said the men believe it was a prank. It is common opinion that you are sweet on Miss Beaton, and someone was trying to make a point of it."

"It does not feel like a prank. The value of those pearls is too costly for someone to risk jail or even extradition to Australia. No, this feels more complicated than a simple prank. What if Miss Beaton had believed I stole them?"

"It is fortunate that she has such confidence in you," Foremaster said with a smile. "Do you have similar confidence?"

"No."

"I feared as much. What has derailed you from your course?"

"Since Maria Luisa, Miss Beaton is the first woman of my acquaintance who has shown determination, bravery, sense, even humility."

"She is too good for you," Foremaster teased.

"Yes, she is. And she deserves better."

"Yes, and you have had the good sense to realize all of her good qualities. She, too, has seen something in you. Pursue her, man."

"I failed her. I saw her sliding across the deck, certain she would be swept out to sea, and I could not save her."

"But that did not happen. Miss Beaton did not die because you saw her slide. And others saw it as well and helped her. She is here, alive, well, and in love with you, I daresay."

Joshua raked his hands through his hair. "I was not even the first to her. You were."

"But she did not ask *me* to stay with her, to comfort her. She asked you." Foremaster stared at him meaningfully, but Joshua could only shake his head. "Wynn, if you continue to blame yourself for Maria Luisa's death, it will eventually claim your whole existence. You cannot change the past; you cannot predict the future. You cannot even choose what Miss Beaton will do." He dropped his hands to his side. "You can only influence the present. I suggest you do so, or you may both end up unhappy. I will see you after my watch."

Joshua lay in his hammock. He did truly ache for Maria Luisa. He did still love her. But now, he loved Miss Beaton as well.

Miss Beaton recognized that part of his heart would always belong to the brief years with Maria Luisa. But he was young. How many years lay ahead? How many of those years could be filled with companionship and love? Pleasant evenings spent with Miguel and, hopefully, Miss Beaton. Perhaps more children would join them. It was the life he wanted—needed.

When Miss Beaton was able to come out of her cabin, he would make his feelings known. He grabbed his coat and headed on deck.

Joshua stood watching the late afternoon sun set. Off the port side, he could see the haze of the Portuguese coast.

"Hrmph." Foremaster cleared his throat.

Joshua turned to see Foremaster, lips pursed. "Is something wrong?"

"I have news. In our cabin."

A minute later, Joshua entered the cabin to see Kernsby and Tom. Foremaster motioned for Tom to step forward. "You must repeat what you told us to Mr. Wynn."

"Cook'll beat me for sure."

"Tom." Foremaster used his stern captain's voice.

But Joshua knelt by the boy. "Tom, I have a son. Did you know that? And what I want most for him is to grow up truthful and honorable. Good men will always help one another. Just as I will help you. Please, tell me what you know."

"I saw Mr. Sallow creep out'a the ladies' room and into your'n."

"When was this?" Joshua still knelt, listening, trying to calm the anger which grew in his chest.

"The afternoon the pearls went missin'." The boy dropped his head.

"You should have told me immediately," Foremaster said.

"Aye, sir, but I was scar't."

"Thank you for telling me now." Joshua stood, but looked at Foremaster. "This is damning but still not proof that he took the pearls."

"Tom," Foremaster said, "tell about Cook."

"Yessir." The boy took a deep breath. "Ol' Salt, I mean Cook, was talkin' with Mr. Sallow about hiding the pearls, and the look on Mr. Wynn's face when they was foun'. They laughed."

Joshua swallowed hard but bit his lip. "Where were you, Tom?"

"I, uh." Tom reddened. "I was hid behin' the potatoes, eating a biscuit. But, please, sir, I dinna' steal it. It was off Miss Beaton's tray when I cleared it. Seems she had no more use for it."

"Thank you, Tom. I think we understand." Joshua put a hand on his shoulder.

"Now, go. And speak of this to no one. We can protect you if your information stays with us. Do you understand? It is for your safety." Foremaster's face was grave.

Tom nodded, wide-eyed.

"Go about your duties."

After the boy left, Joshua raked a hand through his hair. "How do we act?"

"We confront Sallow. Best have Kernsby and Danny with us. Kernsby, bring your pistol. We need to pick our moment. It's nearly dinner time and hard to get him separated. Tomorrow in the daylight. When's he on watch."

Minutes later, Joshua stepped onto the main deck and took a deep breath. He squinted. The sun was beginning to set and the second dog watch was about to begin where half the crew was eating and the other half preparing to. The sea was calm, the sky tinged with red and orange.

"Mr. Wynn?" Miss Beaton stood by the railing, almost hidden by the mainsail. He crossed to her. The sun bathed her face and hair in rosy light. Her light blue gown shone bright against the blue waves. He caught his breath. He had heard of mermaids but believed for the first time that he stood before one. She smiled at him.

"Are you well enough to come above deck?" he asked. It was obvious by the way Miss Beaton held herself stiffly upright that her skin was still irritated.

"You sound like Betty. Yes, I needed to breathe fresh air and give Betty a respite from worrying about me." Miss Beaton motioned toward the bow. Danny and Betty stood on the forecastle deck talking, heads close.

"She feels terribly guilty for my injuries." Miss Beaton traced the railing with her hand. "She believes my aunt will send her away."

"Would she?"

"My aunt? Yes. But I will not let that happen. Betty has become more of a friend than a maid. Being aboard ship has changed me. I believe I would not need a maid at all, if society did not dictate it."

"Careful, you will sound like an American soon."

Miss Beaton's soft laugh warmed his heart. "Besides, Betty will not need employment soon. After Danny's proposal, I… told her that

I intend to stay in Lisbon. This will make it easier to part from her. I will miss her, but I am happy for her."

"I hear Danny and Betty's wedding will be in London." Mr. Wynn chuckled.

"Yes, and Betty has agreed to go to Boston. They discovered that their love for each other trumped any previous dreams or wishes, any fears even. Very wise on their parts." Margaret smiled up at Mr. Wynn.

"Yes?" He swallowed awkwardly.

She gazed into his eyes. "It would be similar to a woman who believed that true love could only exist once in a lifetime and then discovering that love is not so fickle a plant. That it can regrow, as healthy as before."

"Oh?" His eyes widened. "Would a woman worry about such things, that a man may not be able to love again?"

"Yes. Some might, but I am old enough to let go of fairy tales. When I fall in love, it will not matter if my intended has been married before. It will not matter whom he married before. As long as he loves me now, truly, as achingly as I love him."

"*When* you fall in love? I mean, have you found such a man?" Mr. Wynn's eyes held hers. His gaze burned into her soul.

"It would be indelicate of me to declare myself before the man in question has spoken, but I believe—"

Before she could tease him any more with her words, he took her face in both hands and brought his lips to her forehead. She tilted her head upwards. It was enough of a sign. He bent to kiss her—

"Miss Beaton, Mr. Wynn." Captain Foremaster nodded and passed without looking directly at either of them. Margaret blushed to her toes, only to find Mr. Wynn was just as red.

"I would like to speak to you tomorrow, Miss Beaton. I have an important question to ask you. Will you meet me at morning watch?"

"So early?"

"With the rising sun." He bent over her hand, kissed it, and left.

CHAPTER 26

A GLIMMER OF DAWN lit the sky and the waves. The blues and pinks of the clouds were mirrored on the sea. Joshua stood under the main sail, listening to the crew. Some were aloft raising the sail to catch the wind. The flapping of canvas and the song of the men at work would normally calm him. Not this morning. Tomorrow, they would arrive in Lisbon. Today, however, his life would begin again.

He had barely slept, waking at every bell, wanting to arise early enough to greet Margaret on the quarterdeck. He paced the length of the deck again.

The door opened, and she stepped out. Her auburn hair was in a single braid curving around her upswept hair. Her green eyes shone when she caught his gaze.

He stepped toward her and offered his arm. Neither spoke, but they walked the main deck together. "I wish to show you the rising sun from the figurehead."

He helped her climb the steps up to the forecastle deck, mindful of her scraped skin. As she released his arm, he pulled her hand up to his lips. She gazed at him. He placed his arms gently on her upper arms and turned her toward the starboard side until she faced east. A bright glimmer shone on the horizon. The tip of the sun peaked above.

She gasped. "It is so beautiful."

"Do not look directly at the sun, but at the water in front."

For several minutes they stood watching the sun inch up from its watery reflection. Golden light, pinks, and corals tinted the clouds.

Joshua broke the silence. "Miss Beaton, I have walked in darkness for years until I did not realize it was perpetually dark. The light you shone into my soul reminded me for a time of all that I might lose again. But finally, the light banished the dark. Your goodness inspired that."

Miss Beaton blushed. "I have also felt it. The loss of my mother and the distance of my father has weighed on me. Changed me. I wondered if I would find light again." She beamed and shifted toward the rising sun. "And in my darkest moment, I found you."

Joshua paused, his soul filled with tenderness. Touching her arm, she turned her head to him. He gazed into her green eyes and smiled. "Miss Beaton, I wish to ask if I may court you."

She paused. "I am happy to receive your attentions." Her smile faded. "I only hesitate because I know that you are still in love with Maria Luisa. Are you truly ready?"

He shifted his weight and nodded. "Yes, part of me will always be in love with her."

"And I would never ask you to give that up." She dropped her head.

"Margaret, look at me." He used her Christian name for the first time; he could declare himself to her in no other way.

There were tears forming in her eyes.

"You deserve to be loved and cherished. You understand unlike most what it is to suffer without love—and, I daresay, respect. I can offer both if you wish, if you will share a life with me. I devoted myself to Maria Luisa and was faithful to her. She blessed my life." He swallowed and brushed a tear from Margaret's cheek. "But I have many years ahead, I hope, and so much love still to share. I wish to devote myself to another, to love again. I need to—I want to share the coming days—with you."

"Are you asking me to marry you?"

"Not before I speak to your father. But my intention is—"

She leaned into his chest. "Yes, ask my father."

"Three cheers for Mr. Wynn. Hip, hip—"

"Hurrah!"

He stepped away from Margaret and looked up. There in the foremast was a team of riggers, raising the mainsail, cheering for them. Margaret put a hand to her mouth and turned away, but Joshua held her hand up with his, saluting the crew. Another, "Hurrah!"

Joshua lightly put his arm around her and pointed slightly right of the bow. "Lisbon will be there.

"And my father! He will be so happy! Joshua, you must tell me again how he is. I am breathless with excitement. We can have tea together and walk the Oeiras Promenade again. Oh, Joshua, I am so very happy."

Joshua put his hands on her arms, basking in the warmth of her, but careful not to disturb her scratched skin. He sighed. He should feel ecstatic, but his heart was heavy. She deserved to know her father was ill, and he would have to tell her. Joshua stood on the deck, gazing at the sea. If he told her, he would have to break his word to her father. The memory of his last conversation was vivid.

"But yes, Joshua, figure out how that stuffed brocaded-waist shirt, namby-pamby fop of a macaroni intends to make my daughter happy." Mr. Beaton stopped and slumped into his chair. "Promise me. If she is happy, stay for the wedding. If she is not happy, promise to help her." Mr. Beaton gasped for air.

Joshua rushed over and poured a small glass of port. He held it to Mr. Beaton's lips. He sipped a little, gasped for air, and sipped again. Finally, he pushed Joshua's hand away and leaned forward, grasping his stomach.

"Do not tell my daughter how ill I have become. It will do her no good. I would make the journey myself, but the voyage would kill me. I have written my will and leave her as my sole heir. She will have my controlling percent of this business. I have named you in charge of running it. If Pearl does marry a nincompoop, her ownership of this business will fall under her husband's control. I hope you can buy him out.

"Here is a second letter to her explaining my wishes. Deliver it to her only if you hear of my death. Now, go. Catch the next tide."

Mr. Beaton tried to stand, but Joshua bent to hug him. "You have been a father to me. I give you my word to protect your daughter at all costs."

Her voice broke his reverie. "Do you think Father will meet us at the dock? I am so eager to see him again." Miss Beaton looked up and smiled at him. "How wonderful it will be—"

"Margaret."

She beamed at him, wide eyed. Her smile grew. *Blast.* This was not the reaction he wanted. "I need to tell you about your father." He placed his hand fully over hers.

Her brow creased. "What is it?"

"Your father is ill."

"What?" She shuddered.

"Are you in pain?"

"No, but I moved too quickly. My skin itches and burns some. But what do I care about that? What is wrong with my father?" The intensity of her question was matched by the burning look in her eyes.

"He has the sugar sickness."

She looked out at the sea. Her lips formed a straight line. "Then I have come in time to nurse him."

"Yes." It was all he could think to say.

"How far has the illness progressed?"

"I am not a doctor."

"Joshua." The pleading in her eyes broke him.

"He has difficulty with his vision and with walking. He has been put on a strict diet."

"And you knew this. All along." The recrimination in her voice was sharp even though she fought to keep her voice low.

"He made me promise."

"Men and their promises."

She turned to leave, but he caught her arm. "I told Sir Reginald that you should be—"

"Sir Reginald and Lady Frances know?" Her mouth dropped open, and her eyebrows creased.

"Your father—"

She did not allow him to finish. "My father. And you. Men and honor and duty. And you leave your women confused and alone." Head down, she walked away, descending to the main deck. He watched until the sails hid her from view. He finally heard the door to the hallway bounce shut behind her.

He leaned to the rail again and put his head down.

Joshua had paced the deck for an hour, gone in to eat, and returned to pace it more. He could find no peace. He lost track of time. He felt sick. Physically and mentally.

"It is time."

Joshua looked up at Foremaster and Kernsby who joined him on the poop deck. He rolled his shoulders and descended the steps with them.

Sallow, now on duty, strolled the quarter deck, laughing with some of the crew.

The three walked to the forecastle deck where Sallow had stopped with a few sailors coiling ropes. Danny joined them.

"Sallow." Foremaster's voice was clear.

Sallow turned and saw Joshua. Fear flickered in Sallow's eyes. He glanced over Joshua's shoulder.

"Yes, sirs."

"We have proof that you first removed Miss Beaton's pearls and then planted them in Mr. Wynn's cabin." Foremaster's voice boomed. The other sailors on the ship stopped their work and listened.

"That's a—"

"Before you speak, if you will confess your part in the 'prank,' your pay will be docked a week's wages, but you will not be reported to the authorities for theft."

"And ruin my reputation? I will never be hired on a ship again! Not as a mate, at least."

"That well may be," Foremaster continued, "but you will be shown mercy."

"Why?" Joshua said, stepping toward Sallow.

"Why?" Sallow huffed disdainfully, but stepping back. "*You* have the gall to ask *me* that? You are responsible for my brother's death. Then you poisoned Beaton against me and prevented me from rightly being made first mate. Finally, I have a chance to get something back. To destroy some of your happiness. Looks like you did that yourself this morning. At any rate, I'll be paid nicely for my revenge."

"What?" Joshua asked, but before he could get any answer, Sallow ran for the starboard railing and jumped off the main deck into the water below.

All the men ran to the side.

"Sallow, come back!" Foremaster yelled.

But Sallow was swimming toward the distant shore.

"Can he make it?" Joshua said. As much as he wanted justice, he did not prefer it to cost the man his life.

"Possibly, but not probably." Foremaster's lips drew a tight line. "Back to work."

The men glanced at them and back to the ocean. One made the sign of the cross. Another shook his head. Everyone moved silently back to his work. Foremaster, Kernsby, and Joshua headed to the wheel house.

"This is my fault. We should have waited until we reached port." Foremaster cursed.

"No," Joshua said to his friend. "You are the captain. You have the right and the duty to keep order. Besides, if we had waited, he would have escaped into Lisbon Harbor instead."

"That thought does not console me," Foremaster said, climbing the stairs.

Joshua stood another minute looking east until he could barely distinguish the swimming figure. The ship was making good time, and he hoped that Sallow would survive. Perhaps a fishing boat or other vessel might find him.

Seeing the retreating figure fighting through the water against terrible odds made Joshua think of his own predicament. Having lost Margaret's trust and the possibility of her love, Joshua felt just as alone, just as lost as that man swimming to shore.

CHAPTER 27

MARGARET MOVED CLOSER TO the candle and repositioned her mother's journal. She rubbed her neck. Though she had no clock, she could tell it was very late by the lack of sounds on deck. All she could hear was the rhythmic creaking of the ship's wood. The ship slipped calmly through the waves. Looking out the window, she could only see darkness, with no distinction between sky and sea.

Betty lay sleeping soundly, but Margaret was awake. All the fears and feelings she had fought came crashing in on her. Abandonment, disrespect, loss, disappointment. She had cried until she was numb. Now, she read to distract herself.

The love between her mother and father had grown over the course of a few weeks' courtship. Her father's leave had been ending, and he would be sailing off to the Mediterranean. In the meantime, Sir Reginald and Lady Frances had become engaged. Her mother had hoped Reggie would be happy but had not believed it was a love match. After the engagement, the friendship between the four of them faded. Margaret grieved that her mother and father had been ostracized by her aunt and uncle.

April 30, 1796

David received his orders today, and my heart is breaking. He sails in May, first to Lisbon and then Gibraltar. He wants to see my father and make his intentions clear. He will ask Father for my hand. I hesitate because I do not believe my father will allow or approve of our marriage. I am to meet David tomorrow in the square outside my father's house to talk. There is a bench in the park that we love.

Reggie pulled me aside last night and told me I must forget David and find a suitable husband. It would be damaging socially and politically if I were to marry below my station and give him and Lady Frances mean relations. I felt as if I had been struck. I do not understand what has changed in Reggie. I believe Lady Frances is much to blame for his increased pride and self-importance.

I must decide if I truly love David, even if it has only been a short time. Do I trust him? Will I be happier with him—regardless of money or family?

May 1, 18796

When my maid, Sally, and I went out walking this afternoon, we met David a little way off. I was so pleased to see him. But we were suddenly overtaken by Lady Frances. "This will not do. Captain Beaton, you must leave Miss Colborne alone. You have played with her emotions long enough."

I was shocked by her behavior. In the open street, as well. David maintained his demeanor and led us into the park at the center of the square. He was calm, but I was not.

"Frances, how could you accuse him of this?" I demanded.

"He has pretended to seek out my affections as well. I have not told you, Alice, but you are not the only woman with whom he has dallied."

"Lady Frances," David began, barely keeping his voice down. "It may be rude to contradict a lady, but that is a bald-faced lie."

Lady Frances went white. "Do you see how he acts? He may be a captain, but he is 'common.'"

David said, "You threw yurself at me. Tried to pull me into your own little game, missy. When I rebuked you, you went and got yourself engaged to Sir Reginald. I'd hoped you would be content and be happy for yur soon-to-be sister here. But, no, you can't let others be happy where you've failed."

I was shocked. I could see some of the truth in her abashed face, but then it burned with haughtiness. I demanded to know if it was true! And if she loved Reggie at all. If she were trying to sabotage my future with David.

"How could you consider marrying him?" she demanded. "Throwing your life away on a poor sailor. I tried to stop you myself, but now I know how to act."

With that she turned down the street toward my father's house. I began to cry.

"No dear, no tears. Tell me. Where is your father now?"

"At his club, I think."

"Aye, I will go to him now. Don't you worry. If all goes well, we'll be engaged this afternoon. If not, well, I'll get word to you through Sally here."

I am writing and waiting in my room. I have not seen anyone for a few hours. I pray David is successful, but I do not believe my father, Reginald, and Frances will accept us.

May 2, 1796

The worst has occurred. Father called me down to his study as soon as he arrived home yesterday. Reginald was also there. He told me to stop allowing David to see me, dance with me, or even talk with me. Reginald accused David of first seeking Lady Frances's attention for her fortune. And when he failed, he sought after mine.

I was indignant. I told them it was untrue. Perhaps Frances had been mistaken—though I knew in my heart she had flirted with him and failed. And then out of embarrassment or spite tried to destroy our happiness.

Father tried to reason with me as if I were a child, telling me that I did not know how men truly are, how persuasive they could be, but only serving themselves etc.

I dried my tears and listened. Then I asked father if he would disown me if I married David. He stood up and walked to his desk. "Yes," he said quietly. "Please reconsider this course of action."

"Reggie, please." I looked at him, but he said he would disown me, too.

Heartbroken, I ran to my room. Sobbing, I lay on the bed. I do not know how much time passed. Finally, Sally brought me some tea and pulled a note from her pocket. It was from David.

Darling Alice,

I will understand if you choose your family over me, but I offer you my love and my life. If you will marry me, and make me the happiest of men, I will work hard to make our life a beautiful one. I don't want a penny from your father.

We would never ask him for anything. You will not have the comforts that you currently do. I know that yours will be the greater sacrifice. But if you can't see a life without our love, then I will take you to Scotland and marry you.

Put a candle in your window tonight if your answer is yes. Then I will wait for you out back at three o'clock.

My heart is both light and heavy. It is a hard choice, but I know I must go. I must find my happiness with him. I placed a lit candle in my window, and I have packed a bag. Sally knows nothing, so she cannot be accused or dismissed.

Before the others retired to bed, I crept into father's room, and I took Mother's pearls. Perhaps it is beneath me to take them this way, but mother did leave them to me. I need to feel close to her right now. Somehow, touching the pearls helps me to remember her love.

Margaret closed the book and balled her fists. How dare Lady Frances and Sir Reginald and Grandfather make her mother so miserable. She sighed, grateful she was beyond their influence now. She was glad her mother had had the fortitude to elope, to pursue her happiness regardless of what others thought.

Margaret closed her eyes and again wished her mother were alive. She could have held Margaret, could have counseled her. She understood what it was like to be mistreated, misunderstood, disrespected, betrayed. Mother would understand Margaret's distress and how deeply Joshua and Father had hurt her by keeping that secret from her but not from others.

Lady Frances trying to use Father, thinking she was irresistible! Margaret was incensed. But Father had rejected her. No wonder Lady Frances was bitter toward her mother, father, and even *her*.

Margaret replaced the journal in her trunk, blew out the candle, and climbed into bed. She had no idea what would happen now, except that tomorrow, she would be with her father. All other concerns needed to wait until she ascertained how seriously ill he was. He was what mattered most to her. She was proud of herself for not waiting in London, for taking her chances to come to him.

After tonight, she did not have to feel alone anymore.

CHAPTER 28

LISBON

"IT'S TIME." BETTY OPENED the cabin door.

Margaret nodded. She wanted to be among the first off the ship. To distract herself, she kept repeating the actions she would take. She would disembark. Danny would procure a carriage and take her and Betty to her father's office since his living quarters were above it. She would embrace him and call for tea. She would ask to see his doctor and come to an understanding of how ill her father was. Repeating the steps in her mind over again helped her control her sorrow.

Pulling her shawl around her, she stepped onto the quarterdeck. The bright sunlight blinded her momentarily. She had not come out of her cabin since learning the truth from Mr. Wynn. Yesterday afternoon, Betty had invited Danny in for tea of sorts, but Margaret had been poor company.

Joshua had called at their cabin twice, but she had been too angry to see him. Too hurt. Too disappointed. In both Joshua and her father.

How could her father have kept this from her? She was not a child. Why had he not sent for her? Told her the truth? Come to find treatment and doctors in London? These questions had spun in her brain, one after the other, since she had learned of her father's illness.

How could *Joshua* have kept this from her? Clearly, he did not trust her, believe in her abilities, her determination. It crushed her. She had confided in him, had confessed her secrets. She had thought they would face troubles and joys together. She had been wrong.

Margaret straightened her posture and masked her face with the bored, unimpressed look her aunt had taught her, forced her, to wear in society. Margaret would never have dreamed she would choose it of her own accord. But it was her defense. She was desperate to keep from crying. What good would tears do now?

The deck was crowded and busy. She walked quickly, Betty right behind. Margaret descended the gangplank, but halfway down, she heard a child's voice. *Papai! Papai!* A dark-haired boy of five was running up the ramp. A smile lit his entire face, and his brown eyes were wide with excitement. Margaret could not stop the smile which came unbidden to her lips. He was beaming. Below, his Portuguese grandmother watched.

"*Filho!*" a voice behind her called.

Margaret twisted her head. Her jaw dropped. Joshua had spoken, had called the boy, "son."

Briefly, his eyes sought hers as he hugged his son. His eyes reflected a sorrow she had seen in them once before. Turning away, he carried his son up to the quarterdeck.

Bidden or not, the tears began to flow. That beautiful boy was Joshua and Maria Luisa's son. Even now she might have met him, been introduced. She continued down to the dock, head down, past the lady who must be Maria Luisa's mother.

On the dock, Margaret stopped. She could not see.

Betty came to her side and gasped slightly. "Danny!" Betty called. Soon, Danny was at their side. He walked them to the street, placed her and Betty in the carriage, and arranged for their luggage. Margaret had imagined her father meeting her, running to his open arms, just as Miguel had done to Mr. Wynn.

Safely inside the carriage, Margaret laid her head on Betty's lap and sobbed.

"Papa!" Margaret sat on the sofa next to her father and threw her arms around him. He held her as she cried.

Costa and his wife, the butler and housekeeper, withdrew, leaving father and daughter alone. Margaret's sobs broke free. Years of disappointment, separation, worry, spilled out. It was bittersweet—finally reunited only to find her time with her father would be short.

She buried her head in her father's arms. He stroked her hair and kissed her head. Some of his tears fell on her cheek.

When Margaret's sobs gave way to infrequent gulps of air, her father said, "Hush now, my Pearl, hush. Why are you crying?"

"Why did you not tell me of your illness? Why did I have to learn it from—"

"Was it yur aunt or uncle who betrayed me? Those faithless, feckless, irresponsible—"

"It was Mr. Wynn." She sat up and looked at him.

He blinked. "Wynn? Really?" He paused for a moment to wipe away some of her tears with his handkerchief. "I tried to imagine what you would look like, a grown lady. But now, I feel as though I'm lookin' in your mother's eyes. Yes, there, lass, is her flash a' determination."

"Papa, how sick are you?"

He clasped his hands. "I had so many plans for us. I wanted to send for you, but it wasn't safe here. I hoped you were enjoying yourself. Enjoying London. Why would I shackle you with a sick old man who had abandoned you? I wasn't sure you'd forgiven me."

Margaret's tears came forcefully. "Papa! You are more dear to me than anyone or anything in London! All I have wanted for these past years is to be with *you*!"

"Forgive me, forgive me." He rocked forward, his own sobs now coming thick.

Resting her head on his shoulder, they cried together.

That evening alone in bed, Margaret lit a candle and opened her mother's journal. She was near the end of it, which saddened her. Hearing her mother's words, her story, had strengthened Margaret. But she knew she would re-read it over the years.

May 5, 1796

Our wedding was simple. David had purchased a special license, though it was quite costly—imagine me worried now about cost. I laugh at how sheltered I have been, but I am amazed at what I have become—more resilient, more trusting, more hopeful. It is wonderful to be married and to be inspired by my David to do and be more than I ever believed possible.

At our wedding was Mr. Jones, the vicar, and some of David's friends—Captains Scoresby and Waters, and David's first mate, Peterson. It was not the grand wedding of my girlhood imaginings, but we stood together before God. I will remember gazing into his blue eyes all my days. We had a small wedding breakfast after and drove to an inn near St. Giles.

June 24, 1796

I have not written for some weeks. We sailed to Lisbon shortly after our marriage, and I was seasick nearly the entire time. David and members of his crew were very kind to me. Near the end of the voyage, we could walk the deck in the evening without my becoming ill.

Lisbon is all I could wish for. The air is sweet with flowers. The ocean breeze is warmer than London, and the sunshine—I am amazed by the sun. We leave for Gibraltar soon. Living on board with David has been a strange but beautiful experience. The accommodations, companionship, food—all of it is so opposite of what I have experienced in London, but I feel so much more alive. Quite happy and content.

When I think of what I have left behind, I do miss the companionship of my family—the years of happiness when my mother was alive, my friendship with Reggie. Perhaps in the future, we can reclaim that. I do not know, but I hope for a chance to forgive and be forgiven. Those relationships are my only regret. There is so much joy in being with David that I am forever grateful I had the fortitude to act, to seek my happiness, and to be content with the consequences.

Margaret sighed. This is where the journal ended, but for a simple penciled sentence in her mother's hand added at the end.

Margaret, be brave and good. Find love and cling to it. Tears last for a time, but love is forever.

Margaret blew out the candle and lay on her back, staring into the darkness. Could she be the woman her mother wanted her to become? To rise above disappointments as she had? Could she forgive Mr. Wynn? Did she love him enough to follow her heart?

She was here in Lisbon with her father, and she would stay with him for as long as he lived. But that time would be shorter than she had anticipated. This thought constricted her heart painfully. But was being with her father all she wanted, or had her hopes and dreams expanded? She had changed in the past month—her understanding of people, her compassion, her faith in herself and her abilities. How could her dreams not have also grown?

A single image focused in her mind's eye. It was after she had been scraped and torn by the storm and the deck—after she had been brought to her cabin. Joshua Wynn's face peered down at her. His face full of relief, his mouth a slight smile, and his eyes full of love. Love. For her.

She rolled over and sighed. And pulled the coverlet over her shoulders. Thoughts and emotions battled in her head and chest. Sleep would not come quickly tonight.

CHAPTER 29

JOSHUA SAT NEXT TO Miguel on the stone bench and leaned against the wall of their home's enclosed garden. The land was solid beneath him, no give and take of waves. A slight breeze from the ocean blew uphill and cooled him. It blew the broad leaves of the fig tree above them. Joshua sighed. This garden spot had always been one of peace, away from the concerns of business, the sounds of the city, but today, Joshua had not been able to keep his sadness out.

His other home, the sea, was not far away. In truth, he was more comfortable there than on land. On any land. In any country.

He could not bear to be too far away from either place. The harbor sparkled in the distance—over the wall, past the red roofs and white walled houses down the hill to the water. Then outward, a distant darker blue where the sky blue met in a hazy line, was the sea. He had spent the last fifteen years balancing his need for land and sea.

Now, he was torn between two women. Maria Luisa, whose eyes had been passed on to Miguel, tugged at him. When he looked at Miguel, he saw her reflected there, just out of reach. His son was a pure source of joy in his life. One that eternally bound him to Maria Luisa. He would care for Miguel as the last gift that he could give Maria Luisa.

But like the pull of the land when he was at sea, another woman drew him. Margaret, who understood his pain and sympathized with his loss, whose happiness drove his future plans, was down by the harbor, within reach. The shock and disappointment in her eyes haunted him. He had treated her as disrespectfully as her aunt and uncle had by keeping the truth from her.

Joshua rose and walked to the end of the wall and back. He could not get comfortable. His heart ached in his chest. It was visceral, palpable. He stood against the garden wall, watching Miguel, who ran with the carved elephants Joshua had bought him, laughing and trumpeting across the lawn. Joshua smiled as he watched his son's dark, curly hair bounce as he pranced. He had bought this house for Miguel and Benedita a year earlier. He could not make Maria Luisa comfortable anymore, but he could care for her family.

Joshua stepped on the bench and leaned his arms on the wall. His eyes followed the road down to its end at the harbor. To where Margaret was.

"*Papai!*"

Joshua sat back down and clapped as his son danced with his elephants.

Benedita sat beside him. "*Genro,* my son-in-law, let us speak in English while Miguel plays close by. Why are you so sad today? Did your voyage not go well? You are back earlier than expected, no?"

"I brought Mr. Beaton's daughter to him. She was determined to be with him. I was not to tell her that he was sick, but in the end, I had to. I broke faith with him and broke her heart. So, yes, I am sad."

"A girl or a woman?"

"A woman."

"Is she the beautiful lady I saw leaving the ship?"

"Yes."

"The one with tears after she looked at you?"

Joshua's head came up. His mother-in-law's eyes were soft and gentle—and knowing. Just like Maria Luisa's. Just like Miguel's. "I did not see the tears."

"They were there. Like the ones that hide in your own eyes, now."

They sat in silence, watching Miguel.

"*Uma andorinha não faz verão.*" Her eyes were soft and knowing.

"True, one bird does not make the summer by himself. But I have you to help me with Miguel. I have Miguel to live for. I am content."

"Joshua, you have not been content since Maria Luisa's death. You have been breathing, but not alive. It is time for you to make a home for your son—with your son. It is time you fall in love again."

"Benedita—"

"I will not be here forever. I can give Miguel all that is worthy and proud from his Portuguese people, but he must live in your English world as well. *You* must give him the world, *filho*." She took his hand in hers. "Now, tell me of this lady."

"Will that not make you uncomfortable?"

"No. I know of your love for Maria Luisa and your love for me. But I have known that there must be another love for you. I want to hear it from you first. It will be good for you to tell it."

"I met Miss Beaton at the house of her uncle."

He began at the beginning and did not stop until the story was told. Until he knew what he wanted and what he must do.

ℭHAPTER 30

"WYNN! DELIGHTED TO SEE you. Come, sit," Mr. Beaton called from the sofa in his office, his cane nearby and foot propped up on a pillow.

Joshua could hear the soft close of a nearby door and guessed he had just missed Miss Beaton. He had waited two days before coming, wanting to give father and daughter some time. "How are you, sir?"

"Better now that you've done me the greatest service in the world. Please sit."

Joshua smiled as he pulled up an oak chair close to Mr. Beaton. It was a pleasure to be back in his company, to hear the man's Scottish accent again.

"I cannae believe my Pearl is so grown; I had a picture in my mind of her at fourteen, you see." Mr. Beaton fiddled with his cane. Then turned and looked Joshua straight in the eye. "She is lovely and sweet. And you've disappointed her, man!" The man's forehead creased and his lips pursed.

"I?" Joshua's jaw went slack.

"Yes, you! You broke faith with me and tol' her I was ill. She would have known the moment she saw me, but—" the old man sighed. "Now, I cannae get her to stop weepin'. So, I asked more and more questions." He held Joshua's gaze. "She's fallen in love with you and what do you have to say for yourself? How could you lead her into a fool's paradise? You of all men?"

"Sir," Joshua stood abruptly. "I have come here today to ask your blessing—to ask that I be allowed to court her,"

"Well, it's not my permission now that you'll be needin'. Poor girl. Besides, her tears have likely drowned all her looks away."

"Papa!" Miss Beaton burst into the room. "I have not—" She stopped, realizing that she had been caught eavesdropping.

"See, Wynn! We'll have it out. I detest unspoken, unresolved issues. You fancy Pearl, and she you. Now she's as turkey red as a stripe in our Beaton tartan, she is! What do you have to say for yourself, man?"

"Miss Beaton," Joshua closed the distance between her and him, "I have come to apologize for hurting you, for treating you like a child. I also came to ask permission to court you—of you and your father."

"How can I trust you?" She clasped her hands in front of her.

"Because I can trust him!" Her father interjected. Then softer, he said, "I am at fault, Pearl, not Wynn. He was trying to keep both my confidence and your faith. In the end, he chose you over me. That is when I knew he had fallen in love."

Joshua's jaw dropped. Was he that transparent?

"Is that true, Mr. Wynn?" Miss Beaton leaned toward him slightly. Her eyes intent on his face.

Joshua took her hand, cradling it in both of his. Neither had gloves on, and the touch of her skin quickened his pulse. He sought her eyes and dared to caress her cheek. "Miss Beaton, I wish to court you, and I hope in time to convince you to marry me. I am in love with you—"

At that moment, Mr. Beaton cleared his throat.

"But I will say more on that topic when we are alone."

Mr. Beaton raised an eyebrow.

"Alone, in a crowded room, I mean."

Mr. Beaton nodded.

Joshua bowed over her hand and kissed the top of it. He could feel her tremble. He looked up into her glistening eyes. "It is up to you to decide if you can love me."

She smiled and clasped his hand in both of hers, but she withdrew her hand as her father cleared his throat again. Blinking a few times, she dropped her chin and raised an eyebrow.

Joshua nearly laughed aloud at the familiar expression they shared.

"You may court me, Mr. Wynn, and we shall see what comes of it. Good day, Mr. Wynn, Father." She curtsied and left the room.

CHAPTER 31

JOSHUA GLANCED OUT THE dining room window, looking down at the hilly, narrow streets. He wiped his sweaty hands on his pants. The Beaton's carriage would arrive shortly for dinner. Margaret—he was now permitted to call her that—would meet Benedita and Miguel.

Joshua had tried to prepare Miguel for visitors. Miguel, naturally wary of newcomers, did not understand why others had been invited. Joshua hoped with time, his son's fears of outsiders, of Margaret, would be allayed. He stepped away from the window and straightened his coat.

"*Genro,* do not be nervous," Benedita said, entering the room.

"I cannot help it." He tugged at his coat and shirt collars.

"A new jacket, no?"

"No, but I borrowed it from Foremaster." Joshua had realized how worn he had allowed his clothing to become and had made an appointment with a tailor. For now, Foremaster's jacket would have to do, even though Foremaster was slightly shorter in the arms and more fit than Joshua in the waist.

"*Avó.*" Miguel called as he ran to his grandmother who gave him a tight hug. The nursemaid curtseyed to Joshua and left.

"Miguel, let me look at you!" Joshua held out his arms to his son. "You are so handsome."

"*Sim, Papai.*" Miguel beamed. "*Olhar!*"

"Look." Joshua repeated back. Miguel was showing Joshua the carved elephant again and imitated its trumpeting.

The butler announced the Beatons. Mr. Beaton, using two canes, moved slowly across the dining room, but the smile on his face was only surpassed by the one on Margaret's.

Benedita curtseyed to their guests.

"Dear Dona Marques-Abreu," Mr. Beaton said. "I am delighted to see you again."

Benedita greeted Margaret with a kiss to each cheek. "I am pleased to meet you, Miss Beaton."

"And I, you." Margaret curtseyed to Joshua.

"May I also greet you with kisses?" Joshua asked her under his breath as he bowed to her.

"Absolutely not," she whispered. "At least not this time."

His eyes widened, and he hoped she was not teasing him.

"This is my son, Miguel." Joshua bowed first, and Miguel imitated his father.

Margaret curtseyed and then bent down before Miguel. "It is nice to meet you," she said slowly.

"Nice to meet you," Miguel said, then in shyness, he found his grandmother's skirts.

"Please sit," Benedita motioned. "Dinner will come shortly."

AFTER DINNER, PAPA SHOOED Margaret and Joshua out into the garden to enjoy the afternoon. She sat on the stone bench and breathed in the fresh air, tinged by the distant sea. The weather was warmer than London, more humid. Every scent reminded her of her childhood. Joshua pushed Miguel in the swing until Miguel explained he did not need his father's help.

Joshua came back and sat next to her.

"He is a handsome boy. I see your mannerisms in him."

Joshua responded by taking her hand and kissing the back of her fingers.

Miguel stopped swinging and looked at his father and then back at Margaret. She pulled her hand away and stood, making her way to the fig tree.

"Papa, por que você beija a mão dela?" Miguel asked his father quietly. *"Vou explicar isso mais tarde."*

Margaret wondered exactly *how* Joshua would explain later to his son why he was kissing her hand. She wondered if Miguel would be pleased to have another woman in his life or if he would resent her.

Miguel jumped off the swing and walked into the house. *"Avó?"* he called as he entered.

"Will he accept me? I do not mean as a mother—"

"He will come to love you, yes, as a mother. He does not remember his mother, of course, but he has heard of her from his grandmother. He knows that she died protecting him. You will become his English mama."

"His *mãe inglesa*?" She smiled at Joshua. "If I decide to marry his father, I would be quite pleased with that."

"If? I sense a challenge, to which I will rise."

"You may begin by asking me for the first two dances."

"First—oh yes, your father's ball. He wishes to show you off to all of Lisbon, to his friends and acquaintances." He looked into her eyes and caught his breath. She kept his gaze and began to blush. "I understand his sentiment."

"Mr. Wynn, I am asking you to dance. And it is becoming quite awkward." She raised an eyebrow.

"I accept." He winked at her.

CHAPTER 32

"FATHER, YOU ARE WORSE this morning." Margaret came to her father's bed side. She placed a hand on his forehead. No fever, but he was clammy.

"I just take longer to wake up these days."

"Let me send for your doctor or for Dr. Giles."

She expected a refusal but was surprised when he said, "Aye, you may call Dr. Giles. But first, sit next to me."

Margaret pulled up a chair.

He took her hand. "Come closer, lass. My eyesight is not as good as it once were. You are so beautiful, so grown up. I have missed so much time with you."

"Father—"

"No, I should have found a way. I should have quit the war and come for you."

"Father, I missed you incredibly, but I was proud of you for serving. I did not—do not—see any other way you could have behaved. Besides, that is in the past."

"But the past is all I have, my dear. Very soon I will join your mother."

Tears began to flow down Margaret's cheeks. "Perhaps Dr. Giles… "

"Pearl, listen. When I heard that your mother had died, I was distraught. I felt turrible guilt for not being able to come to her, to you, even to the funeral. I did not know what had transpired until a month after, when I finally received your letters. Even now, that regret is still fresh. I have missed her every day since. I have tried for the past year to build a successful business and find a house for us, intending to bring you back here. After learning my prognosis, I decided to send for you. That is when I received yur uncle's letter. He implied that you were all but engaged. Since you had not mentioned this *Sir Edgar* in any of yur letters, I was concerned. I ken the Colbornes and their tricks too well." He coughed. "Water, please."

She poured a glass for him from the pitcher on the nightstand.

"Thank you. You cannae comprehend how pleased I am that you're here now. Wynn told me how you stormed his office and demanded a berth to Lisbon."

"Is that how he truly described it?"

"Well, the wording is my own."

Margaret smiled through her tears.

"I'll miss you, Pearl, my Pearl. I'm sorry that yur mother and I were not given more time with you. But we will watch over you, lass. If there is a loving God in heaven, and I believe there is, we'll not be far from you."

Margaret began to sob into her handkerchief. Her father pulled her from the chair to sit on the bed next to him. She lay her head on his chest, sobbing, letting him shush her. After a few moments, she sat up, wiped her eyes with her handkerchief, and regained her composure.

Her father patted her hand. When he spoke next, his voice broke. "You see, Pearl, there'll be tears for a season, but love for all time. True love often requires true sorrow until God will wipe away our tears. It also requires true strength to walk on in life, to find love and happiness, not by forgetting but by remembering. When we remember our lost loved ones, we remember how to love. And then we ken how to find it again." He coughed.

She watched him swallow and close his eyes.

Margaret waited, happy to sit with him, pondering what he had taught her.

Her father opened his eyes. "Now, we need to send you out shopping. You need a new gown since I am throwing you the grandest ball this port has seen in years! I have arranged for Wynn to accompany you today. Now, take Betty, a'course, and buy her a new gown, too. It will be my wedding present to her."

"Oh, papa!" Margaret hugged him and kissed his forehead.

She rose to leave, but her father added, "And I expect a detailed account of the excursion! Wynn had best behave."

"Of course, Papa, or you will fight him and beat him!"

Her father laughed as she left the room.

CHAPTER 33

JOSHUA HAD NEVER ENJOYED shopping, but today he happily walked with Margaret and Betty up and down the *Rua do Loreto*. The rain of the morning had cleared, and warm sunshine highlighted the wisps of Margaret's auburn curls, some of which, lifted by the ocean breeze, escaped the confines of her bonnet. Her muff and pelisse were the color of a stormy sea. Again, he felt as if a mermaid had bewitched him.

Nodding to a passing acquaintance—another ship merchant and his wife—Joshua stood straighter with Margaret's hand on his arm. The sun and her touch warmed him. Portuguese ladies noticed them and nodded. The men noticed Margaret's unique hair and then met Joshua's steely gaze.

They passed a milliner's shop, and both Margaret and Betty stopped to admire a bonnet in the window and the orange and gold nasturtiums which had begun to bloom.

"It is time to rejoin Danny." Joshua held his arm to Margaret.

"Oh, and not a word to 'im. I want my gown to be a surprise." Betty giggled a little.

"We promise," Margaret said, looking up into Joshua's eyes.

They had left Danny minding the carriage a few blocks ahead on the next street over. Joshua put his hand in his pocket and rubbed the receipt to be sure it was there. While the ladies had ordered gowns at the dressmakers, he had visited a jeweler. The order slip for a ring was secure in his pocket.

Joshua spun around at the sound of shouting, one hand holding Margaret behind him and the other searching for his sword, which he was not wearing. *Blast!* From down the street came men shouting, carrying guns. Laborers and sailors mostly, their white shirt sleeves a contrast to the gray and brown guns they carried. One waved a red flag. They spilled onto the street. Chaos erupted. The ladies they had just passed screamed and scrambled to enter the dressmaker's. Shopkeepers were slamming doors and locking them.

Abaixo o domínio estrangeiro! Malditos sejam os britânicos! The protestors yelled again.

"Joshua, what are—"

Joshua turned and took Margaret and Betty by the arms. "They yell, 'Down with foreign rule.'" They rushed to the jewelers. It was already closed, but Joshua yelled to the shopkeeper in Portuguese. The man opened the door long enough for the three to enter.

"Get down." Joshua pulled Margaret and Betty to the floor behind the counter.

The shopkeeper pulled on Joshua's shoulder, and said, *"Você trouxe mulheres britânicas para minha loja. Por favor, você deve sair. Por trás. Por aqui."*

"He wants us to leave?" Margaret looked up at Joshua. Her eyes darted between him and the owner.

"João!" The jeweler's wife yelled her husband's name. Her terrified face peeked down the upper floor staircase.

"We cannot stay. We are putting them in danger. This way." Joshua moved Margaret and Betty ahead of him toward the back door. Betty choked back a sob, and Margaret put an arm around her shoulder.

Joshua's throat went dry. The shouting was growing closer. He grabbed Margaret's hand and ran out the back door.

"Joshua, you are hurting my hand." Margaret peered into his eyes tenderly.

He tried to relax it.

"This will end differently," she said. "You are here."

His pounding heart jumped in his chest. She understood.

They stumbled out into the alley where horses and carts were kept. A groom was trying to quiet the horses sheltered across from the shop.

"Quickly, here." Margaret said as she stepped across to a stall.

"Yes, we can hide with the horses." Joshua spoke with the groom and handed him money. The groom ran away. He joined Margaret and Betty. Margaret had wisely chosen a mare. She shushed the frightened horse, patting its brown foreleg, careful to keep to the side of its hooves. It whinnied and stamped. Joining the women, he huddled against the wall, holding Margaret close.

Betty trembled but remained silent. Margaret held Betty's hand while leaning into Joshua's chest.

Within a minute, protestors rushed out the back of the jewelers. The noise broke like a dam on the quiet alley. Joshua could see very little through the stall slats, but he saw enough to know they had barely escaped. The men pushed the jeweler, who was gesticulating wildly, backward onto the ground. Men shouted and ran both directions up and down.

One man paused. Even with his lower face partially covered, Joshua recognized Sallow. Joshua's face reddened; he balled the fist of his free hand. Sallow did not move, but looked up and down, searching the area.

Joshua held his breath as Sallow stepped toward the horse stalls.

The sound of British drums, beating the quick cadence of charge, echoed up the alleyway.

The mare neighed and whinnied. Joshua pulled Margaret closer, cradling her head in his hand. He scraped his cheek against the rough wood.

Sallow ran. A few other rioters flew up the street away from the British regulars.

Soon, they heard the sound of British troops, the high-pitched calls of the fife and the sound of boots clacking on the cobbles. Joshua kissed the top of Margaret's head and stood. "We can go now." He gently pulled her to him. Then offered a hand to Betty.

"Are ya sure, sir?" Betty's voice trembled.

"Yes, no harm will come to us."

"But who were those men? What did they want?" Betty asked.

Joshua sighed. "The British are not popular here. Beresford has been very heavy-handed with his 'regency' administration. The Portuguese want self-rule. I believe at some future time, they will succeed. But as yet, they are not truly organized. And you see how quickly our troops were able to respond. We are not in danger now."

"Thank the Lord for that," Betty said.

Margaret turned and smiled at Joshua. "Thank you."

Joshua's heart swelled, but a cold sweat trickled between his shoulder blades. It was a close thing. Too close. He let out his breath and pulled her close. Feeling the wild thump of his heart. He was not leaning over Margaret's dead body. Together, they had escaped.

One thing he knew. The Portuguese wanted the British to leave. And if their monarch remained in Brazil, eventually, the people would take matters into their own hands. Joshua and Margaret could not remain here much longer.

"Officer," Joshua called out. An officer at the back ran over to them. "There is a British sailor who was with the rioters. Tawny hair, wiry, about five foot six. Goes by the name of Sallow. He ran there."

"Yes, sir. Special eye on him, then." The officer ran and rejoined his men.

"Betty, me love." Danny jumped down from the carriage and caught Betty in his embrace. He kissed her face and neck and buried his hands in her hair.

"Thank you, Danny." Joshua lifted Margaret into the carriage.

"I came as soon as I could." Danny spoke directly to Betty, then handed her up. "Double time, sir."

Joshua climbed in, and Danny cracked the whip. The horses started up the alley. Joshua held Margaret. Betty clutched Danny's coat while he drove. Joshua's heart only slowed when the horses slowed near the Beaton's house.

Joshua finally relaxed as he closed the front door and all four were safely inside the office. Margaret ran to her father's room. Danny caught Betty in his arms again. Joshua slumped against the door.

Sallow! That man would never work in Lisbon again. Joshua would make sure his reputation as a traitor was known.

Joshua stood and walked toward Beaton's rooms. He cracked his neck and rolled his shoulders. All was well. And he would never allow a woman he loved to be in danger again.

CHAPTER 34

"I AM AWESTRUCK!" MARGARET had her first glimpse of the *Rainha Maria* from the carriage as they approached the dock. The lantern-lit ship glowed against the dark harbor. Many of their guests were also arriving.

A week had passed since their frightful experience with the rioters, and in response, British soldiers had doubled patrols through the city and General Beresford had reassured the public of their safety.

Under these conditions, her father insisted on holding her ball onboard, but Margaret knew extra men had been hired to watch the dock and the ships nearby. And they had passed a patrol of British regulars on their way to the dock.

Holding her father's hand as the carriage approached the glowing ship, she was happy and at ease. It would be a night to remember. She touched her mother's pearls and beamed. They matched her cream and pink ballgown.

At her insistence, Danny and Betty had joined them in the carriage. They would dance the first two dances, and then escort her father home. Both were uncharacteristically quiet. Danny tugged at his cravat, handsome in his new dress coat. Betty's arms stiffly lay by the sides of her beautiful rose-colored gown. Margaret worried that she had erred, that being invited had only made them uncomfortable. Then Betty gave Margaret a full smile.

Margaret relaxed. Some of society may raise an eyebrow at Danny and Betty's inclusion tonight, but Margaret could not care less. She was surrounded by those she loved.

As they got closer, the ship shone and the reflection of both lantern light and starlight undulated on the dark harbor. Margaret caught her breath. "Oh, Father, Joshua, it is perfect." Her eyes were on Joshua, who sat facing her. "Yes, it is perfect," he said without taking his eyes off her face.

She blushed but smiled.

They exited their carriage and Father was placed in a sedan chair carried by four men. The rest walked down the dock toward the ship.

Margaret turned her head, captivated by the people around the ship. It was full of both British and Portuguese gentlemen and ladies, her father's acquaintances and friends, waiting to board the *Rainha Maria*. The night was full of happy chatter and the sound of a quartet tuning up by the wheelhouse.

Breaking the sounds of visitors and music, a monkey screeched. Margaret looked along the dock to see a small crowd gathered around an organ grinder. His back to her, she watched the organ grinder sway and his monkey climb up the next ship's mooring ropes and swing about.

Father used two canes to make his way up the gangway to an arm-chair, placed just for him so he could greet his guests. "It is marvelous! Just what my bonny lass deserves. Thank you, Wynn."

"My pleasure, sir." Joshua winked at Margaret, whose blush deepened.

Margaret stood next to her father and Joshua. The guests were announced by Costa, who had been brought for that important job. After greeting their guests, Joshua took Margaret's hand. She would lead out the first set of dances.

The chill of the night air was no comparison to the tingle that ran up her arm as her gloved hand met his. They spoke little during the country dance, but their eyes rarely left each other's gaze. Their second was a Scotch reel in honor of her father. Margaret was breathless with the steps and her laughter by the end.

"I've seen you happy at last," her father said, as he prepared to leave.

"Thank you. I could never have dreamed of such a night." She kissed him.

He patted her cheek. Turning to Danny, he said, "Devine, take me home and tell me of your plans with Betty."

"Gladly, sir." Danny grinned and nodded. "We're to be married in London, you know."

His happy chatter trailed off as the sedan chair carried her father away, Danny and Betty walking by his side.

The ball was delightful. A dream. She met many of her father's friends, much of Lisbon's society. She was praised, complimented, and never wanted for a dance partner. Above all of that, she caught Joshua's eye, over and over again—each glance a reassurance of faith and future joy.

"The Lady Frances Colborne. Sir Reginald Colborne, baronet, and Sir Edgar Fortescue, baronet." Costa's voice rang out above the music.

Margaret nearly tripped in the middle of her dance with Dr. Giles. Her head spun toward Costa's voice. *It could not be.* The music stopped to allow their entrance. Margaret's heart plummeted, her stomach in knots.

Lady Frances and Sir Reginald stood near the railing, self-satisfied looks upon their faces. Their heads bent slightly, acknowledging others as they made eye contact with many in the now quiet crowd. Sir Edgar did not move. His knuckles were white on the railing. Margaret wondered how he had survived the voyage over.

"Are you all right, Miss Beaton?" Dr. Giles asked.

"Yes, but I should greet my aunt and uncle."

Dr. Giles led her toward them, and Joshua met her part way. The crease between his eyes deepened, but he smiled at her and raised one eyebrow moments before they reached the three newcomers. Warmth flooded into her cheeks. Confidence flowed into her heart.

With a wave of Joshua's hand, the quartet continued the music for the dancers.

"Aunt and Uncle Colborne," Margaret said. It came out as more of a question than Margaret wanted. Her mouth was dry. She could think of nothing more to say.

"Manners, Margaret," Lady Frances hissed.

"Welcome, Lady Frances, Sir Reginald, and Sir Edgar," Joshua said. "We are surprised but honored by your attendance tonight."

Sir Reginald gave Joshua a slight nod, but Lady Frances ignored him completely. Sir Edgar bowed to Margaret.

Margaret took a deep breath. She would not have to face them alone. She had Joshua here and her father at home. A real smile flickered on her lips.

"It is vulgar to smile so," Aunt Frances whispered.

Margaret's smile faded, but then she let it blossom as she saw Foremaster approach.

"Lady Frances, I believe we have had the pleasure of dancing before. Would you do so again?" Captain Foremaster's timing, as well as his cravat, was impeccable. With a low bow and a dashing smile, he led the lady to the main deck.

Uncle Reginald cleared his throat. "Niece, would you dance?"

Joshua caught her eye. A silent question passed between them. She nodded to reassure Joshua. "Yes, thank you."

As Margaret and her uncle moved up and down the line of the country dance, Margaret kept a neutral, but pleasant look on her face, her churning feelings hidden beneath.

"We called on your father first, hoping to find you both at home," Sir Reginald said as the dance brought them to the middle. The hair on top of his head flopped back and forth, like a rooster's comb.

She bit her lip and did not respond.

"He told us you were here."

Margaret could imagine how her father had given them an earful. His pride in her and a desire to show her aunt and uncle her success must have been the reason he'd allowed them to come.

"Yes, I am very happy living with Father. We are enjoying Lisbon." She found her voice and her manners.

"But the riot. We heard of it as soon as we docked, just hours ago."

"We are not in danger."

"Every British citizen is in danger. Lady Frances and I feel it would be best—" He completed the sentence on the next pass. "For you to return home with us as soon as possible.

She fumed, but politely responded, "Thank you for your concern, but I will remain in Lisbon with my father."

Sir Reginald's lips pursed, beak-like, and his brow lowered. She barely caught her laugh. It would not be kind to laugh at him. He had to live with Lady Frances, after all. Perhaps that was what had turned him against her.

On the next turn, Sir Reginald spoke more politely. It nearly threw Margaret off her step. "We are here to escort you home. We offer you our protection and care. Your father does not have long—"

"Please do not speak of it. Not here. Not tonight."

They said no more during their dance. The rest of the evening, Margaret danced and enjoyed the company of many. Propriety required that at the end of each dance, Margaret be returned to her aunt. Margaret tried not to look at her, but always felt the weight of Lady Frances's gaze. Her tight lips and haughty demeanor left no doubt as to her opinion of the evening. More unsettling, Margaret often caught Sir Edgar's scrutinizing eyes.

Joshua joined Margaret when he could, making conversation with others who had come to make the Colbornes' acquaintance. His faith and strength imbued her with confidence. She began to understand the combined power of a united couple. Perhaps she would not have to do everything for herself, by herself anymore.

The moon set in the early morning hours as the dance was coming to a close. Joshua and Foremaster were speaking with Sir Reginald when Sir Edgar touched her arm.

She shuddered, but nodded at him with a calm countenance.

"Would you do me the honor?" he asked.

"Yes," Margaret said. He led her out to the dance floor. It was the Quadrille, which meant she would be closer to him longer, but she could endure it.

At first, he said nothing, but near the end of the dance, he began. "Miss Colborne—"

"Miss Beaton is my name." She smiled, trying to reign in her anxiety, which grew with each dance step.

"Margaret." His voice was low and respectful, yet he used her Christian name. "We have known each other for many years, please. I wish to speak to you as an equal."

Margaret raised her eyebrows. She was speechless.

"I wish to apologize for the way I treated you at the beginning of your voyage. I was ill and… fearful."

"Thank you," she said, but she shuddered. She had not expected kindness, let alone an apology.

"I have heard stories about your crossing. You were in a terrible storm and injured. I am sorry."

Again, Margaret was unable to account for his sympathy. Here was a different version of Sir Edgar than she had ever known. "Thank you. I am recovered." Her back still itched in a few places, but less each day.

"I have never wanted to marry, but I know that it is expected of me." His voice was even and calm, the way he might comment on the weather or ask where the refreshments were.

Her mouth dropped open slightly. She closed it, but her knotted brow still betrayed her confusion.

"I wish to live my life more freely. To love freely. That is why I crossed an ocean, seasick every day, to find you. I believe we would do well together. I would not control you. You would not control me. Together, we could face Lady Frances. She could no longer control either of us."

Margaret breathed out, startled. "Sir, I had not thought you felt—"

"Felt as you do about Lady Frances? I have watched you and her together." He paused. "She is pressuring me to marry. For the good of the family. Last year, it is she who prevented my alliance with—I see you are shocked. That is not my desire. Please, reconsider and allow me to find a more appropriate time to ask for your hand. I believe it would serve both of us well."

The dance ended. Margaret pulled her lips together and swallowed. "Thank you for confiding in me and treating me so respectfully. It is impossible, however, for me to consider your offer. I have fallen in love—"

"Please, do not be so hasty." A bead of sweat was showing on his forehead. As he walked her back to Lady Frances, he whispered quickly. "We would be wealthy, admired, and free. We could have a child if you wish. Or none. Or if you are discreet, I could accept a child from you. Just one."

Margaret shook her head, but Sir Edgar pushed on, his hushed tone growing more frantic. "I am afraid you are compromised. Consider my offer carefully before your reputation is tainted." He would not meet her gaze.

She stopped and turned to face him. "I assure you, sir, that you are misinformed. I have done nothing that I have to be ashamed of."

"That is not what Lisbon and London will hear."

She pulled her lips into a tight line.

"You were alone in a cabin with a man for a full half-hour."

Margaret reflected but shook her head. "From whom have you received this information? I was injured aboard ship, and Dr. Giles attended to me *with* my maid, Betty. Both will renounce this slander."

"Hm." Sir Edgar smirked. "And what of the time Betty left to change her clothes? Who was with you then?"

Margaret blushed. Sir Edgar had hit his mark. "Sir Edgar, why are you telling me this? If your object is to sully my name, why warn me of it?"

"So that you might prevent it. Lady Frances has a source. Perhaps I can stop it before it is known. The easiest way to quell rumors is to marry. I have had my own dalliances, of course. Almost a scandal last year. I wish to continue with a certain lady, but I need a wife to secure my standing in society. It would never do to embarrass Lady Frances or Sir Reginald. At first, I believed you to be too naive to be that wife, and I hesitated. But now, I know we are more alike than I thought."

"We have nothing in common. You wish me to marry you so you can continue on with your infidelity without consequence? You are mad." She whispered as loudly as she dared.

"You will be able to do what you like, when you like."

Joshua was at her side. She sighed and felt her soul relax. Margaret took Joshua's arm and said, "Sir Edgar, may I introduce you to my betrothed?"

Sir Edgar's mouth dropped open then snapped shut.

Joshua nodded and pulled her to his side as they walked away. "I have watched your face for a full ten minutes. Are you all right?" he asked, rubbing the back of her hand with his thumb.

"Yes, but surprised… and dismayed," she whispered.

"You must tell me about this after we say goodnight to our guests."

Joshua and Margaret stood on one side with the Colbornes to wish their guests goodnight. Sir Edgar was the first to leave. The guests were very complimentary, and Margaret was grateful for a reminder of how much of the night had truly been pleasant.

After the last goodbye, Margaret could barely wait to return home to her father. She rubbed her temple when she heard a screech. She looked up to see the monkey from earlier baring its teeth at her and hanging from the main mast lines above her. It jumped onto her shoulder. Margaret ducked her head and placed her hands over her face. She sank to the deck in an effort to shake the monkey loose. She heard Joshua's voice and felt his hands yanking at the monkey. "Help me, Sir Reginald." Another set of hands. With a final screech, the monkey retreated off the deck, the boat, and into the darkness of the dock.

"Margaret, your neck is scratched." She turned and found Joshua's face next to hers. He helped her to her feet, then pulled her into a gentle embrace.

Lady Frances, who had backed away to a safe distance, said, "Mr. Wynn, unhand my niece at once. You should not—"

Joshua pulled Margaret in close. She could feel the intense beat of his heart. "Lady Frances, do not lecture me on the care of my future wife."

"Your—"

"What was that?" Foremaster asked as he ran up the gangway. Other sailors were appearing from their berths below deck.

Joshua said, "The monkey was trying to tear off the pearl necklace."

Margaret's hand flew to her neck. The pearls were still there. She sighed. "Thank you, Joshua."

"The pearls," Lady Frances repeated. She looked off the ship toward the dock. "Come, Sir Reginald."

"Thank you for your help, Uncle." Margaret touched his arm.

Sir Reginald nodded, and wrapping his scratched hand in a handkerchief, led Lady Frances off the ship.

Foremaster gave orders to Kernsby and some of the sailors to secure the ship. Then, he followed Joshua and Margaret.

In a minute's time, Margaret was in a carriage with Joshua at her side, who had not released her from his embrace.

Foremaster sat across. "It is as we suspected. As the guests were leaving, I saw Sallow on board another ship, across from us. Then I heard the screeching, so I ran back. He must be involved."

"Why would he—" Margaret began.

"He is angry and wishes to pay me back. But we will have the law on him now." Joshua gently guided her head to rest on his chest.

"Joshua, the monkey bit you! There is blood on your glove."

"I had not noticed."

"A flesh wound. Tosh, it is nothing compared to what I have seen Wynn endure." Foremaster nodded at them both.

Margaret smiled in spite of her worry. "Clearly, you both need looking after."

"Miss Beaton, you will be entirely occupied looking after this one," Foremaster joked. "I fare well enough on my own," he said, relaxing back into his seat and stretching out a leg.

"You are every bit the Corinthian, Foremaster," Margaret teased. Then exhaling, she added, "But I believe Sallow intends to spread gossip and ruin my reputation."

"What?" both men exclaimed.

She repeated what Sir Edgar had told her. "I believe he has offered to pay if Sallow will keep quiet. Who else would have known? Who else would wish to ruin me?"

Joshua turned and bent his face toward Margaret's. In a soft whisper, he said, "I swear, no harm will come to you."

"I trust you, Joshua." She closed her eyes. Between Joshua's warmth and the sway of the carriage, her nerves calmed and her breath returned to normal.

CHAPTER 35

"WE HAD BEST WAKE your father." Joshua held Margaret's hand at the bottom of the stairs. He noticed the table clock showed a quarter past four.

"I am afraid it is for the best." Foremaster handed his hat and gloves to the butler.

"I wish I could spare him." Margaret placed her other hand on Joshua's.

"Miss, you're scratched somethin' awful." Betty's voice echoed in the entrance way. She stood at the bottom stair, hands to her open mouth. "Costa, is your wife still awake? Could she make some tea?"

"Betty, good, just what we need. Take Marg—Miss Beaton up to her room and tend to her, please." Joshua caressed Margaret's cheek with the back of his fingers. "I will take care of your father. Trust me."

She nodded, holding back her tears. "Thank you. Good night."

Joshua watched as Betty began to escort Margaret upstairs. "Oh, miss, there's been such a clinkum-clankum! Lady Frances showed up unexpected and said to me, 'You have been a profligate and lazy servant.' But I've always been Episcopalian, and she knows it. Then she dismissed me! But your father engaged my services as a lady's maid on the spot. And wasn't she in high dudgeon, then! Then Sir Reginald wished to see you. That's when I notic'd Sir Edgar. He looked positively ill. I hated to see the three of them head to your ball. Did they disturb it? Oh, that is a nasty scratch. What happened?"

"Shall we, Wynn?" Foremaster interrupted Joshua's concentration on Margaret and motioned toward the ground floor rooms that Mr. Beaton was occupying due to his illness. "Danny, please alert us as soon as Kernsby arrives"

Joshua pulled his eyes back to the men beside him and nodded. Foremaster and he waited at the door for Costa to let them in.

"Sallow, you say?" Mr. Beaton motioned for Costa to help him sit up in bed, his eyes ablaze. "That bacon-faced bamboozler! What has been done to apprehend him? The devil take him; he's probably half-way to England by now, the white-livered coward. Where are my dueling pistols?" Mr. Beaton's cough overcame the rest of his rant.

A knock sounded at the door. Foremaster was summoned by Kernsby.

Joshua lifted the glass of water to Mr. Beaton's lips. "Sir, sir. Please, I will defend Margaret's honor if and when the time comes. Rest assured. We have alerted the harbor, our employees, the British authorities—we will find him."

"If I were ten years younger and had my health again." Mr. Beaton breathed deeply and laid his head back on the pillow.

Foremaster rejoined them. "We have intelligence concerning our ships the *Invicta* and *Próspera*. The harbor master reports sightings of privateers to the south. We fear they will be attacked."

"Oh, it must be prevented. Always the unscrupulous grab power where they can. Foremaster, can you take the *Rainha Maria* and a crew to escort them in?"

"I will sail with the next tide. Mr. Beaton, Wynn." Foremaster was calling for Costa before he exited the room.

"Promise me." Mr. Beaton grabbed Joshua's arm.

Joshua was surprised to hear his first name and the pleading in Mr. Beaton's tone. "Anything," he said.

"Promise me that you will take Margaret away from here. It's not safe, nor will it ever be for her."

"I have been thinking about that very subject. As soon as you are well enough, we will travel to London."

"No, no. I will never be well enough. That is why you must promise me. Not London. They rejected me, they will reject your son. No, take her to the Colonies. Take her to Boston and set up our offices as we originally planned."

"Sir, you must—"

"Joshua, we are men of action, men of truth. Help her when my time comes. Comfort her. How I wish I could have seen you two married."

Joshua nodded, taking a moment to carefully consider. "Sir, about that. I have an idea."

CHAPTER 36

"LADY FRANCES COLBORNE, MISS."

Margaret stood as Costa opened the drawing room door further for Lady Frances. It had been two days since the ball. Margaret knew that *she* should have visited her aunt and uncle first, out of respect, but her father was ill. She would not leave him. She bit her lip. She should have known that Lady Frances would not wait long to come to her.

"I should go," Betty said.

"No, please stay." Margaret took her arm.

Lady Frances swept into the room. "Good. Betty, gather Miss Colborne's hat and gloves so she can accompany me. We have quite a few calls to make. Most importantly to Lady Beresford. I wish to know what her husband is doing about these uprisings."

"No, thank you, Aunt Colborne, I need to remain with my father, who is quite ill."

Lady Frances froze, only her reticule swung slightly on her arm. "My dear, please refer to me in *public*," here she bent her head in Betty's direction, "as Lady Frances. I am aware of your father's condition; however, it will do you no good when your father dies for you to be unknown and friendless. Fortunately, Sir Reginald and I arrived in time."

Margaret held her balled fists behind her. "Lady Frances, thank you for the honor of your visit. I am sorry I cannot join you this morning." She nodded at Betty, who pulled the bell for Costa.

Lady Frances took a step forward, an angry crease between her eyes. "You are my niece and will not dismiss me."

Margaret attempted a smile at her aunt as Costa opened the door. "Send my regards to my uncle. Costa, please show *Lady* Frances Colborne out.

Lady Frances adjusted her gloves but did not move. "I can either discuss things with you or with your father. Which do you choose?"

Margaret eyed her aunt, knowing full well what she was capable of. "Thank you, Costa, but remain outside the door. Betty, will you check on my father?" After Betty left, Margaret faced her aunt. "What is it you wish to discuss?"

"You could have called for tea," Lady Frances said, sitting down on the couch.

Margaret stared straight at her. She could think of nothing lady-like to say, and so said nothing. She did not sit and hoped Lady Frances would take the hint. This interview would be short.

"Margaret, Sir Reginald and I have come all this way to support you during this trying time. I have spent two weeks onboard a ship full of stinking sailors. Sir Edgar, as you know, is extremely sensitive to the motion of the sea. Yet, he came out of a desire to make you an offer. To show his contrition. To do the honorable thing."

Margaret had nothing to say to this but wondered she had not seen how Lady Frances had controlled Sir Edgar as well.

"We came just to be here when you need us the most. Your father is dying. And you pretend to dismiss me? How ungrateful. I remember your tears, your behavior after your mother died. I am the only one who knows what losing your father will be like for you. You are acting like a spoiled child instead of an accomplished young lady."

Margaret's mouth parted. She was speechless. "How dare you speak of my mother or my father's… condition."

Lady Frances's head came up. "I have not finished. It is bad manners to interrupt me. Margaret, dear, your father will die, and soon. You must face that reality. And other realities."

Margaret went to the window, throwing it open, using the moment to control the angry tears which threatened. But here, under her father's roof, with her friends nearby, she did not weep. Calmer, she turned. "Lady Frances, you will not be needed this time. I am older. I am not friendless. And I am well cared for here."

"Here?" Lady Frances said. "There are riots. You are British; you would not last three days! A single woman, unprotected, unable to independently control your inheritance—it is preposterous. How would you, a mere girl, run your father's business? You need a man, a husband, for all of that. Which is why we had hoped Sir Edgar—"

"Sir Edgar?" Margaret's voice rose to an angry pitch. With a moment of concerted effort, she controlled it again. "Sir Edgar recently tried to blackmail me into marrying him. I read the paper now in fear that his slander will appear. Sir Edgar is not interested in a life *with* me. He has his own pursuits, as well you know. You did not spend two weeks aboard a stinking ship for me, but for your own interests and reputation."

Lady Frances bit her lip. "Our reputation. Ours. You are a Colborne, and you know how to act like one. Unfortunately, mingling with the lower classes, as I warned you, has caused you to lose all sense of decorum and even your reputation. I know you were alone with that sailor, Mr. Wynn."

"You know something about this, I do not doubt. You told me before I left London that you would *know* how I behaved on ship. Did you pay that man Sallow to be a spy? To discredit Mr. Wynn, to steal the pearls? Is he your source of information? How could you?"

"This is an outrage. Look at yourself. Your behavior. You are throwing a tantrum."

"Like the one you threw when my father chose to court my mother and not you?"

"Whatever stories your father has told you—"

"My father would never stoop to discuss how you betrayed my mother. How you twisted the circumstances to hide your embarrassment, your jealousy. I read about it in my mother's journal."

Lady Frances arose. Only the twitch of her left eyebrow revealed her anger. "I have been the one woman who has held this family together for twenty years. *I* have protected our reputation, our good name. Your grandfather and uncle would have welcomed your parents back in their indigent circumstances with such low connections." She scoffed. "A Scottish last name like Beaton? Why, your father could not even afford to keep a separate house for your mother at first. She lived with him on his ship."

Margaret tried to pass Lady Frances to reach the door. "You have no right to speak of—"

Lady Frances caught her arm. "I am not done. I, *I*, stayed and kept the family in order, kept our name, our standing. What did I ever receive? Praise, respect? No, all I heard was 'Poor Alice.' Your grandfather even allowed her to keep the pearls *you* now wear. Pearls that were meant to be inherited. She was disowned; they should have passed to me."

"You are incorrect, Lady Frances. My mother was never *poor*, not in the things that truly mattered. My father has done very well for himself."

"But he will not be here forever to protect you. What will you do then? Where will you go? I cannot have a niece who—" Lady Frances stood up straighter. "Do not dare to marry that *sailor*!"

Margaret winced but raised her chin. "Lady Frances, that *sailor* is a gentleman who has given noble service to the crown and who has acquired the means to support—"

"His half-British son, yes, I know about his marriage. Hah, a gentleman who continues to work as a merchant? You would not be accepted in London, not by the *ton*. This is exactly our objection. You would be humiliated at every turn."

"No, I will not feel humiliation, but you may. That is your real reason for concern." Margaret brushed past her aunt as she moved to the door. Holding it open herself, to the surprise of both Lady Frances and Costa, she said, "We do not have anything further to discuss. Costa, please show Lady Colborne out." Without waiting for Lady Frances to pass first, Margaret descended the stairs.

"You have not heard the end of this," Lady Frances called after her.

Margaret did not look back. She entered her father's room and shut the door behind her.

CHAPTER 37

JOSHUA CALLED ON MARGARET the next afternoon. She was playing the piano with the door to the drawing room wide open. He paused and studied her before entering. Her head slightly bent, she swayed with the music. His heart beat faster and not just from the Scottish dance that she played.

He stepped to her and sat on the bench backward, leaning toward her.

"Joshua! I am so glad to see you." She stopped playing. "Tell me, what have you heard about Foremaster?"

"Nothing as yet, which is good. Why are you playing with the door open?"

"Father wants to hear 'Bony's Finale' by Gow." She played the last few measures, ending on dramatic chords.

"Have I ever told you how beautiful you are?" Joshua traced her chin with a single finger. "Or that you blush the sweetest shade of pink."

"Have I ever told *you* that you have a tender heart?" She gazed at him, a slight smile on her lips.

He cleared his throat and stood up. "I was hoping you would come with me."

"Oh," she blinked several times. "I cannot leave Father."

"What if we go outside without leaving the house?"

She gave him a confused smile. "How could we do that?"

"I will show you."

Joshua used both hands to help Margaret ascend the last few stairs. Now standing on the widow's walk—a small fenced platform on the roof overlooking the harbor—he turned her to look to the west across the ocean.

She clung to him. "I did not realize how high up we would be. It makes me dizzy to look down."

He did not mind the way she grasped his coat. Placing his arm around her waist, he said, "Do not look down, look across."

She glanced up at him and relaxed into his arms, pulling them around her.

He placed his head lightly on top of hers. Her hair tickled his cheek. Swaying, they looked out in companionable silence. Small fishing boats dotted the coast, their white sails full of wind. The sea was not a solid blue but varied and lightened as it came closer to the small strip of beach and rocks that rimmed the harbor.

Joshua whispered into her ear. "I wished to take you somewhere different today. To the promenade where you walked with your parents or to my garden. But perhaps this is best after all. When I look at the ocean stretching away from us, unbroken, shining. I am full of the future, Margaret. Thank you."

"Thank you for what?"

"For helping me see what is still ahead. Restoring my faith. For helping me to love, again."

She reached up and touched his lips with her hand. "You gave *me* a future—this precious time with my father. *I* cannot thank *you* enough. You gave me hope." She turned and folded herself into his chest.

He held her. Breathing in the sea air, feeling her warmth, her breath on his neck.

Pulling back so he could look into her eyes, he said, "Margaret, I love you more than my own life. I love you beyond what my heart can hold. I cannot imagine a future without you. Will you do me the honor of becoming my wife?

"Yes. Oh, yes!" She placed her hands on his chest as tears glistened in her eyes. Her lips parted in a smile.

He placed his lips over hers. A gentle first kiss.

She buried her head in his shirt. "Your heart is pounding, Joshua."

"You have awakened it."

"Then, may it always match mine." She tilted her head up.

He kissed her again.

CHAPTER 38

"FATHER?" MARGARET PEEKED INTO the darkened bedroom.

"Come, child." Mr. Beaton raised a tired hand to Margaret.

"How are you feeling?" She sat on the chair next to his bed.

"Better now that you are here. Have you brought them?"

"Yes." Margaret set the case with her mother's pearls near his hand.

"Open the curtains so we can see better."

When Margaret returned from the window, her father reached for her hand.

"My eyesight is going more rapidly. But I can still see, you understand, your smile, your mother's smile, and these pearls. Hold them in your hand."

Margaret removed them from the case and held the beautiful necklace in her hand.

He placed his hand on top of hers to touch them.

"They were a present from her mother, you see. Alice brought them when we eloped. I could not give her anything this beautiful for years, but that did not matter to her. She said that her mother gave her the necklace, but I gave her the Pearl she loved most. You." His lip quivered.

A tear slid down Margaret's cheek.

He lowered his hand. "These pearls were the last thread to connect your mother with her own mother and father. She believed her father may have relented, but Lady Frances, Sir Reginald—ah, there is repentance needed in my soul still. For those two."

"Papa, you—"

"No, let me finish. Your mother loved these pearls and wore them for me. She knew that I loved to look at her. In time our circumstances improved, and I bought our first ship. The early days of the war made this possible. Yet, it meant I was away from your mother more often. Then you came. We were overjoyed. You were worth more to us than any pearls, any ships." He closed his eyes for a moment but smiled.

Margaret choked back the tears. "I have always known this, Father."

"I should have been with you. I should have moved my business to London. I should—" a sob and a cough rang from him.

Margaret dabbed his mouth with her handkerchief. "I understood."

"Do not repeat my mistakes." He closed his hand over hers. "Do not be separated from Wynn. It is not good for a marriage. You *must* leave here. It is not safe enough for my precious Pearl."

"Yes, Father, you are right. But we still have time."

"Of course, we do. Memory is the perfect preserver of time. Do you remember walking on the *Oeiras Promenade*? The three of us?"

"We went nearly every Sunday after church."

"I can see it now. I can be in the past and here with you at the same time. Do you understand?"

"Yes, Father." Tears now freely flowed down her cheeks.

"We can be together as often as it is helpful to you, sweet lass. Do not let the pain of the past keep you away from the present too long, though. But know that your mother and I will be waiting, in your memory and in heaven."

"Yes." Margaret buried her head in his chest. She began to sob.

"Here, here." Her father lifted her head. "This is not how a bride should look on her wedding day."

She laughed. "No, I expect not."

"Now, go change. Quickly. It will soon be time."

CHAPTER 39

JOSHUA PULLED AT HIS sleeves. His hands shook slightly, but he patted the pocket where he had placed Margaret's ring. He cleared his throat.

"Goodness man, you're as nervous as a mouse during harvest time." Mr. Beaton chuckled. He was also dressed in his very best, but lying on his bed, propped up by pillows. His hat lay next to him. The rest of the furniture in his bedroom had been removed so the guests could attend. Sunlight streamed through the open window.

"Were you this nervous, sir, on your wedding day?"

"All wise men are." Mr. Beaton sighed and closed his eyes.

"Any advice for me?"

"Always take care of her. And be thoughtful of her feelings. Speak gently. The rest will work itself out."

"Yes sir, I will. Thank you."

The door opened and Mr. Sheppard, the vicar of St. George's, entered. "A beautiful day for a wedding," Mr. Sheppard said. "But then, every wedding is a beautiful day." He beamed and nodded. "Should I invite the other guests in?"

"When Miss Beaton is ready," Joshua said.

"Ah," said the vicar.

As if on cue, Costa opened the door. "She is ready, sir."

"Thank you, Costa. Please."

Costa motioned for others to enter. Benedita came first. She kissed Joshua and moved toward the window. Next came Dr. Giles, Kernsby, and Danny and Betty, who was already crying into her handkerchief. Costa and his wife entered last.

Joshua placed a hand on his stomach and tried to stand up straighter. He focused his gaze on the door. Then, Miguel and finally Margaret stepped into view. He caught his breath and his heart stopped for a moment. Her auburn hair was accented with blue scilla and white rose buds. Her pale green gown accentuated her blushing cheeks and blue eyes.

She caught his gaze and smiled at him. She held Miguel's hand, and together they walked in. Miguel, producing a shy smile, stepped to Joshua's side. Joshua placed a hand on his son's shoulder.

Margaret stood at the side of the bed between her father and Joshua. His heart raced as he took her hand.

Mr. Sheppard stepped in front of them and, smiling and nodding at everyone, opened his book. "Dearly beloved, we are gathered together here in the sight of God, and in the face of this congregation, to join together this man and this woman in holy matrimony."

Joshua looked into Margaret's shimmering eyes. He smiled.

"… which is an honorable estate, instituted of God—"

Boom! A distant explosion, the sound of cannon shot in the harbor, reverberated through the room.

CHAPTER 40

"HOW RELIABLE IS THIS report?" Father asked Joshua. "What of the cannon shot and the damage to the *Minerva?* Are Foremaster and our incoming ships from London and Boston truly at risk?" He coughed

Margaret handed a glass of water to her father, which he drank. He was propped up in bed, still in his formal attire. His brow was sweating, but he was still sitting upright, leaning on the nightstand for support. He sipped the water and thanked her. What a confusing past few hours they had spent. What a sad ending to a wedding day.

"Danny has returned from the harbor. The cannon fire earlier today and evidence of sabotage on the *Minerva* is irrefutable." Joshua spoke quietly. "We believe the sailors who heard rumors of sabotage on Foremaster's ship are reliable, but it was second or third hand information. We cannot ascertain if the report is from Foremaster himself."

"But is it caused by rioters?" Father handed her back the glass.

"No, this was a very small, very targeted event." Joshua rubbed his forehead.

Margaret's eyes darted from Joshua to her father. Her trembling hands were clasped in front of her.

Joshua took her hand. "I need to sail with the tide."

"The *Liberty* is our last boat in harbor. It's not safe practice to have them all gone. If you become endangered... " Father did not choose to finish his sentence.

"Of course, you must go to Foremaster." Margaret rose and crossed to Joshua. She took his hands. "And we will wait for you here. Miguel is with Benedita, and I will stay here with Father." Her lower lip trembled, but she willed her tears back. It was her first test—letting him go, possibly into danger—and she would not fail him.

He kissed her hands. "I promise to make this day up to you."

She nodded as two tears escaped her eyes. She turned. "Now, Father, you should rest so you have your strength when the next wave of news comes and decisions must be made."

"I'll not argue with you." He sighed. "I'd like to argue with you. I'd like to sail in Wynn's place. However... " He lay back down.

Margaret removed his shoes and covered him with a light blanket. She tucked it around his shoulders.

"Just half an hour. Then wake me." Father touched her cheek.

"Yes, Father."

Betty was waiting in the hallway as Joshua and Margaret emerged. "Oh, miss, you look pale. Mr. Wynn, I have a fire in the office, and tea."

"Thank you, Betty," Margaret said. Joshua led her to the office. She loved the feel of his protective arm around her.

Joshua asked, "Oh, Betty, is that Margaret's shawl? She is cold, and I need to warm her." He took the shawl from Betty.

"Yes, sir." Betty sighed deeply, head cocked to the side while she handed him the shawl. She looked at Margaret as she left, a dreamy smile on her face. Margaret smiled back.

Margaret went to the couch by the fire while Joshua quietly closed the door behind them. Then he tucked the shawl, a bit awkwardly, but gently folding it around her, brushing her neck with his fingers.

A pleasant heat rose to color her neck and face.

Then he cradled her neck in one hand and pulled her in close. His lips closed on hers tenderly, but fervently.

"The crew will be ready within—pardon me." Danny's voice broke the kiss. Margaret opened her eyes.

Joshua pulled back but continued to look at Margaret. "Danny, I will join you outside in a minute."

"O' course, sir, ma'am." Danny closed the door.

"I am sorry—" Joshua began.

Margaret placed her fingertips on his lips. "Do not be. This is the life I want, a life with you."

He kissed both of her hands, raked a hand through his hair, and pulled her to him again, his lips seeking hers briefly—too briefly. Stepping toward the front door, he said, "I will be back as soon as possible. Two days. Three days."

"God bless you, Joshua."

"And you." He left, closing the door to the office.

Margaret wrapped the shawl in her hands. Her head dropped forward, and her tears fell freely.

Betty came back into the room. "Now, now. You and I must console each other." Betty put her arm around Margaret and led her out of the office and up the stairs. "You have a rest. I will alert you when your father wakes or if any news comes. I will take care of you, and Danny will take care of Mr. Wynn."

Margaret nodded and allowed herself to be led, the disappointment of the day welling up inside her chest and spilling out as tears.

CHAPTER 41

THE NEWSPAPER ACCOUNT WAS in the morning paper. "Miss B—, recently of London, was compromised on a recent voyage as a Mr. W— was seen leaving her cabin unchaperoned."

Margaret was stunned. She had not thought Sir Edgar would go through with it. Embarrassment coursed up her body and burned her cheeks. Tears formed in her eyes. What she had been taught to fear most by Lady Frances had happened. She sank onto the drawing room sofa. She was disgraced. She swallowed twice, but it did not help the knot forming in her stomach. With shaking hands, she lay the paper down. Was she ruined?

No. She clasped her hands in front of her. Held them and willed them to stop. She had done nothing wrong. The circumstances—her injuries and the storm—Joshua and she would not have been alone together except for these. No. She rejected this evaluation of her character, just as she had rejected Lady Frances's mocking head shakes and Sir Reginald's judgmental glares.

It was unfortunate. She could not change it. But she would not be defined by this implied misconduct.

Betty wanted to burn it, but Margaret asked for scissors. She moved to the writing desk, clipped out the "article," and sent it with a short correspondence to her uncle. Leaning back in the chair, she shook her head. She was shocked that Sir Edgar had actually told the newspapers. Even though he had implied it would come out, she did not believe he wanted to hurt her as much as he wanted a solution to his own predicament. It was entirely out of character for him since it also hurt his and the Colbornes' reputations. Lady Frances might be capable, but she would never damage her own reputation.

Embarrassment crept back in with one thought. She rose and crossed to the window. She peered out, but her eyes focused on nothing. What would Benedita and Miguel think of her? While *she* knew what was true about the incident, she worried what Maria Luisa's family would think. Had she brought shame to that family? What would Joshua's family in England think of her? They had not met her, but from Joshua's account, she believed some of them held the same beliefs and prejudices as Lady Frances. She walked back and sank onto the sofa.

How would it negatively affect her father's business associates? Who now would shun her? Certainly, the gossip would find its way to England within a few weeks. She would never be admitted to Almack's again. Or to many of the balls and musicales of the past.

Fortunately, she never intended to return to London. And her marriage to Joshua would restore some of her reputation. She rose, determined to put this foolishness out of her mind. Her father was ill, Joshua was out at sea—she had more important cares than what people may believe about her. She went to find her father.

In the afternoon as she sat watching her father sleep, she heard Costa answer the front door. Costa entered and announced that Dona Marques-Abreu was waiting in the sitting room.

When Margaret entered, Benedita stood and greeted her with a kiss on the cheek. "I have heard of—the English newspaper. I have come—are you all right?"

Tears began to flow down Margaret's cheeks. "I am so sorry that this scandal has reached you. I would never have done anything to embarrass or discredit you and your family."

"Have peace. No tears" Benedita pulled her into a hug.

Margaret nodded as she calmed herself.

"Please, sit down." Margaret pulled out her handkerchief and wiped her eyes. She sat next to Benedita on the sofa.

"When Joshua courted Maria Luisa, many disapproved. An Englishman marry our daughter? He wants only money. He may abandon her. But we have a saying, *Quem vê cara não vê coração.* Who sees the face does not see the heart. We saw his heart. Now I see your heart." She reached out and took Margaret's hand. "Joshua told me about the voyage. All. I believe him. People who know you and Joshua will believe the truth. Those who gossip, their hearts are heavy with their own doubts."

"Thank you," Margaret said. "It has troubled me—what you and Miguel might think. What the rest of Maria Luisa's family might think."

"We understand." Benedita shifted so she could look at Margaret. "Have you heard news from Joshua?"

"Nothing yet. It is probably too early for him to have reached the *Rainha Maria.* But I will let you know as soon as I hear anything."

"Thank you. And how are you?"

"I am... sad for my father and frightened for Joshua."

Maria exhaled slowly and patted Margaret's hand. "It is difficult to be a woman. We are left behind to care and worry. Men fight on the outside. Women fight on the inside. I am sorry you are learning this. You are so young. Can I help?"

Margaret reached and took Benedita's hand.

"Thank you. I will let you know what kind of assistance I will need. But you are helping. Simply by being here with me." Margaret squeezed Benedita's hand.

Margaret received a letter from her uncle that afternoon. Sir Reginald insisted that Sir Edgar had not carried through with his threat, stating that Sir Edgar denied it vehemently. They could only imagine someone else had contacted the papers. Then he shared his belief that Margaret had been wronged. She nearly dropped the letter in shock that her uncle would take her side.

Margaret wondered who, then, would have contacted the papers? Sallow? Another member of the crew? But no one knew beyond Dr. Giles, Betty, and Joshua. None of them would betray her. She read the rest of his letter. To Margaret's surprise, Sir Reginald actually apologized to her for Sir Edgar's behavior and informed her that Sir Edgar had decided to sail on the next ship back to England, but that Sir Reginald and Lady Frances would remain until after her father's death.

It was common knowledge, then, that her father was reaching the end. Even though she knew it, reading those words struck her. She sat by her father for most of the afternoon. She wanted to be near the office as well. Kernsby was handling all correspondence and business matters, and she wanted to be close in case there was news. Hours went by without any.

Betty tried to get Margaret to rest. Finally, Margaret agreed after her father was asleep for the night. "But wake me at midnight. I wish to sit with him." Betty agreed.

Alone in her room, Margaret knelt by the bed. The tears poured out of her. Muffling her sobs with a pillow, she cried and prayed until the emotion had spent itself. Her prayer, "Oh, God, please give my father peace and rest," tore her heart open again. Later, the prayer that Joshua be returned safely was followed by more quiet tears. Still, she had great hope that they would be reunited.

It was only after these concerns that she had any time to ponder her embarrassment over the newspapers. Lying on her bed, she remembered Benedita's kindness and her counsel. Those who truly mattered—Benedita, Miguel, Betty, Danny, Kernsby, Foremaster, Dr.

Giles, her father, and Joshua. They knew and believed in her. They would not abandon her.

At midnight, she went down to her father's room surprised to find him awake. And talkative.

The next morning, Margaret awoke in the chair next to her father's bed. The house was still and the morning sky gray. She looked at her father, snoring slightly, and smiled. They had talked most of the night until he had fallen asleep about four in the morning. She rubbed her neck and stretched. Sleeping in the chair, even for an hour, had made her stiff. She quietly leaned over him. His breathing was steady. Needing some fresh air, she slipped out of her father's room.

It had been two days since Joshua had sailed in search of Foremaster. Two days of worry, two nights of fitful sleep. Fortunately, no other disturbances had been heard of in the harbor. Her father had immediately ordered repairs on the *Minerva*. That was a relief to Margaret. It would take a week before they were completed, but the ship could sail as soon as two days' time if needed. She did not know how long it would take Joshua to find the *Rainha Maria* and return. No one could tell her.

Without calling for Betty, Margaret put on a clean day dress and pulled her hair into a quick bun. Quietly, she grabbed her pelisse and climbed the stairs to the roof. The breeze tugged at her hair as she stood on the widow's walk. She looked out at the ocean. A glimmer of sunrise from behind her revealed details of the houses surrounding her. Memories of Joshua holding her there just a few days before, asking him to marry her, comforted her. She closed her eyes and remembered their shared sunrise onboard the *Rainha Maria*. Beautiful memories.

In the quiet of morning, she prayed until the slight chill of March finally permeated her pelisse. Taking in another deep breath, she descended the stairs. Pausing by her father's rooms and hearing no sound, she continued to the kitchen below. Costa was coming up. "Costa, any word, any news?"

"I am sorry, but no."

"I will go check on my father. Please let me know if you hear anything or if we have visitors."

"Yes, ma'am."

She slipped into her father's bedroom and paused by the door. He did not stir. She sighed and her shoulders relaxed. She smiled as she remembered. Last night, Margaret had been surprised at her father's energy. They had talked for hours, or rather, he had. Margaret had listened, delighted as Father had recounted details about his life—meeting her mother, their first married year together, Margaret's birth, her childhood. Margaret had beamed. This was the life she had imagined in Lisbon—a life with her father.

Since he had talked late, he would be tired this morning. She turned to leave but stopped. The room was still. Too still. She took a few steps closer. The realization came suddenly. "Father?" She lightly shook his arm. It was cold. She lit the candle on his nightstand. He looked peacefully asleep. She bent over him, her ear to his mouth. *It could not be. Not yet. Not yet.*

"Costa!" she called loudly and pulled the bell three times.

Costa appeared at the door. Seeing her face, he crossed to the bed.

Her hands covered her mouth. "Call for Dr. Giles. No, go for him yourself, quickly. Please."

Costa ran from the room.

Margaret fell to her knees by her father's bed.

Dr. Giles confirmed it. Her father had passed peacefully in his sleep. His suffering was over. Dr. Giles would help her make arrangements, but for now, she knelt by his bed, resting her head against the side. Alone now in the candlelight, she sobbed. The bed covers served as her handkerchief.

Time passed. And yet it did not. Margaret cried and remembered. She relived her father's tearful welcome when she came from London. His accent and booming voice. His laugh. His smile. The smell of his soap. The gentle touch of his large, rough hands. Hands that had worked for her and her mother—worked his whole life. She reached up and touched his hand.

She remembered each story from the night before. Memorizing them. Someday, she would tell Joshua, their children, her grandchildren—about David and Alice, the unlikely pair, who had wed, and loved, and lived. And now?

It was as her father had promised. Her memories were real. There they were, the three of them walking the promenade after church, she holding a hand of each parent. Fishing with her father. Sitting by her mother at the pianoforte. Through her memories, she could relive the precious moments with them, regardless of how much time had passed. It had all happened. She had been loved, cared for, protected—and she would never forget.

She emerged from his room an hour later to find Mr. Kernsby and Betty waiting.

Kernsby took her hand. "I am so sorry for your loss, so soon after being reunited. Your father was a good man. May I sit with him for a while?"

"Thank you, yes." Margaret blinked, exhaled a shaky breath as Kernsby entered the door to her father's bedroom.

"Margaret." Betty entwined their arms. "I have a tray for you in the drawing room. Please, come eat somethin'," Betty said.

Margaret allowed Betty to lead her upstairs.

"Come sit and let me serve you? Would you like water, tea, or something stronger?" Betty asked.

"Thank you. A sandwich, please. But only if you will eat with me."

"Of course." Betty smiled and picked up a plate.

"Is there any news of Joshua?"

"Not yet."

Margaret yearned for news of Joshua, waiting for his return, wanting to share her grief, to feel his comforting arms about her. She worried for his safety. She took the plate from Betty, and took a bite of cucumber sandwich. She had no interest in food, and set the plate down. She rubbed her temples. There was so much to do.

The next hours were a blur.

Benedita came that afternoon supplying Margaret with a motherly hug and a black dress.

As Betty helped her change, Margaret stood looking into her open closet where her ballgown and wedding dress both hung. She was grateful her father had seen her in both. She turned toward the door, smoothing the black skirt. Looking down at her dress, she remembered wearing black for the first time when her mother had passed. The emotions overtook her, and she fell on the bed, sobs racking her body. Betty sat next to her, rubbing her back and handing her a second handkerchief.

Half an hour later, Margaret took three deep breaths and sat up. So much needed to be done to properly honor her father. That would quell her emotions for now. Together, the Margaret, Benedita, and Betty washed and dressed her father's body. The bedroom curtains were closed and lit candles were placed throughout. Margaret placed fresh flowers around him. As her father's friends arrived, chairs were brought in. The vigil began. Margaret sighed. Her father would not be left alone.

Keeping busy helped Margaret to channel her grief, to keep her mind occupied. How she longed for Joshua. Her heart ached for his comfort most of all, but in the drawing room, Benedita tied sprigs of rosemary with black silk to be given to the mourners. Betty was busy cleaning, and Senhora Costa began preparing food for luncheon to be served after the funeral. Dr. Giles brought Mr. Sheppard to make funeral arrangements. When she found a moment to herself, Margaret pondered these acts of support.

Reading the letters of condolence often brought her to tears. Margaret had not realized the extent of her father's influence in Lisbon until letters began flooding in. Many contained stories of her father's kindness. Flowers arrived by the dozens. She was overwhelmed by the outpouring of respect and love.

Deep in her heart, she was grateful that the newspaper account of her alleged impropriety had not deterred people from honoring her father. In fact, she realized how unimportant it was what Lisbon, London, or anyone else believed of her. It paled in comparison to losing her father.

The vigil continued. And Margaret thanked the sailors and friends who came to her father's bedside. He was not left alone. And neither was she.

CHAPTER 42

MARGARET SLEPT FITFULLY. SHE arose early and from her window could see dark clouds billowing in from the sea. A light rain was falling. First, she checked the preparations for the luncheon. All was in order, so she dressed for the funeral and then waited by her father's body. In silence, she looked at his peaceful face, recounting his life and her gratitude for it. Too soon, the carriage arrived to take him away. She rode in her father's carriage behind.

Against tradition and in spite of any danger, Margaret insisted on walking in the funeral procession for the half-mile along the Avenida Infante Santo leading to St. George's Church. If Joshua were here or if Margaret had had a brother, they would have walked it. But she could not bear that her father would not have family, not have her, to be with him, to honor him, to walk one last time with him.

To Margaret's surprise, Sir Reginald was waiting to accompany her at the start of the procession. Together, in silence, they followed the carriage carrying his coffin. Her veil and the rain disguised her tears. She touched her pearl necklace for comfort, and thoughts of her father and mother flooded her mind.

Sir Reginald sat on the pew with her at the funeral and later held her umbrella as they watched the burial from the doorway of the church. The heavens were weeping with her.

That afternoon, after three hours of visiting at the luncheon, Margaret said goodbye to her father's friends and acquaintances. Exhausted, she retired to her father's room, needing a few moments of quiet. She stood in the room, which now felt terribly empty. The curtains were open, and sunlight was streaming in. At his dressing table, she fingered the brush of his shaving kit, stared at his comb. She closed her eyes, and as he had said, she was with him again, recalling her childhood. Yes, memory was a precious gift.

Betty entered quietly. "Sir Reginald and Lady Frances have remained behind. They wish to speak with you."

Margaret sighed and made her way up the stairs to the drawing room. Before entering, she could hear a disagreement.

"Today is not the right time." Sir Reginald's voice.

"We do not have time to wait." Lady Frances's higher, shriller voice.

Margaret entered. "Thank you for coming today. Uncle, I am grateful for your kindness earlier when you walked with me."

"Of course. I… it was for your mother," he said.

Lady Frances fiddled with her reticule.

Weariness settled on Margaret. The activity and tension of the past few days was over. She made her way to the sofa and sat. Looking expectantly at her aunt and uncle, she realized they were just that: two people, related to her, looking at her. She no longer had any fear of them. They were family, but they did not love her. That was the real tragedy. At this moment when she craved gentleness and kindness, she could not expect it. They were family, but she did not feel it.

"Margaret—" Lady Frances began, but Sir Reginald gently pulled her to sit on the sofa opposite Margaret.

"We are truly sorry, Margaret," her uncle said quietly.

"Yes—" Again Lady Frances started to speak, but Sir Reginald's hand on her arm stopped her. Margaret believed her aunt stopped more from the shock that he would interfere with her wishes than from respect for him.

Her uncle leaned forward. "Margaret, you see, it is unsafe for you to remain here, single and alone. It is not good for you physically or for your reputation. Especially after the newspaper article. We would like you to sail home with us. We believe we can mend your reputation." Her uncle's voice was quiet and measured. He looked at her intently, as men do if they fear a woman will cry and make them uncomfortable. No. Margaret looked again. He was sincere.

Margaret took a deep breath and relaxed her shoulders. "That is kind of you—"

"Good," Lady Frances rose to ring the bell. "You see reason. I will send for Betty to pack your things. I understand she is to be wed soon, so we must engage a new maid for you. We are working even now to quell reports of the *incident* on board the ship. With our combined efforts, we will find you another suitable match since Sir Edgar—"

"Aunt, I have not finished. Please sit." Margaret stared at her and motioned for her to return to the couch.

Lady Frances was nonplussed and paused. When Margaret did not retract her extended arm, Lady Frances returned to the sofa. "Well, then?"

"Sir Reginald, Lady Frances, I want to thank you for taking me in after my mother's passing, for caring for me until I was able to reunite with my father. I will be remaining here with—"

"That will not do," Lady Frances said. She pulled her arm away from her husband's touch. "We told everyone in London that you were coming to care for your dying father. That will be understood, admired even. But remaining here alone will not, especially after your conduct onboard ship. You will become the target of gossip, and your reputation will be tarnished beyond what we can repair."

Margaret was much too tired to guard her emotions or her words. "I was injured during a storm and under Dr. Giles's care when this *incident* occurred. But the conduct I find worse is that you told everyone in London that my father was dying but kept that information from me. That was unkind. I should not be surprised, however, since you wrote to my father that Sir Edgar wished to marry me before he had even made an offer to me. And Sir Edgar only wants to marry so he can carry on with his affair with a married woman. What about *his* reputation tarnishing yours? Let me be clear. I no longer care what London, Sir Edgar, or you think of me or my behavior."

"Just like her mother. We offer everything noble and proper, and she throws it in our faces." Lady Frances scowled.

"Frances!"

Margaret was shocked to hear her uncle address her aunt in such a familiar way.

He turned to Margaret. "You are set to inherit your mother's money, which was set aside by your grandfather. You should return to London to meet with the solicitors. The money is to come to you at twenty-five if you remain a spinster or at nineteen if you marry a gentleman who is approved of by your family."

"Meaning you? You decide whom I may or may not marry?" Margaret slapped both hands on her lap. "No wonder you tried to foist Sir Edgar on me. You could control me and my money through him."

"You ungrateful brat," Lady Frances said. "Marriage to Sir Edgar would have provided for your lifetime and that of your children. That is not an evil or unkind situation. Most young ladies in England would be overjoyed to receive such an offer."

"But you did not consider my feelings, my inclinations—or even his. Besides, I have chosen my own husband with my *father's* approval."

"You would choose a man with no title and little fortune over Sir Edgar? You are a fool." Lady Frances folded her arms and turned away from Margaret.

"I have chosen the grandson of a Lord, a gentleman in his own right, a decorated naval hero, and a man able to provide for me." Margaret rose. "And further, what you have not allowed me to explain is that I married him here, in this house, not four days ago. If he does not meet with your approval, I forfeit my inheritance."

Sir Reginald's jaw dropped, proof that he was dumbfounded by the news.

Lady Frances coolly stood and adjusted her gloves. "Congratulations. We accept your terms. If you will kindly turn over the pearls, we will leave."

Margaret's hand went to her neck. "What?"

"They are part of the inheritance," Lady Frances said. Her face was a mask of bored indifference, the trained London society face she wore amongst strangers. Only the streak of red blush on her neck belied her true emotion: anger.

"That is not necessary." Sir Reginald said to his wife. His face had reddened, from either anger or embarrassment or both. His fists were balled.

"If that is what it takes to buy my freedom from you, from London, I will part with them." Hands shaking, Margaret reached to undo the clasp. "Their true worth, you can never buy nor sell. These pearls bear my memory of a loving mother, a doting father, the pride in his eyes when he saw me wear these on my wedding day. You can never take that happiness from me." She placed the pearls, not into Lady Frances's outstretched hand, but into Sir Reginald's reluctant one.

Margaret rang the bell and moved to the door, determined to be polite this time as she dismissed Lady Frances. Costa opened it.

Margaret curtseyed as her aunt and uncle passed. "If you need to contact me in the future, please send your correspondence to Mrs. Joshua Wynn, Boston, Massachusetts. The office of Beaton and Wynn."

Lady Frances passed without looking at her, but Sir Reginald paused and said, "I truly am sorry."

Margaret waited until she heard the Colbornes leave and Costa close the front door. Then she sank onto the drawing room sofa and buried her sobs in its cushions.

CHAPTER 43

JOSHUA SAT IN THE pinnace of the *Liberty,* the small boat used to convey him between the ships. He waved at Foremaster, who was standing on deck of the *Rainha Maria.* As soon as the boat was near enough to the ship, Joshua caught and climbed up the rigging. Swinging over the side, he crossed the main deck to Foremaster.

"Wynn, I am astonished to see you. What has happened?" Foremaster clasped his hand. "Come to my cabin."

Joshua stopped him. "Did you not send word of distress? We heard reports of privateers attacking you. You sent a distress message."

"No, our voyage has been routine so far. We met up with the *Invicta* and now wait for the *Próspera.* She will join us tomorrow. We will sail into Lisbon together; three ships together should be enough to ward off any privateers. Come inside and get warm."

"We have been tricked." Joshua slapped his hat against his thigh.

"I do not understand."

"I have been tricked into leaving port, leaving Margaret alone with her ailing father. Of all the feather-headed—"

"If that is true, I can only think of one man who would have reason to orchestrate this. You must return—"

But Joshua was already headed over the railing. "Signal the *Liberty*, Foremaster. Tell them to ready full sail at once. We will sail as soon as I reach her. And follow as soon as you are able."

"Be careful," Joshua heard Foremaster yell over the sound of slapping waves.

"You as well."

CHAPTER 44

"THANK YOU, BENEDITA," MARGARET said, "for taking me and Betty in."

Benedita crossed the drawing room of Joshua's house and kissed her on the cheek. "Of course. We are family now. It is proper that you wait for Joshua here."

Benedita showed Margaret to Joshua's room, now her room. Betty followed and began arranging some of Margaret's things. Margaret smiled as she touched Joshua's brush, smelled his shaving soap, and watched Betty hang her dresses next to his suit in the closet.

Benedita's invitation to stay with her had come during the luncheon after the funeral. Margaret had eagerly accepted it, but it had taken two days for Margaret to set her father's house in order. She'd arranged for Kernsby to take over the business for the time being, then helped Betty to pack their things. She had not heard from her aunt and uncle again but learned from Kernsby that they would soon sail for London.

Margaret left Costa to run the house and send her any correspondence. Soon, Joshua would return, and then all would be well. Then she could begin to mend.

Her grief had been intense—at times uncontrollable. Eating was a chore. Sleep brought some respite, until she awoke each morning to the knowledge of her father's passing and the pain filling her chest again. Margaret had another reason to look forward to staying with Benedita. It would allow Margaret to get to know Miguel better. She was still nervous about her role as a stepmother. Having Benedita there would, she hoped, help her find her way.

The next afternoon, Betty was mending clothes while Benedita napped, leaving Margaret alone with her thoughts, her grief, and her worries. The following week, they expected Benedita's son, Rafael, and his wife for a visit. Margaret hoped she would make a favorable impression. She also hoped Joshua would return by then.

Fighting her nerves, Margaret went out into the garden. She watched Miguel swinging and playing with his carved elephants for a while. He said he did not want or need help but soon became bored.

"Quando meu pai vai voltar?"

"I expect your father any day now."

"Devemos sair de Lisboa?"

"We will ask your father, but yes, I believe we must leave Lisbon." Miguel dug his toe into the grass.

"Come, teach me how to sword fight."

"Que?"

"Luta de espadas." To demonstrate, she picked up two sticks from under the tree. She peeled off a few leaves and twigs and then threw one to Miguel, holding her own "sword" aloft. She pointed it at him and said, *"En garde."*

Miguel bent over laughing.

Margaret stood one hand on her hip. "What? Am I doing it wrong? Do we not just swirl our swords at each other?" She swished her stick wildly. Miguel dropped to the ground, giggling harder than she had ever seen.

"Ensine-me; teach me."

For the next quarter of an hour, Miguel showed her the correct stance and posture to hold her sword, punctuated by laughing fits from both of them. Finally, he agreed she was ready.

Facing each other, they bowed. Margaret turned her body to the side, raised her left arm behind her head, and extended her stick in with her fright hand. *"En garde."*

Miguel stared over her shoulder and gave a slight cry. He dropped his stick and stepped back. Margaret whirled around to see Sallow jump to the ground from the top of the garden wall.

CHAPTER 45

MARGARET STEPPED TO HER left to shield Miguel who was now behind her. Her fist tightened around the stick.

Sallow brandished a knife. "Stick won't help ya." He slowly walked toward her.

"*Corra!*" she yelled to Miguel without taking her eyes off Sallow. "Run!"

Sallow pointed the knife at Miguel and yelled, "*Pare!*"

Margaret heard Miguel's footfalls stop.

"One more word and I will stick him with this." Sallow took a step toward Miguel.

Taking in a shaky breath, Margaret's whole being was consumed with anger and indignation since Miguel had been threatened. The anger emboldened her. She stepped again to her left, keeping her body between Sallow and Miguel. "*Corra!*" she yelled again and heard Miguel run to the door.

Sallow growled and ran toward her, but she feinted left and threw the stick at him. He deflected it as she ran for the gate, but he caught her.

Grabbing her about the waist from behind, he stuck the knife under her chin. "You are not so haughty now. And I won't keep my distance. On board you treated me like your servant. Like a dog you ordered around. Ha. You wish to leave. Well, so do I."

As he moved toward the gate, she struggled to get free. Unable to escape his grasp, she dragged her feet. In response, he growled and thrust the knife closer. A trickle of blood moved down her neck. She recoiled, pushing her neck as far back as she could and took a few hesitant steps.

"Why?" she asked in a ragged whisper. Her breathing was shallow and her throat constricted.

"Hmpf. You're not too bright. It's simple. Your husband ruined me, and now I will ruin him."

They were nearing the gate. She grimaced. "You brought that on yourself."

He jabbed the knife a little.

A small whimper of pain escaped her lips.

He pushed against the gate. "First, your fine aunt wishes to pay me to act as valet to that buffoon and to ruin Wynn's chances with you. Fine by me. Wynn is responsible for my brother's death. The only family I had left. He deserves to suffer. On board, Wynn figures it out and threatens to destroy my ability to earn a living. I swim, barely making it to shore, but there I vow to ruin you both." Holding her secure with his left arm, he said, "Undo the latch."

Even with the pressure of the knife against her skin, she purposely fumbled with the latch. Surely Miguel would bring help. If she could just delay another minute more. "Lady Judith?"

"Aye! Your aunt shows up but won't pay me, says I didn't finish the job. At least the newspaper paid me for details of your conduct onboard. But not enough. So, I try and steal her precious pearls at your ball, but that doesn't work. And I am left with NOTHING!" he shouted. "You and I will settle the debt. If I am to go through life in sorrow, so will he. He'll never touch you again." He pulled her body to one side and with his left leg kicked open the gate, busting the latch.

"Stop!"

Sallow wheeled Margaret around toward the voice, hiding behind her, the knife nicking her again.

There stood Benedita with a flintlock pistol held in both hands, raised at eye level. Her face was a mask of anger.

"Careful, woman, or you'll shoot her, eh?" He laughed, leaning his head behind Margaret's ear. He took a step backward.

"I said STOP!" Benedita yelled.

"Now, now, woman. I will return this lady when I've had a nice visit. Then we'll see if Wynn wants her."

He turned his head to find the opening as the shot rang out.

Margaret fell to the ground.

CHAPTER 46

JOSHUA WAS RIDING AT full gallop when he heard the shot. He had nearly reached his house when he reigned in his horse. The sound had come from his garden. Who had fired a gun? If only he had known that Margaret was staying with Benedita and Miguel, he would not have stopped at Beaton's first. He had come as fast as he was able, but was he too late? His heart sank. Eternally, too late.

Directing his horse to the stone wall, he stepped onto the saddle seat and pulled himself over the wall. He landed in his garden, fists balled in front of him. Where was the gun? Had someone been shot?

Near the partially opened gate, Margaret lay on the ground with Sallow on top of her. Neither moved. He bolted to her and threw Sallow off, kicking him in the ribs. Only then did Joshua realize Sallow was dead, blood pouring out of his head wound.

"Joshua." Margaret's eyes opened.

He knelt next to her, and lifting her in his arms, he pulled her to him. "My love." Feeling a sticky wetness, he pulled back to see the splatter of blood in her hair and a trickle of blood down her neck. "You are bleeding." He placed his handkerchief to her throat and picked her up, turning for the house.

Benedita was kneeling near the door, tears streaming down her face, a pistol lying on the ground next to her. She cradled Miguel in her arms.

"*Papai!*" Miguel ran to him.

Joshua knelt, placing Margaret on the ground next to him, and hugged Miguel. Joshua reached out for Benedita, who staggered to join them. Placing an arm around Benedita, he said, "Thank you."

Benedita looked up, her face tight as she blinked back tears. "The last time wicked men came, I saved Miguel, but not Maria Luisa. I was *not* going to lose another daughter to another man *implacável.*"

Joshua placed his forehead against Benedita's and whispered, "*Obrigado.*"

"SHARE YOUR THOUGHTS?" MARGARET asked.

Joshua breathed out slowly. He had one arm around Margaret and the other around Miguel, who had fallen asleep. They sat in the drawing room. The only light came from the flickering fire. They were alone. Safe. Margaret rested against his shoulder.

He sighed and leaned into her. "I was thinking about Benedita." While the British officer in charge had asked Benedita a number of questions, Sallow's body had been removed from the premises. A Portuguese lady killing an Englishman was not likely to go over well. If Joshua had not returned when he had, they may have taken Benedita away.

"I am glad the officer agreed to let her stay with us. Will they be satisfied with Foremaster's evidence?" Margaret asked.

He nodded and sighed. Once Joshua had reported Sallow's actions to the officer and gave guarantee of further verification from Foremaster, the British officer became more polite. He examined Margaret's wound and cautioned Benedita to stay in Lisbon. "I believe Benedita will be questioned at the inquest. But, yes. Benedita should be cleared."

Joshua intended to ask Benedita to come to Boston for a few months, if not a year, for Miguel's sake. Now, it may be beneficial for Benedita as well. Tomorrow, he would ask her. She had been too upset to talk. Her maid had helped Benedita to her room to lie down.

"I do not know what Miguel would do without her," Margaret said.

"I know." Joshua brushed Miguel's hair. The sleeping boy did not wake. He had not left Joshua's side since the shooting. After dinner, Miguel had refused to go to bed, so Joshua had brought him into the drawing room where they had sat by the fire while Dr. Giles and Betty attended to Margaret.

After a bath, Margaret had joined Joshua and Miguel. Soon, Miguel had fallen asleep. Margaret sat quietly next to Joshua, tracing his arm with her fingers. He noticed her hands still shook.

"Thank you," Margaret whispered.

"For what? I was too late," he said.

"Joshua, look at me."

Margaret moved from his side to face him. His eyes went directly to the bandage on her neck. He shook his head.

She raised his chin to meet her eyes. "You may not have saved me from this small injury, but you saved me, more importantly, from sadness, from loneliness. You have given me love and hope. And a son." She smiled. "Here we sit, together as a family—I have not known this joy in a very long time. I will treasure this memory forever."

He kissed her hand and caressed it. "For us, there will be love for all time."

Eyes glistening, she leaned in and kissed his lips tenderly. The fire of her touch consumed him. He released her hand and moved his to the back of her neck, kissing her more deeply.

She pulled back and smiled. "Now, Mr. Wynn. It is time for you to put your son to bed. And then perhaps we should retire?"

A blush spread across her face only matched by his own. "Yes, wife." He picked up Miguel, careful not to wake him.

"Call me by my name," she said. They crossed the drawing room. "Yes, Pearl."

She giggled, picking up a lighted candle and holding it in front of them. "Not my middle name."

"But you are just that. A precious Pearl lent to me by your father. I promised to cherish you, and I will."

They made their way down the hall to Miguel's bedroom. "That is beautiful, and you may call me that in private. But say my other name. My new one."

"Which name is that, Mrs. Wynn?" he asked, raising an eyebrow.

"Precisely," she said.

EPILOGUE

MARGARET STOOD AT THE stern of the *Rainha Maria,* leaning against the taffrail and watching the coast of Portugal grow smaller. The wind whipped her eyes, creating tears or adding to the ones already there. She would never return. Somehow, she knew that.

Steadying her bonnet on her head with one hand and dabbing a handkerchief to her face with the other, she let the tears flow. It was a strange mixture of loss, forgiveness, and joy. Yesterday, she had visited her father's grave one last time. She only regretted leaving him behind, but he had taught her to carry memories with her. She would always cherish the memories of her parents and now ones of Joshua.

Oh, Joshua. The memory of him arriving at her uncle's London house, deeply tanned, in his faded jacket, having come straight from his ship to discharge his duty, stirred her soul. She blushed at how she had arrived at his London office and demanded he take her to Lisbon, but she sighed with relief as well. She was more blessed than any woman she could think of.

"Margaret," Joshua called above the sound of the ship's wake.

She turned to see him coming to her, holding his hat against the wind. In a moment, he had his arm around her shoulder.

"Foremaster said all is ready for Danny and Betty's ceremony now that we are safely underway. Look, they are trimming the sail to calm the ship. However, the vicar looks slightly seasick, so we had best hurry." She heard the calls and songs of the sailors aloft. She and Joshua crossed to the wheelhouse, nodding at Jonesy, and took the steps down to the quarter deck.

Joshua helped her down carefully. "I saw you sliding across this deck from here. I thought I had lost you."

She shuddered and leaned into him, but tossed her head back to catch his eye. "Such a trivial incident could hardly separate us."

He shook his head but smiled.

She moved toward the door to the interior cabins. "A wedding at sea. I am glad for Betty. It is truly romantic."

"Romantic may well be the name for it. We are running away to America."

"Do you think Boston society will welcome us?"

"Absolutely. What Americans admire most is resolve and independent will. And money does not hurt. And you, my dear, have all three." He stopped her before she entered the door.

"Most importantly, I have love," she said. She embraced him, slipping her hand into his coat to warm it. They remained a moment, gently rocked by the sea.

Clearing his throat, he stepped back. "First, immediately, we need to be married." His voice cracked a little.

She smiled at him, but then her eyes grew wide. "Joshua, we are already married."

"True, but the ceremony was rushed after that cannon explosion, and then I left abruptly. I have an idea that may restore some of the tenderness our wedding lacked. As well as this." Joshua pulled from his coat pocket a mahogany wooden box with a single bee carved on a rose.

"How?" Margaret's voice broke and tears escaped her eyes.

"Sir Reginald left it with Costa before they sailed. In his letter, he said that I was everything his father would have wanted for a grandson-in-law. He said it was his duty to right a wrong."

"I hope he and Lady Frances had separate cabins on the way home." She laughed. "But truly, thank you."

Margaret carefully held the box as he unclasped the necklace. She turned, and he secured the pearls around her neck.

He lightly turned her shoulders to see the pearls and then gazed into her eyes.

Looking up at him, she fingered the pearls. "These pearls will always remind me of true love. My mother's, my father's, and yours."

"And one day, you can give them to our daughter."

She blushed and folded herself into his arms. "I hope they will bring her true love and happiness."

He kissed her lips gently. "Now, we have a wedding to attend." Taking her hand, he led her down to the main deck.

MARGARET STOOD IN THE captain's cabin, placing a few roses in Betty's hair. She handed Betty the bouquet of flowers—lilac, white roses, and eucalyptus—which Danny had bought before leaving shore.

"Thank you, miss. I mean ma'am. Can you believe we are both about to be ma'amed for the rest of our lives?"

"Yes, and you will enjoy every minute you are called Mrs. Devine."

"Mrs. Devine," Betty sighed. "And I will meet his family in Boston."

"And become my housekeeper, if you want."

"Even though I'm married?"

"Absolutely. We will brave America together."

There was a knock at the door. "It is time, Betty." Joshua offered Betty his arm.

Margaret slipped out ahead of Betty and Joshua and onto the

quarter deck, which had been scrubbed and cleaned. A breeze pulled at her hat and cooled her from the brightly shining sun. The blue sea glinted its shiny reflection, almost too bright to look upon. Margaret joined Benedita and Miguel standing in the crowd. They were near the vicar, a Mr. Stoney, who was also immigrating. Danny, whose legs were shaking, tugged at the sleeve of his new suit, a gift from Joshua and Margaret. He would need it in his new role as assistant manager of the Boston office.

Betty and Joshua walked forward. She was beaming and beautiful in her gown. Many of Danny's friends in the crew were standing respectfully nearby. After delivering Betty to her place next to Danny, Joshua stepped to Margaret and then pulled her back a few steps more toward the railing. She looked up at him in wonder. He winked.

Mr. Stoney began. "Dearly beloved, we are gathered together here in the sight of God, and in the face of this congregation, to join together this man and this woman in holy matrimony; which is an honorable estate, instituted of God… "

This time, no cannon fire interrupted, and Margaret relaxed. But Joshua moved in closer. She could feel his breath on her neck, which caused her pulse to quicken.

The ceremony continued and Betty began to tear up, but to everyone's surprise, Danny began to sob.

"Wilt thou have this woman to thy wedded wife," Joshua whispered in Margaret's ear word for word with Mr. Stoney. ". . . to live together after God's ordinance in the holy estate of matrimony?"

Margaret leaned back into her husband's embrace, grateful for his love and tenderness. The sea rocked them, and its spray cleansed them. As if newly baptized, they would head for a new land and life.

"Wilt thou love her, comfort her, honor, and keep her in sickness and in health; and, forsaking all others, keep thee only unto her, so long as ye both shall live?" Mr. Stoney asked.

"Yes, Pearl. I will," Joshua whispered.

Acknowledgements

I owe some amazing people much appreciation and thanks.

My parents, Richard and Mary, instilled in me a love of reading and gave me a supportive and loving environment in which to grow. They read this novel with excitement and support! Thank you, mom and dad.

Kathleen Eddy Cummings, sister and fellow author, started writing with me when I was too insecure to try it myself. Her friendship and confidence have been invaluable.

My writing group (Book Babes all) have read, re-read, suggested, questioned, congratulated, and supported throughout this process. Thank you, Jenny Webb, Rachel Camp, Shelly Powell, and Kathleen Cummings.

The talented Emily Poole, who caught my mistakes as well as the essence of Margaret and Joshua! Thank you, Midnight Owl Editors.

For the gorgeous book cover, my niece-turned-model, Mary Cummings, and designer Stephanie Anderson at Alt 19 Creative Services for Indie Authors. Stephanie patiently answered my many, many questions.

Beta readers Elizabeth Watson-Barnes, Deborah E. Fairbanks, Jessica E. Brousseau, Mary S. Eddy, Margaret "Peggy" Black, and the incomparable marketing consultant and friend, Helen J. Stoddard.

The Storymakers Guild for holding amazing conferences to help me hone and build my skills. UVU's Capitol Reef Writer's Weekend attendees (love you guys) and Lisa Mangum for their advice and confidence.

And, most importantly, Don J. Harris, husband extraordinaire, dream believer, and enthusiastic supporter. He heard the story first, read its early drafts, listened to verbose explanations, and gave honest reactions and solid advice. I could not have completed this without his help, support, and excitement.

Thank you, Jane Austen, who started it all.

About the Author

Marjorie Eddy Harris loves a good story. She's been known to stay up all night reading to find out the how and why. Her undying love of Jane Austen's novels began in high school. In her twenties she discovered contemporary authors writing about the Regency era and became a devoted fan. Wishing to tell her own stories, she started learning the craft. After many rough drafts, conferences, and a supportive writers' group, she is happy to present her first novel.

A former English teacher turned author, Marjorie lives with her husband and their dog and writes in her office with 32 overflowing bookshelves. You can visit her at www.janeaustenlegacyromance.com.

Made in the USA
Monee, IL
13 January 2023

25204684R00159